NIBBLE & KUHN

NIBBLE & KUHN

David Schmahmann

ACADEMY
CHICAGO

Published in 2009 by
Academy Chicago Publishers
363 West Erie Street
Chicago, Illinois 60654

© 2009 David Schmahmann

Printed in the U.S.A.

Library of Congress Cataloging-in-Publication Data on file with the publisher

• • •

To my mentor and friend Robert W. Sparks, whose store of
courtroom stories is surpassed only by the number of juries he
has persuaded to go along with him; to my friends in the Johnson
& Johnson Law Department who bear not even a smidgen of
resemblance to the characters in this book; to Francisca, who
knows why; and mostly, of course, to Sheila, Olivia, and
Annabel, the sum of my good fortune.

A good lawyer would tell me I need to say that any similarity
between characters in this novel and actual people living
or dead is entirely coincidental. All right.

MARIA WAITS ON ONE SIDE OF THE NEWSSTAND AND I ON THE OTHER.
We are trying to look casual, unhurried, but we are watching
the lobby carefully. Harry Cabot walks by, a rolled *Boston Globe*
under his arm. He is wearing his usual gray suit and olive green
fishing hat, and as he passes his crepe-soled shoes squeak on the
granite. Many Nibble & Kuhn partners display this kind of odd-
ity of dress, a formal suit, for instance, under a shabby, waist-
length parka, or sober pin-striped trousers that end in beige
socks and scuffed penny loafers.

Cabot passes without looking at either of us. His face is expres-
sionless, as if minding one's own business were an important
mark of character. He may have a thyroid condition too. Without wishing to be gratuitous there is something bug-eyed about
him, how he always looks vaguely startled though always, of
course, in a perfectly good-natured way. If you didn't know who
he was you might mistake him for a simpleton. He stands by the
elevator doors waiting for them to open and when they do he
steps forward and disappears.

The lobby is now empty and we cross it, Maria and I, quickly
but nonchalantly. We step into an open elevator and Maria
presses the button.

"Close, doggone it," she commands.

I have been sitting beside her in a small room all morning, feeling her knee against mine, catching glimpses of her face, the fragrance of her skin when I lean over to whisper advice, and it has driven me half crazy. Mercifully I seem to have had the same effect on her. As the elevator rises we begin to kiss and she holds my face in a manner that is almost rough. The ride slows and she tries to pull away but I will not release her. We are almost at a stop before I do.

She breaks free and straightens her shirt.

"You're looking for trouble, bucko," she says when she sees that no one is waiting at the doors. "We would have been gonners for sure."

"To say nothing of the fact that someone might have told Alfonso," I say, taunting her.

"Don't be like that," she says. "You know how it is."

She goes into her office and I continue on to the men's room. I do, indeed, know how it is. How it is is the bane of my life. My most intimate moments with her—my *only* intimate moments with her if you discount the rubbing knees and the incidental touches—are in the elevator. The elevator has become, for want of an alternative, our love motel.

Everything else is Alfonso's. And she's not even married to him. Not even close.

• • •

There have been moments in my life which I knew in an instant were significant, but none more so than when I first spoke to her. Every June a small troop of law students arrive at Nibble & Kuhn for the summer, each of them brimming with an artificial, easily punctured ease. They are given simple assignments, invited to ball games and partners' homes for dinner, and of course are carefully watched all the time. The best of them are offered permanent jobs after graduation and those who are not well, something happens to them because we never see them again. I had been through it myself seven years before. By the time Maria's class arrived I had all but forgotten what a miserable experience it had been.

The firm distributes an amateurish brochure with photographs before the interns arrive, and I recognized her as soon as I saw her: Maria Parma. Wellesley High School. Harvard College (Art History). Columbia Law School. Her looks were unprepossessing, or at least they were then, before I paid attention. She was tall with narrow hips, straight legs, a pageboy haircut. I did not, not then, notice more. What rubbed me the wrong way was how little she seemed to be affected by the anxiety around her. Her manner was jaunty, reckless. I saw her once singing in the corridor, came across her laughing as she slapped a messenger on the arm. Perhaps, and I am not sure if I remember this accurately, I caught her hoisting her nylons behind a library stack and when she saw me she shrugged, laughed, and said something like: "What's a girl to do?" I know I risk sounding stuffy, but it seemed to me at the time that she was not paying her dues, not starting out where everyone else had. One expected a little deference, a little sobriety.

Who knows what I was thinking?

But I did ignore her, and all summer long. I might pass her in the hallway or sit across the table from her at a meeting, but nothing more. I treated her as lightly, in short, as she seemed to be treating us.

• • •

Sometime toward the end of August, on a night when I had to stay late to finish a brief, I ran into her in the copy room. She was about to use the machine and I stood back and prepared to wait.

"You go first," she volunteered.

"No," I said. "Please finish."

"No," she insisted, taking her paper from the glass and moving out of the way.

She pressed back against the wall.

"I'll stand here."

I may have paused for a moment but then I fed my document into the machine and pressed a billing code on the monitor. The machine whirred unevenly, snatched the paper, and then pushed it out crumpled.

"It did that to mine too," she said.

"You knew it would do that?" I said.

"I thought I was doing it wrong. I'm new here, you know."

"You could've warned me."

"You've never told me your name," she said.

I told her then, but with an edge of coldness.

"I'm Maria," she said, and held out her hand.

She had olive green eyes, tawny hair, and very white, straight teeth. As I say, I had hardly seen her before that moment. Her hand was quite warm, soft.

"You've ruined my document," I said.

"*I've* ruined your document?" she exclaimed. "Why is it, do you think, that boys always blame someone else when they break a machine?"

"You broke this machine before I got here," I said, and then I remember laughing because there seemed no other thing to do. Her eyes were filled with challenge, and as I tried to straighten the damaged paper I knew that she was watching me. I also knew, instantly, that I wanted something more of her, that there was chemistry between us.

"Where do you go to law school?" I asked.

"Columbia."

"Did you have a good summer?"

She shrugged.

"Did you?"

Much later, after she had gone back to complete her studies and then returned to the firm, after months of clever patter between us as we discussed ordinary matters in a manner laced with pretense and ambiguity, we both agreed that something extraordinary, entirely physical, entirely unsaid, had passed between us that night. And when she returned suntanned after a month in Spain, her hair longer, as offbeat and jaunty as before, I was thrilled to see that she had been assigned an office near mine.

If I wanted an office romance in the year I was up for partner, there was not much more I needed to help me drift into one. Nobody would dispute that this would not have been a good idea.

• • •

To my dismay, as I enter the men's room I see Cabot, still in his green hat, standing at the urinal. His head is tilted back and he is staring up, perhaps examining the ceiling tiles.

"Had time for any fishing lately?" he asks when he notices me.

"Not really," I say. "How about yourself?"

"Caught a marlin off Key West early in the summer," he says. "I've told you about that, haven't I?"

"Twice," I answer, and we both laugh.

Among fishermen, apparently, it is acceptable to be vaguely disrespectful, even to a senior partner who is urinating, on the subject of boring others with fishing stories.

"It's a good story, though," I add quickly, just to be safe. "And you never brought in the photographs you said you had."

"Got to remember to do that," he says as he zips his fly.

I watch him walk to the washstand and begin the process of brushing his teeth. I look away. This is something I don't need to see.

...

One has to wonder whether anyone would ever set out to name a business, let alone a law firm, Nibble & Kuhn. The people who run the place seem to think nothing of it, to accept the cartoon name as quaint and historic, even *valuable*. And if Alfred Nibble and Lionel Kuhn once practiced law together, and a hundred and ten years later the firm they founded still exists, who will take issue with the continued use of their names? It would be childish to giggle. The name in context is no more remarkable than that of the Smuckers' whose jelly is a staple, or that of the Philadelphia Mayflower family who rejoice in the name of Biddle.

Nibble & Kuhn may seem at first glance to be just another old law firm, indistinct except for the oddness of its name, mired in tradition, as seamless and hidebound as an institution can possibly be. To outsiders such an impression would be almost compelled. But it is not an accurate picture and does not do justice to the firm.

Take Harry Cabot, for instance, he with the green fishing hat and loping, distracted walk. I interviewed with him when I first applied for a job here, back before I knew anything about him. What I remember most vividly about the interview is not Cabot himself but the mounted fish on his wall, a great, macabre, painted thing of astonishing ugliness.

"Did you catch that?" I remember asking, pausing to read the little brass plate below.

"I certainly did," he replied proudly. "Off Marblehead. Mounted it myself, too."

"It's quite a specimen," I said, craning my neck to examine the fish, my expression, I hoped, adequately admiring. "It must have put up quite a fight."

"You can say that again," Cabot said. "She fought like the dickens. Almost knocked me off my hoo hoo. But boy, when I hauled her in, how sweet it was."

I could guess from the context where Cabot's "hoo hoo" was, but I learned afterwards that Cabot substituted "hoo hoo" for any word that was distasteful to him. To "step on your hoo hoo" meant to ask a stupid question and to be surprised by the answer. To "hand someone a bunch of hoo hoo" meant to talk nonsense, and so on. One way or another his use of the word was Harry Cabot's notion of swearing, and it seemed as well to encapsulate his view of life; the world as a great big benign place and he, Harry Cabot, treating everyone with the same kind of genial detachment, simply along for the ride. Not surprisingly his clients were fiercely loyal to him.

"Do you get to fish often?" I asked politely.

"Every chance I get," he answered.

On the credenza behind him I saw a plastic box filled with feathery flies and two photographs in silver frames, one of a powerboat and the other of Cabot, a strikingly plain middle aged woman, and several teenage children. Attached to his office window with plastic suction cups was a plaque which read: "Boat: *(n)* A hole in the water surrounded by wood into which you pour money."

"I'd love to fish again," I said, to my lasting regret. "I haven't had the opportunity in a long time."

It is this lie that seven years later continues to follow me. I had never been fishing in my life. I was only trying to make conversation, to find common ground with Harry Cabot.

"You fish?" Cabot had exclaimed. "Not many of the young fellers here do, to say nothing of the ladies."

"My father used to take us every Sunday," I think I said, or something like that, thus beginning the complex story I would have to continue. "My favorite book in high school," I added, trying now for a measure of authenticity and a literary credit at the same time, "was *Islands in the Stream.*"

"I haven't heard of that one," Cabot said. "I like that you fish, though. In my book it shows qualities of perseverance and patience. We can always use those around here."

When the interview was over I was left with the odd feeling that it had been too easy. It even crossed my mind that Cabot had actually disqualified me early on for some reason and was merely passing the time on irrelevancies until my half hour was up. How else could one explain the banal tone of our discussion? But before long a letter arrived offering me a summer position and I accepted the offer without hesitation. Nibble is, Nibble was, one of Boston's leading firms. And when they offered me a permanent job at the end of the summer, I accepted that too.

"Done any fishing lately?" Cabot has asked me at least once a week in the years that have followed.

I always make up something, pray that no one is listening.

"What was all that about?" Stanley Lioce asked once when he overheard us.

Stanley and I shared an office as summer clerks. For whatever reason we do not see each other away from work, but he is one of the most genuine people I know. Stanley's father hangs wallpaper in the Bronx. Mine owns a small cheese shop in Toronto. Perhaps we share something deeper than either of us knows, here among the Brahmins.

"Oh what a tangled web," he said dryly when I told him.

The irony is that of all the senior lawyers in the firm, I do believe Harry Cabot is the most decent. He heads the firm's Business Law Department and runs things in a manner that leaves no room for complaint. I would have been glad to work for him forever had business law not been quite so dull. I decided early on, you see, that my life was going to be in the courtroom. I did not know then that for firms like Nibble, courtrooms are mythic and abstract places. Nibble lawyers do not try cases. Nibble lawyers threaten to try cases, and then they settle.

Who knew?

•••

I reach my office and Kay, my secretary, comes in after me. She is a woman in her sixties who wears a little pillbox hat every day, something like the pink one Jackie was wearing the day JFK was shot. I also seem to remember that Kay used to wear white cotton gloves to work, but Stanley insists this is a figment of my imagination.

"She'd have to be mental to wear white gloves to work in this day and age," he says. "You're casting her in some quaint little movie you once saw."

"I'm telling you I remember it," I say, though in the face of his resolute ridicule I do think there is some chance, perhaps, that the white gloves are an overlay all my own.

"May I speak with you, Mr. Dover?" she asks.

I have asked her several times to call me Derek. She has said she prefers not to.

"Of course," I say.

"It's about the move," she says.

"Yes."

"Mrs. Buckles insists that only the moving company can pack your office because it has to be done in a certain way, but I'm most reluctant to have a stranger rifling through your belongings."

"I don't have anything personal here," I say, opening a drawer to demonstrate the point. "A few paper clips. Some empty notebooks."

"It's the principle of it," she insists. "I never permit anyone to go through your drawers."

"Please, Kay," I say. "Don't make an issue of this."

"Well if it doesn't bother you, I don't see why I should take the trouble," she says and walks out.

• • •

The firm had tripled in size since I'd arrived and by all accounts the partners were making loads of money, but there was nothing about the offices themselves that suggested it. Instead, Nibble's chipped wooden panels, mismatched college chairs, framed photographs of tall ships parading through Boston Harbor, suggested an old confidence, a stolid view of the future, a disregard of money, even, that seemed to be a part of the firm's character. Perhaps it was inevitable that it not last. Nothing lasts forever. But in Nibble's case change came very abruptly indeed.

We underestimated Mrs. Buckles, when she first arrived, the associates did. We all assumed that she was just another in a series of office managers the firm seemed to dabble in from time to time. They'd arrive filled with high ideals and complex plans but the firm's inertia kicked in each time leaving everyone free to continue doing things pretty much as they always had. Eventually, buried somewhere in a notice, we'd learn that the new manager had left "to pursue other opportunities" and the subdued tone of it always suggested just a tinge of ignominy. A hundred and ten years of doing things a certain way creates all sorts of habits that are hard to break.

This time it was different. For one thing it was obvious that Mrs. Buckles had far more authority than the hapless procession that had preceded her. Not only did she call Tony Olwine, the firm's gruesome managing partner, "Tony," forcefully and without a hint of self consciousness, but instead of being stuck off in a corner with the accounting types and the title examiners she had her own partner-sized office right next door to Olwine's, even her own secretary.

"A secretary with a secretary?" Lioce mused when he heard it. "Do the lawyers get lawyers?"

To be fair, perhaps the firm's old ways were a touch archaic, but almost overnight it was as if a team of strangers had landed on us with the single-minded mission of jettisoning all traces of the past. At one time the firm's only visible bureaucrat was a dear old thing who was rumored to have known the original Mr. Nibble. Stuck in a cubicle that always smelled somehow of powder, she handled everything from petty cash to Blue Cross forms, and even if she couldn't answer the simplest question, or more accurately could, but not correctly, there was something endearing about her. And then, without notice, she was gone, replaced by a swarm of "staffers" each of whom, or so it seemed, was tasked with a small corner of what the old dear had once mishandled. There was no being stuck in a cubicle for this lot either. They were everywhere, usually following Mrs. Buckles about like a line of ducklings.

That we would be moving as well began as a rumor, but eventually it was confirmed and once it was not a day passed without a memorandum or two from someone on Mrs. Buckles's staff revealing some innovation or other that would greet us in our new offices. It was as if these people, whom we'd never seen until three months before, had actually invented *us*, as if without them we had scarcely existed. I suppose change is always hard, but there was something particularly unsettling about how eagerly the firm's management seemed to embrace it. Rumor had it—there was always an associate who had been in a partner's office and overheard something, or a confidential memorandum lying indiscreetly somewhere—that the offices into which we were moving were very lavish indeed. One couldn't help but be apprehensive.

I was actually in Mrs. Buckles's office once. She wasn't there, but I was passing by and looked in. I saw a piece of calligraphy she has hanging on the wall behind her desk. It read:

None of us is smarter than all of us.

I must admit that I disagreed with every single syllable of that notion. I mean, hasn't Communism been discredited?

• • •

Maria had problems of her own with Mrs. Buckles and I suppose they were trivial, but it does seem to me that if you take a whole lot of trivial things together they can, in the end, add up to something that is less than, or more than, trivial.

"They changed my chair overnight," she said one morning, "because the old one doesn't meet some sort of fire code. But the new one doesn't fit under my desk. The arms are too high. If I don't sit right on the edge of it I can barely reach the keyboard."

It's not exactly death or famine, as I say, but if it irked her it irked her. She did, after all, sit in the darn thing all day.

"Are you perfectly sure you're not overreacting?" I said. "You do have to pick your battles in this world."

"Mrs. Buckles's minions insist that it's a regulation chair and a regulation desk. So I took one of them across the hall and showed them a chair that slid under a desk and she said she'd look into it. That was the last I heard."

"We could cut an inch off the legs," I said. "I'll bring a saw."

"You'd cut your hands off before you did any damage to the chair," she said.

I started to leave but this simple act was always difficult for me. The air in her office held me back. Sometimes I felt as if I was bending backwards as my legs carried me away.

"May I make a comment, Mr. Dover?" Kay had said.

"Of course."

"I don't think it seemly that the new associate, Maria, spends as much time in your office as she does. People will notice."

"It's perfectly innocent, Kay," I told her, trying to think of what I could say that might convey some reason for my strong interest in this new lawyer without conveying too much. "She's an interesting person, you know. She studied art history at Harvard and spends every summer in Spain."

"Be that as it may, Mr. Dover," Kay said, clearly not convinced. "I'm talking about appearances. This is not the year to ignore that aspect of things."

"Don't worry, Kay," I told her. "Nobody even notices."

"I've been around offices a long time," Kay insisted. "I wouldn't say that."

• • •

My phone rings. It is Tony Olwine, thin lipped, elegant, silver haired. It is a fairly firm rule of thumb among the associates that it is never good news to hear from Tony Olwine. He is too powerful, too acerbic, too critical, for an associate to emerge unscathed from just about any encounter with him. If he calls, it is because there is a typographical error in a letter to one of his clients, or something in a brief that he happens not to like.

"I would like to see you in my office," Olwine says.

He never identifies himself when he calls, simply assumes you recognize his voice. On the phone he sounds younger than he is, not at all menacing, if you disregard what he is saying, that is. The voice is always calm, boyish, very precise. I once heard John Updike on the radio. Olwine's a dead ringer.

"Now?" I ask.

"Unless you have something more pressing," he responds.

This is classic Olwine. His answer contemplates that there might be something more pressing than answering his summons, but that this is inconceivable.

"I'll be right up," I say as a sense of foreboding engulfs me.

"Where are you going?" Kay calls after me as I take my jacket off a hanger behind the door. "If you leave your office without telling me where you're going and someone calls for you, you make me look very foolish."

"Mr. Olwine," I say, and she leaves it at that.

Stan's office is next to mine and as I pass he calls me in.

"I heard that," he says. "What does he want?"

"Who knows?" I say.

As I turn to go I see in his face a trace of concern. It's impossible to ignore how close Stan and I are to the partnership decision. At this point, despite all the years of work, an ostensibly innocuous event could take one of us over the top, or just as easily sink us. I'm not in competition with Stan. I couldn't be. And yet, by definition, I am.

Who knows what Olwine wants from me. If I knew I'd tell Stan and put him out of his misery. But I don't know so I can't.

II

TONY OLWINE'S OFFICE, THOUGH THE LARGEST IN THE FIRM, IS QUITE ordinary in most respects. There are no mounted fish on the wall or fly-fishing paraphernalia, of course, though there is a large U.S. Navy flag in the corner for some reason. (Perhaps he was in the Navy at some point. It would be easy enough to look it up on the firm's website, but why bother?) He lives, so they say, in a large brownstone on Beacon Hill, sits on the boards of the Museum and the Perkins School, and I can't begin to picture him in wading boots or carrying a tackle box. On his coffee table stands a marble statue of seagulls in flight, and on the wall is a collection of photographs, several of his yacht, a quite inhospitable looking vessel from my perspective, and others of people one instantly recognizes. He appears to be on reasonable terms with Tom DeLay and Bob Dole, but who knows how such photographs come about.

I hope, as I climb the stairs, that his secretary will not be at her post outside his office. Matters between us have been unresolved for months. It is, without question, a situation I have brought upon myself. It predates, of course, Maria's return to the firm and Maria knows nothing about it.

"You did what?" Stan asked incredulously when I first confided in him.

"Close the door if you're going to yell."

"You slept with Olwine's secretary?" he said, his voice rising. "She's attractive enough if you like the type, but that you actually did this in the year we're up for partnership is staggering. You're a *kamikaze* man. The only problem is that you didn't die."

I didn't reply. Everything is explicable, I suppose, if you see it in context. It's just that after the fact the context is sometimes a little difficult to see.

"Was it worth it?" he asked. "Were they memories you will cherish as you stand behind your hot dog wagon counting change?"

"I didn't sleep with her," I said. "She invited me to an aerobics class she teaches and then we went to her apartment. We made out but items of clothing remained in place. She kept saying that she didn't expect anything from me."

"You're the bravest man I know," he said, coming around his desk and trying to shake my hand. "But assume for a moment this girl decides that she does expect something from you."

"Don't call her *this girl*," I said. "You know her name. It's Cindy."

"Assume for a moment," he said, overriding my interruption, "that *Cindy* is under the illusion, I'm sure not encouraged by anything you said, that you are open to having a serious relationship with her."

I started to say something but he kept talking.

"Please," he said. "My question is, what happens *vis a vis* Anthony Olwine if there are hard feelings on Miss Hardbody's part when you fail to follow up?"

I said nothing.

"That is," he added, "provided she doesn't come to her senses first when she realizes that you are nothing more than an overweight, oversexed, balding lecher."

"I'm not overweight and I'm not balding," I said and left the room.

• • •

As I make my way down the corridor toward Olwine's office I see that she is at her desk, facing her computer screen, her back straight, her hair in a pony tail. As I approach and see her delicate profile and smooth forehead, her perfect nose, her shining lips moving as she reads off her screen, I remember with great clarity what it was that made me so reckless. One of her legs is hidden under her desk, the other is folded beneath her. Beside her chair in a neat row are sneakers and a pair of blue shoes.

She looks up and sees me, and then she smiles and I realize with relief that she appears to harbor no resentment. These things can be touch and go.

"This is a nice surprise," she says. "How are you?"

"Fine," I say. "You look good."

The neighboring secretaries are watching us and I ask: "Is Mr. Olwine in?"

"They're expecting you," she replies, and as she turns back to her screen she adds, "I like your suit."

"They?" I say.

"Margaret Kelly's with him," she says off-handedly.

"What now?" I mutter as I knock on the door.

• • •

Tony Olwine is sitting in a red armchair, his half-glasses on the end of his nose, his legs crossed, a pile of papers in his lap. Margaret Kelly is on a couch by the window. As I enter the office he looks up and gestures to me to sit. Margaret asks how I am and I say I'm fine and somehow, in Olwine's office, even this amount of small talk seems inappropriate and excessive.

Notwithstanding her avalanche of idiosyncrasies I don't mind

Margaret Kelly. I wouldn't want to spend a whole lot of time with her, but deep down you can see that she's a decent sort. She is in her mid-forties, unmarried, a partner in the Litigation Department, and though everyone knows that she's disorganized, frenetic and ill-tempered, whatever people say she doesn't have fangs.

Margaret came to the firm at about the same time I did. I came straight from law school while she had worked for the government for years and so she's ahead of me in the firm's arcane hierarchy. She is also a regular on continuing legal education panels as if she has some great wisdom about trying cases to impart, and what makes this sort of funny is that she has never tried a case in front of a jury. That isn't so unusual, as I've said. There is more than one trial lawyer at Nibble & Kuhn who has never in his life, except perhaps in front of a mirror or in some lame training exercise, uttered the words: "Ladies and gentlemen of the jury."

Something else about Margaret Kelly, something almost comical, is that while she professes to be both inflexibly liberal and a feminist, she is so rough on secretaries that no secretary who knows anything will work for her. In fact, refusing to do so isn't even considered insubordination, as far as I know. The secretarial station outside her office is therefore perennially vacant, or, if occupied, filled with one of the elderly floaters who move from station to station with neither the skills nor the direction to take a permanent assignment. The closest the firm ever came to finding her a permanent secretary was when someone had the bright idea to assign her a gay black man, needless to say the only male secretary in the firm, one of the very few black ones, and the only openly gay person in the place. Somehow Margaret found it harder, with him, to stand snorting at his station and to yell reprimands from her office. He'd stayed for only six months anyway, though he did make a point of saying that his departure was not related to anything she'd done. You'd have to walk quite far to find someone who believed it.

Judging by the solicitations she is constantly sending around the office she is active in a whole range of charities that have very little in common; a battered women's shelter, for instance, and a fund for migrant farm workers, of which there are probably four in all of Massachusetts. I am about to learn that there has been method in her madness.

• • •

Margaret leans into the couch, swings an arm over its back, and waits for Olwine to finish whatever it is he is doing. She has a strange smile on her face, something that should tip me off. One doesn't look quite so comfortable, throw one's arm over the back of a sofa, in Tony Olwine's office.

Finally Olwine turns his attention to me.

"We will shortly be announcing to the firm," he says, omitting any extraneous greetings, "that the Governor has nominated Margaret to be a justice of the Massachusetts Superior Court. In preparation for that, I have been going through her caseload in order to assign to other lawyers responsibility for her cases."

"What great news," I say. "Congratulations."

"Thank you," Margaret says, and turns back to Olwine who has paused as if frozen while my congratulatory diversion runs its course.

Clever Margaret, I think. All the supposed good works, the fundraising for orphans, the late nights lecturing, the apparently thankless public spiritedness, wasn't entirely random after all. Margaret was after something and she has attained it, has succeeded in meeting whatever test it is that the political operatives who make judicial appointments value. I wouldn't have thought she had it in her, that the instincts that make her what she is would have done her in long before she grasped that brass ring. Apparently not. Now she is in line for a lifetime sinecure on the bench, and while it isn't a job I would want, one can see why she would. There's no money in it but there is job security, and to some people—I'm almost certain to Margaret Kelly—having a stream of lawyers oozing deference and a little band of court officers looking after one's whims has merit.

One would have to be a lawyer at Nibble & Kuhn to understand why this news would cause someone like me to raise the edges of his ears. What matters at the firm really isn't how good a lawyer you are, though I suppose it does count for something, nor how hard you work. Rather, the determinant of success at Nibble—which means as it does everywhere, money and power—is whether you have your own clients. The more juniors you have droning away for your clients, the more clout you have at compensation time. It's called, in the Nibble idiom, killing more than you eat. There's no huge leap required, and it's hardly a secret, to conclude that there's fierce competition among partners for clients. People have done horrible things to secure prospects in the face of competition from their supposed colleagues. So when Olwine suggests that Margaret Kelly is jumping ship one has to wonder right away what is going to become of her clients, what few of them there are. I'd like to think that my interest has less to do with greed than with wanting a chit in my column when the firm gets around to deciding whether or not I am going to be voted in as a partner, but one never can be quite sure about one's motivation in matters such as this.

I should have defined "client." A client is a business, preferably a large and busy one with lots of problems—enough need of lawyers, in short—to ensure that a steady stream of revenue flows into the coffers of the deal and peacemakers at Nibble & Kuhn. A client is not a group of bereaved families on whose behalf one may collect a one time fee, if, and only if, one wins a lawsuit. There are no legs in that, not at a firm like Nibble & Kuhn. In fact, until very recently the firm didn't even take contingency cases for injured plaintiffs, though they do seem to be doing it more frequently now.

As it turns out, I already know more than I ever wanted to know about the "client" Olwine has in mind for me. Margaret Kelly is one of those dreaded lawyers who insist on discussing their cases with others, which is one of the reasons to stay away from firm functions, or if you must attend a firm function for some reason to stay away from Margaret Kelly. The better element, the people I spend time with at work, never so much as mention law when they don't have to. Lawsuits, despite what one might see on television, aren't that interesting. Mostly it's people fighting about money and this is not riveting stuff, not at least unless you find the Rule against Perpetuities or the FDA's latex glove regulations good reading.

Margaret has already told me about the seven little boys who have come down with cancer. It's her position that some sort of substance leaked from a nearby factory, the owner of which she has sued, and polluted the groundwater and swimming hole near their homes. She insists that there's proof of this, that she has spoken with chemists and toxicologists and who knows who else, and that they support her theories. My view has always been, as I say: I don't care. It's not my case. My cases also aren't that contentious, by and large. It's not that I'm a particularly peaceable person, but as I've said more than once to my opponents, I don't get paid extra to take things personally. Generally speaking, most of the lawyers I work with on the other side are professional enough to realize this as well, though there are always exceptions.

By all accounts, Margaret's case is a war zone, like a day in Baghdad, and no one assumes that the contentiousness is all the other lawyer's fault. It's not at all difficult to see how a lawsuit with Margaret Kelly could become unpleasant and the lawyer for the factory, which is owned by Morganic Continental, has by all accounts risen to the occasion, or so the snippets of her stories I have overheard from time to time suggest. I have not given a moment's thought to the possibility that one day I would have to decipher the complexities Margaret has tried more than once to explain so poorly and at such horrible length. A few years ago they made a movie about a case more or less like Margaret's called *A Civil Action*. I didn't see the movie but every lawyer in Boston knows something about the case. It didn't end happily for anyone, as I recall. Now, apparently, it's my turn to wade into the thankless sinkhole of a case with no assurance the outcome will be any better.

Didn't anybody think about this when they took the thing on, I want to ask. Of course I don't. I'm disgruntled, not suicidal.

• • •

"I am given to understand," Olwine says, "that a trial date is imminent."

He pauses and stares at me over his glasses.

"If there is any reason why you cannot give this matter your undivided attention over the next several months, speak now because I will hear no excuses later."

"I'm sure I'll find whatever time is needed," I say.

What else can I say? The matter is clearly already decided. Olwine has the monthly run-offs and knows exactly how much time I do and don't have. My billable hours are adequate, but not spectacular. I can fit almost anything in provided I don't quibble about an evening here and a weekend there. And with the partnership vote a few months off, I'm not about to.

Olwine stands and walks to the window. I may be wrong about this, but it seems to me that there is something unusually menacing in his mood, something that causes even Margaret Kelly, Nibble partner *emerita*, to shift uncomfortably on the couch.

"I suggest," he says, "that you spend the rest of the day doing what you can to reschedule or delegate your other matters. In the morning, once you have reviewed the entire file, I would like to know what you believe remains to be done, and a time-table on which you intend to see that it is."

I look across at Margaret Kelly. She is quietly and indiscernibly, but nevertheless palpably, breathing a sigh of relief. As I look at her I remember something that happened not long after we both came to the firm, perhaps seven or eight years ago. I had come into the office late on a Sunday night to get something, perhaps to make a Xerox copy or to retrieve my running shoes, I can't remember which, when I saw a light in a conference room at the end of the corridor. I remember walking down to see who was there and finding Margaret Kelly alone at the head of a table piled high with papers, eating a large piece of very gummy chocolate cake with a plastic fork. I looked up at the clock on the wall and it was ten o'clock. She had her lenses out and was wearing Coke bottle thick glasses, and then for some reason she began telling me a long story about trying to find a home for an aunt who had Parkinson's when all I wanted to do was to get my sneakers and leave. Somehow I surrendered to her story and ended up sitting down and trying to cheer her up.

Margaret Kelly is leaving to become, God help us, God help the poor people of Massachusetts, a judge. The only real beneficiaries of this, other than Margaret of course who may now function for a lifetime free of the normal constraints of social intercourse, ("Yes, your Honor. No, Your Honor. How very insightful you are, Your Honor") are the lawyers at Nibble & Kuhn. Conflict of interest rules require that we never appear before her in court.

"One final thing," Olwine says. "Mrs. Buckles has informed me that her staff now occupy, and will continue to occupy until the move from this building, the two largest conference rooms for move-related activities. My understanding is that there is a great deal of paper that has already been generated by this case, and this should be accumulated in one location. I understand from Mrs. Buckles that this cannot be accomplished in this building."

"Mrs. Buckles can't find space in the office for one of the firm's most complicated cases?" I ask.

Olwine looks at me blankly, even coldly, and then continues without acknowledging that I have spoken.

"She does tell me, however, that although the move of the entire firm into our new space at Triumph Plaza isn't contemplated for another month, the floor on which this department will be located is essentially completed. You and your secretary will, therefore, be moving next week."

"Will there be telephones and copy machines and the rest of it over there?" I ask.

"I have every confidence in Mrs. Buckles," Olwine answers, and begins to read something on his desk.

Mastering the intricacies of other people's lives, other people's businesses, is what I do for a living, after all, but suddenly in the back of my head I can hear the sounds of paper, can picture myself surrounded by boxes of documents and millions of words about people and events to which I feel no connection and which I now own in their entirety.

I don't want to be too dramatic, but the thing of one's life flashing before one's eyes does happen, I discover.

• • •

Cindy is still at her desk.

"So you're on the great Morganic team," she says as I pass her.

"I'm afraid so," I say.

"Say goodbye to your free time," she says. "I just arranged to have the files brought to your office. They told me there were forty boxes of them."

"Thank you," I say. "I have until tomorrow to read them."

"You can do it," she says. "You'd work quicker if you were in shape. Are you still doing aerobics?"

"No," I say.

"You should," she says. "I had a sense you'd be good at it."

I laugh, as do the secretaries on either side of her, and then I get the feeling that I am being mocked. It occurs to me that they know everything, they and perhaps others too, and that what I have rather blindly assumed is our secret is no secret at all.

• • •

It's my lucky day, a Trifecta of good luck. First Olwine, then Cindy, and now I run into Mrs. Buckles in the stairwell.

"Oh, Mr. Dover," she says, and I suspect that this is not a random matter, our paths crossing. Is it possible that she runs the whole firm from a bank of hidden video screens in a secret office somewhere? I hate the way she cuts her hair, like a poodle, fluffy on top and shorn at the back.

"I was just coming to talk to you," she says. "Mr. Olwine has asked me to arrange your early move to Triumph Plaza. I assume I will have your secretary's cooperation in this."

"Miss Parsons is always cooperative," I say. "I would hope you could accommodate her by the same token. In fact, you may find her suggestions useful. Her input," I add, choosing a Bucklesian word.

"Mr. Dover," Mrs. Buckles replies, too loudly for the small stairwell. "We have been planning this move for months. It is a carefully orchestrated campaign designed to ensure that on a Friday the lawyers will leave this building for the weekend, and on the following Monday they will return to work in their offices at Triumph Plaza with each office as completely furnished and arranged as it was here. Everyone must cooperate for it to work."

One of Mrs. Buckles's retinue's tasks has been to put little numbered stickers on things, on everything, vases, chairs, desks, even staplers and Dictaphones, and then to list the stick-ered items on their clipboards. The notion of their putting stick-ers on my potted plant and behind the framed photograph of my parents on my bookshelf had struck me as funny in its perfect pointlessness. Perhaps it was a mistake to express the sentiment quite as boldly as I had.

"My secretary and I always do cooperate," I say, but my heart isn't in it.

For the second time in five minutes, I find myself staring into a blank face, as if I have just said something ridiculous to a Martian.

• • •

The afternoon has shot by. It is almost five. Kay is not at her desk and my guess is that she is in the break room giving her tea cup its final wash of the day and wiping off the counter, a task to which she has appointed herself. ("Keep this room tidy!!! It's yours too," she has posted above the sink.) I walk into my office, drop the folders Olwine has given me on the floor, and am almost immediately aware that someone is crouching under my desk.

A head appears, and it is Maria.

"What are you doing?" I ask.

"Promise you won't laugh," she says, a sheepish look on her face.

She stands up and I see that she is holding a tape measure.

"I don't promise anything," I say, but the truth is that I am so happy to see her I can barely restrain myself. I want more than anything else to take her in my arms and squeeze her until she yells.

"I don't even want to guess," I say instead.

"I'm measuring your chair," she says

I pause for a moment and then begin to laugh.

"It's no laughing matter," she says.

"How will measuring my chair advance your position?" I ask.

"It's because of the Buckles," Maria says. "She now says that everyone's chairs are the same height. But you see, yours slides under the desk and mine doesn't. There's an important principle involved now."

"What principle?" I ask.

"The principle of having to prove her wrong," she says. "But do you know what the odd thing is? Your chair and your desk are exactly the same measurements as mine, but your chair slides zippy fast right in underneath, and mine doesn't."

"Give me the tape measure," I say, and hang my coat behind the door.

As I crouch on the floor behind the desk and begin to measure, Kay walks into the office. She pauses for only a moment.

"Good evening, Mr. Dover," she says. "Miss Parma. I'll be in at the usual time."

III

Now the atmosphere, and our spirits, are quite changed. We sit in my car parked three blocks from Maria's parents' house in Wellesley, the lights off, in silence. When I offer to drive her home despite the knowledge that I will probably have to work all night to meet Olwine's deadline, we are still laughing, at Kay's strange show of discretion, at the absurdity of our quest, at the absurdity of other things too.

"If Mr. Dover chooses to sit under his desk," Maria says, trying to mimic Kay's soft, measured speech, "I have no doubt he has the most solid reasons for doing so."

"Not likely," I respond. "I imagine her clucking with severe disapproval as she discusses my indiscretions."

"That just shows how little you know," she says. "Kay would stab herself with her nail file for you. Everyone knows that."

We are parked near a driveway. A woman comes out of a nearby house, enters a car, drives away.

"That's Helen," Maria says. "She used to babysit me."

"So?"

"So nothing. She'll tell my parents if she remembers to."

We are silent. A car drives by, its lights flashing across the seats, and then it is dark again.

29

"At twenty seven," I say, "it shouldn't make much difference to you what your babysitter or anyone else for that matter tells your parents."

"Well that's the way it is," she says sharply. "I've never hidden the way my family is. They're unusual, not American, old-fashioned, however you want to describe it. You just choose not to believe me."

The streak of sadness that runs through this affair between us returns heavily. Even after all that has passed I have yet to meet her parents. So here we are again, parked a discreet distance from the driveway, sitting in the car, in the dark. Somewhere in the house, which is just partly visible through the trees, her mother is cooking dinner. Her father and sister Emma are there too, people about whom I have now heard a fair deal, who have even entered my dreams, but whose faces I have never seen. She has shown me a picture of Emma, but it is old, taken somewhere by the sea in Spain when they were girls, and Emma remains faceless.

It has not always seemed so hopeless, but now it does again, and especially so.

"If I could, I would drop you like a brick," I say as she sits silently beside me stroking my hand. "But I can't. And so we're stuck."

The thing about this sadness is that it always somehow goes away. I know how we will part—with caring and tenderness—and that I will look forward to the morning and to seeing her walk past my office. She will stop and greet Kay and then come in to talk with me. There will be two conversations, of course, the loud one for Kay's benefit, the *sotto voce,* in the manner that has now become almost second-nature to us, a tantalizing contrast. For months we have made plans, discussed colleagues, talked about our families, all in two-track conversations with enough said about work or on topics that do not betray our intimacy, to keep the suspicion of those who overhear us at bay. It is distracting and at times irritating, but it is also a spice of our romance.

Even this, the chance to sit alone with her in the dark, to talk of love, to acknowledge what is sad about it all, is recent. It took a long time for the first crack in the ice to be made, the act that we were just colleagues, maybe friends, to come to an end. And until the crack was made it was even worse, each interaction a complex waltz between business, friendship, and feelings each of us seemed forbidden to express.

Let me step back a moment. It will be clear.

• • •

After Maria finished law school and passed the Bar Exam she went to Spain. She'd said there were all sorts of family traditions associated with her summers and I didn't think much of it at the time, but whatever the explanation she was the last in her class to begin work. When she arrived back at Nibble in September she came to find me, apparently before she'd even been assigned an office or gone through the usual rounds of orientation and introduction.

"They made me an offer," she said gleefully.

"That would explain why you're here," I said. "Apparently they liked you."

"I liked them too," she said. "I couldn't believe I was looking forward to starting work."

"We'll cure you of that."

"They already started," she said. "Do you know how many forms you have to fill out? And all the personal questions they ask. I lied like a rug."

"What personal questions?" I asked.

"They're personal," she said.

"In any event, for someone who couldn't wait to start, you did take your time getting here," I pointed out.

"I said I was looking forward to it," she said. "You can do that on vacation without doing anything about it."

I asked her to have lunch with me, and then again, and then she asked me. In October I told her I had an extra ticket to the Harvard-Yale game (which I had bought, of course, because I planned to invite her), but she said that a cousin was getting married and the family was going out of town. In November, I told her I had tickets to a concert at Symphony Hall, and she said she had promised her father she would go with him to some event he had to attend.

"Does your family book every free hour you have?" I asked.

"We do a lot of stuff together," she said. "That's just the way we are."

"I'll tell you what I'm going to do," I said. "I'm going to ask you out one more time. It may be this week or it may be the next. It may be in the day or it may not. And when it comes, if you say no, that'll be three strikes and then you'll be out and I won't ask you again."

She had looked unhappy and troubled, but she had not argued.

"All right," she said. "If you've got to do it that way, we'll see. Everyone's gotta do what they gotta do."

• • •

"She works for me," I said to Lioce over lunch. "For all I know, I may be sealing my fate in a sexual harassment suit."

"From what I've seen you're nowhere close to it," he replied. "The girl has practically chosen to live in your office. They should switch her entry in the office directory."

"Yes, but there's something European about her," I said. "I may not know the rules of this game, whatever it is, and get caught offsides. She's sort of noncommittal when I get really personal with her and casually moves off the subject of romance no matter how lightly I touch on it."

"She's sucking you in, that's all," he said. "If you're determined to proceed on this course of intra-office immolation, you might as well stop torturing both yourself and her."

"That's a bit hard-headed of you, isn't it?" I said. "Are you jealous of my romances?"

"It just seems from your exploits," Lioce said, "first with Olwine's little nymphet and now with Ms. Parma, that you are determined not to miss any opportunity to place in jeopardy your chances of partnership. That's all."

• • •

On a Sunday afternoon not long after that I came into the office to complete some work and, as had become my custom, I walked to my office the long way around the floor, past Maria's. I was thrilled to see that her light was on and that she was there. She was wearing black sweat pants and an oversized, cream-colored sweater with a design of musical notes on it.

"I'm stunned," I said, standing in her doorway. "Maria works on weekends."

"Not by choice," she said, riffling through her papers. "Sheinburg gave me an assignment on Friday afternoon and he expects an answer by Monday. Do you think that's fair?"

"You do know that David Sheinburg is one of the firm's three managing partners?" I said.

"I don't care who he is," she said. "His assignment makes no sense."

"You could go on strike," I suggested.

"Will you help me with it?" she asked. "That way you can do my work and I can go home, and then you can do your own work later."

"I'm not sure how anyone could pass up an offer like that," I said. "What *are* you doing anyway?"

I walked behind her desk and looked over her shoulder at the papers spread before her. I could smell her, a sweet, unscented, rich air, and breathed deeply, slowly, wished I could stand there all afternoon.

"The first thing you must do is organize these," I said finally. "It looks like you've shuffled them."

"Yes," she said, nodding. "That's exactly what I've done. Shuffled them."

She glared at me, laughing too, and pushed the papers across at me.

"So sort them, Copernicus," she said.

Maybe I am simply deluded but I welcomed the chance to stay there with her. As I sorted the papers into piles, put paper clips on the important ones and moved others out of the way, I was aware that she was watching me—more, seemed to be absorbed by me—that she was not listening to anything I was saying.

"You're not concentrating," I said, not critically but to draw her out, to force a declaration, any declaration.

To some extent I succeeded.

"I know," she said. "I'm just watching you work."

There was now a long silence between us, a measure of new shyness. I knew that I could make my statement now, come out and say something to breach the gap that still stretched between us, the bridge between friendship—a glowing, sparring, feeling of amity, even longing—and the love I felt and believed she returned. Instead I said, as I continued to go through the motions of sorting her papers, we were still in the office, after all: "Tonight I want to take you to dinner."

"I can't," she said at once. "I have to be home."

"It's my third invitation," I reminded her. "Call them. They won't miss you."

"You don't understand," she said again. "I can't."

I dropped the papers on the desk and walked from the room. The air about me seemed to singe my face as I moved. I was stunned by the rebuff, the inconsistency between what my senses told me was true and what kept happening. I returned to my office and sat at my desk, read and reread a reference book without comprehension, stared for a long time out the window.

I was not aware how long she had been standing in the door-way before I noticed her.

"What time are we going?" she asked.

• • •

The dinner was not a success. It was, instead, a skittish, uncomfortable exercise that left more unresolved when it was over than had been before. We walked to the North End and ate in a little restaurant in a basement, but throughout dinner she acted as if she were trapped, and while it had always felt as if we had too much to say to each other, now we had noth-ing. She fidgeted and wouldn't more than glance at me, jumped from one subject to another, moved her silverware around con-stantly, hardly ate.

"Why are you so nervous?" I kept asking.

"I just am," she said.

She had a way of disguising herself behind a childlike goofi-ness, a rolling of her eyes. It had been funny before, but now it was exasperating.

At nine o'clock she said she had to leave and I was not sorry. We had not laughed and, it seemed, for the first time had dif-ficulty finding things to talk about. It had been awkward, in short, even a mistake. Perhaps there was something odd about this, dating or trying to date a subordinate, however easy her manner.

She clearly was ambivalent now.

"Why are you in such a rush?" I asked as we hurried to my car.

"Got to get home."

"Maria, you're twenty-seven," I said. "Practically middle-aged. You behave as if both you and your family live in the nineteenth century. Are you secretly indentured or something?"

"I know how old I am," she said sharply. "And you're not the first person to say that bit about the nineteenth century either. My family is just different for a whole lot of reasons I can't go into, and anybody who is friends with me just has to accept it. One summer in Spain, when I was still in high school, my parents grounded me for a week because I danced too close to a boy at a fair. Now they go through the motions and I understand why they do, but in the end they let me be."

For a moment she paused.

"I don't *have* to go home," she said. "I *want* to go home. *Fini.*"

Even so, the next morning there she was in my office, holding her coffee mug, and it was almost as if she was separate enough from the Maria of the night before that I would have been comfortable telling her about it, as if we had both been on bad dates and could now laugh about it with an old friend. We made our whispered comments, we were lighthearted, we were once again, in the end, reluctant to separate.

Even when I asked if she'd had a problem with her parents when she got home the question was asked and answered without awkwardness, as if we had not ever had a bad moment, been relieved, perhaps for the first time, to go our separate ways.

• • •

For Christmas I bought her a goldfish and a bowl with plastic seaweed, and left it on her desk with a note about which I had thought for hours. "Progeny," I wrote, meaning, of course, what it means, that she and I somehow now had offspring, but also taking cover under its legal meaning, one ruling that flows from another.

We danced together at Nibble's Christmas party. Afterwards Lioce remarked that to all but the blind we had danced one dance too many and one inch too close.

"Anyone can see you've been sleeping together," he said.

"I've told you a dozen times we're not," I insisted.

"Tell that to the marines," Lioce replied, and acted as if he was offended by my lack of candor.

Dancing with her, touching her, moving with her, gave me my first moments of tranquility in many months.

• • •

For New Year's she bought me a bonsai tree and left it on my desk. We did not discuss our plans for New Year's Eve. I stayed home and watched videotapes until I fell asleep; Benny Hill, Monty Python, episodes of Star Trek. I do not know what she did and I did not ask her out again, but as time passed our looks became more unabashed, what was unspoken took clearer definition, and it was obvious that something was reaching an end and that something else must begin. Even as I took a paper from her she would hold it a touch too long, and when we worked together late, as we did from time to time, and ordered food from a deli or from the Chinese restaurant on the waterfront, she would sample from my plate and I from hers in a manner not fitting two colleagues. We agreed on everything we discussed, almost as if each could anticipate the other, and she made such profound sense to me that there were times when, listening to her, I would watch her almost in awe.

We were in love. Of course we were in love. Can there be any doubt? Talking to her was like coming home, like finding refuge or getting one's bearings. This is all, I suppose, the standard cant of a person in love. And yet when I mentioned love, or romance, even when veiled in stories of others, or of my past, she reacted as if she did not fully hear me.

• • •

I searched hard for a Valentine's Day card, looked at dozens before I found the one I gave her. There were no words on it, only a drawing of two people, a drab man in a business suit carrying a briefcase and walking toward the corner of a building, and a plain woman in a tweedy suit with a bun approaching the corner from another direction, neither yet aware of the other. I left it on her desk after everyone had gone on February 13, and then went home.

In the morning she did not stop in with her coffee cup, nor did I see her during the day. She seemed to have gone to ground in her office, and though I longed to see for myself what she would do next, I stayed away. It was a very long day.

After most people had gone, when it was already dark and the corridors were quiet, she came to my office, closed the door, and sank into a chair across the desk.

"We've got to talk," she said.

"I think so," I said. "It's time."

"Thanks for the card," she said, and made a face, clenched and unclenched her hands, ran her fingers through her hair.

"We've got to talk," I said. "I've fallen in love with you, and you know it."

She cringed, sank further into the chair, acknowledged what I had said by not reacting to me.

"But throughout this all," I added, "you've been so elusive it's hard to tell what you think and really want. So now I'm asking you directly, Maria. What do you feel? What do you want?"

There was a silence, one I was not prepared to break. Twice she looked up, raised her eyebrows, looked down again.

"It's going to snow tomorrow," she said.

"Maria."

"About four inches."

"Maria."

Now there were tears in her eyes.

"You're the boy of my dreams," she said at last. "And yet I can't have you."

For a moment I sat in silence, uncomprehending, and then I stood, turned my back to her, looked out the window and over the darkened city. My heart was sinking and I did not understand at all.

"Why can't you have me?" I asked. "What is this great mystery of Maria's elusiveness?"

"I thought this would end some other way and I wouldn't ever be in this position," she said after a while. "I thought we were just flirting and would get tired of it."

"You thought we would get tired of it?" I repeated in amazement. "How could you ever have thought that?"

"I just did," she said.

We were both silent again.

"And?" I said when she gave no sign of continuing.

"I wish you hadn't given me that stupid card," she said abruptly. "I have to tell you something and I thought I had more time to do it. Now I don't."

"Go on," I said. "You have a terminal illness. You're a lesbian. You're married. What could there possibly be?"

"I'm not married," she said at last. "But I'm supposed to be getting married to Alfonso when he comes back from Spain."

"Alfonso?" I exclaimed. "You tell me now, after all this time, that you're engaged to someone called *Alfonso*. That all these supposed family commitments were a charade on account of some character called *Alfonso*?"

"I'm not engaged, they weren't a charade, and he's not some character," Maria said defiantly, sitting up straight. "I've known him since we were children."

"So where is Fonzie tonight?" I asked.

"Alfonso," she corrected. "And don't do that. He's studying architecture in Barcelona."

"Break up with him," I said.

I knew as I spoke that I was up against something new in her, something more inflexible than I could have imagined just a few minutes before.

She did not reply.

"How long have you and Fonzie been planning this?" I asked at last.

"Alfonso," she corrected. "There's nothing specific. Everyone in my family and everyone in his just knows it's supposed to happen. We even had a feast day last summer in Spain. It's supposed to be some sort of precursor."

"Precursor to what?" I demanded.

For a moment she said nothing.

"I don't have to spell it out," she said at last. "I feel bad enough that we're having this conversation at all. There is so much involved that I don't even know where to start."

"Let me get this straight then," I said. "First they have this feast for you and Fonzie. I'm sure they carried you about on a table and threw olives at you and I hope they stung. And then you come straight back to Boston and spend the next six months flirting your head off and you don't see fit to say a word about the fact that you're precursed. Am I right so far?"

She examined the hem of her skirt and then looked up and saw that I was smiling.

"You think you're very funny," she said. "They don't throw olives. We're Spaniards, not imbeciles."

"What am I supposed to do?" I asked. "You know as well as I do that you hid stuff from me. I can even guess why. My problem is that I don't like you any the less for it."

"And I like you," she said simply.

"Do you want to marry him?" I asked, my voice suddenly quite cold.

"Of course I do," she said, though without enthusiasm. "It's inevitable."

She looked up shyly, saw the hard expression on my face. "Your card wasn't stupid," she said at last.

• • •

Even if I had known what lay ahead I do not know that I would have done anything differently. At first, that night, it had seemed inconceivable that Alfonso, holed away in some moldy medieval university, could keep her in the face of my onslaught, that feelings as strong as ours would not simply sweep him aside. It happened all the time, didn't it, in books if nowhere else? But I did not know, sitting across the desk from her, the rest of the building wholly still, that what lay ahead instead were months of ambiguity and heartache I never dreamed I could endure. Even as she tore at me in private, kissed me with an unrestrained passion in elevators and in the shadows of doorways, she remained steadfast in her loyalty to Alfonso, would not even be with me on the same block as her house in case her parents should see us.

"What are you afraid of?" I asked. "You'll introduce me, I'll shake their hands, and that'll be that."

"They know me," she said. "I wouldn't be skulking about with you if something wasn't going on."

"Something isn't going on."

"They know me," she insisted.

"I was wrong about something," I said. "It's not them. It's you. You're turning them into proxies for your conscience."

"My mother told me that even if I didn't marry Alfonso he'd always be a son to them," she said. "Our families go way back, way, way back. And in any event, who anointed you psychotherapist in residence?"

"So let him be a son," I answered. "Fonzie can chip in with the chores."

"*Alfonso*," she said.

• • •

At Easter she went to visit him in Barcelona, only for five days though it did seem much longer. I took her to the airport—call me a sap if you will; some things are beyond one's self control—and she stepped from my car, took her case from the trunk, kissed me passionately goodbye, and then flew across the ocean to be with Alfonso, unsuspecting, comforting, familiar Alfonso, as I drove off back to the office, angry with myself, wholly impotent.

I would have been distant and restrained with her when she returned had it not happened that the night before her departure from Spain an identical flight, a Boeing from Madrid that had the same flight number and left at the same time, crashed and all aboard were killed. It was on both our minds as I stood at the gate waiting for her, as she rushed through the doors toward me, as we clung to each other there in the arrivals hall.

If I was restrained with her in the days after her return, it was she who was effusive, insistent, not permitting any chance that I might slip away.

• • •

And so we sit in the shadows again, the streak of sadness back, Maria's formless and alien family going about their lives in their rambling house behind the trees, unaware of my existence. I know that she is reluctant to get out of the car and to walk the couple of blocks home, have already now watched her trudge slowly away on more nights than I care to remember. How different it is from the first night, that Valentine's Day, when I drove her home. Nothing has been resolved since then, but that night I drove home joyously and with an unbounded energy. I found her comb on the car seat and took it into my bedroom. It was plastic, but inhaling it I smelled her fragrance, the clean shine of her hair, the rich touch of her skin.

Months have passed and now these unsatisfying brushes with her have developed a routine of their own. Soon she will leave, I will watch her until she disappears, I will start the engine and drive back to town. Everything is empty, cold, lifeless, after I have watched her walk away into the shadows that cover her parents' house.

"I love you Derek," she whispers. "I have since the moment I first spoke to you. I love that you're crazy about your family, and so prickly and facetious on the outside. And that your father owns a cheese shop, and how you describe your parents, as if they were juvenile delinquents and you the one who goes off to school every morning with your sandwiches in your lunch box and your homework all done. And I love the way you treat me, how happy you look when you see me, how kind you are and how funny. You're the perfect boy."

"But not perfect enough," I say disconsolately, staring ahead, not willing for the moment to accept her or to release her from her anguish.

"This is torture for me, too," she says. "It can't go on but I can't stop it either. I keep thinking of this piazza in the center of my grandfather's village, where the cobblestones have been there so long they're almost smooth. When we were kids, every time it rained we used to run down there and wait at the edge of the fountain because no matter how hard they tried almost every grownup who came by would slip. We almost died laughing, me, my sister Emma, my cousins, Alfonso, Alfonso's brothers. We still go down there just to tell stories about it, and we still almost die laughing. Emma's probably going to marry Alfonso's brother, and when we got engaged the whole village came to the feast in my grandfather's chapel. I can't just push it all away. It's how I have understood my life for too long."

"Your grandfather has a chapel?" I say, but she doesn't respond.

We sit in silence, a car passes, its headlights flashing across her face. I run my finger around and around the emblem in the center of the steering wheel.

"I suppose I should be going in," she says. "They're waiting for me for supper."

"Sure," I say. "You wouldn't want to keep anyone waiting."

"Don't be like that," she says. "This is not my fault either. I didn't ask you to pursue me like you did, and now that you've hooked me I can't do anything more than tell you the truth. When you drop me off like this I go inside and act like a zombie. My parents don't know what to make of it, but I'm doing what I have to do, and whatever you do, I'll respect that too. But I never asked for this, and I never welcomed it. It just happened."

•••

When she is gone, out of sight in the shadow of the giant oak and fir trees that line the road, I start the car and drive back to the city. What had once seemed a burden—having to go back to the office and work until all hours—becomes lighter. The alternative—going home, parking in the alley behind the building, going up in the elevator to my deathly quiet apartment—is too depressing to contemplate. I will walk into the kitchen, open the refrigerator, eat. The only sounds will be the clink of cutlery on my plate, the rustle of my book, the sounds of my feet on the carpet. It will be, again, unbearable, another of those nights I have lived through all too frequently; long, without focus, isolated.

Any other woman is unthinkable and so there is nothing for it but to wait. Something will happen. Something must. Only the dawn, the thought that I will see her soon, that she will be so openly joyful to see me, so sure of my tolerance and patience, so clearly in love with me, liking me, admiring me, will allow a glimmer of hope and energy to return.

"I'm doing something wrong," I say out loud. "This is not how things ought to be."

I am not bound to her, could always set a limit after which I could say enough, stop this. And yet I would say that at most I lose patience with her, and then regain it. But is it truly my role to be her defender when I am also, as Stan Lioce has put it more than once, her road kill.

• • •

I take the turnpike, park my car, and walk across the bridge to the office. A crew is going from office to office emptying trash cans and running desultory cloths over credenza surfaces. Maria, who is the only person in the firm who routinely talks to these people, always in Spanish and always with great animation, calls them the Sandinistas, and they find the label funny. Their machines whirr in the hallways.

If there is a silver lining to what I am about to spend the night doing, it is that Olwine could have asked someone else to do it. There are others in the firm who would doubtless have welcomed the work. For years everything seemed to be humming along as if nothing could ever change and then suddenly, even before the whole economy started falling apart, something began to change at the firm, almost imperceptibly at first, but then quite plainly. Lately more than one person has remarked that there does not seem to be enough work to go around, and I know that some lawyers are having difficulty finding the eight or nine billable hours each day that the firm demands. How much time you have to bill has become a preoccupation, padding diary entries as unremarkable as daydreaming. Perverse as it may seem, in some ways I am fortunate that Olwine has chosen me as his victim.

I do want this, to be a Nibble partner.

Occasionally my father mocks my single mindedness. "Money is not for hoarding," he says. "One doesn't need much, and may live better with little. But if you have it, relish it. Too much money, or too many possessions, is corrosive."

But that's my father. As I've said, he owns a specialty cheese shop on Bloor Street in Toronto, and to this day he is unable to tell me whether it makes money or not. It's a fabulous place, really it is, tightly packed with the most exotic, odd, pungent cheeses, but it is very disorganized. My father seems to know where most things are, and of course his regular customers love the place exactly the way it is. My father was in more businesses than I can remember before he decided to open a cheese shop, arguably his most productive enterprise. He's grown a pencil moustache, wears a little blue beret, at all times carries a silver paring knife on a chain around his neck so as to be constantly prepared to provide samples to his customers. I am like him in many ways, but in others not like him at all.

We are both cynics, I would say, and view the world around us with what we hope is a wry humor. But unlike my father, I am no rebel. I have somehow grown up to be entirely conventional. I did not like, when I was young, how impotent he seemed to be when things went wrong in his ventures and the walls threatened to close in around us. Men like my father, it seemed to me, honest, optimistic, making their decisions on something less than a solid knowledge of the rules, were just pawns of larger interests, and it was this impotence that I determined to avoid by becoming a lawyer. At the time I had no idea—though I did begin to suspect it already in law school—how inadequate my analysis was.

But I stayed with it, and here I am.

• • •

Before opening the first of the Morganic folders I call to order a pizza, and as I am replacing the receiver a vision of Margaret Kelly, alone in a conference room, crosses my mind. I close the door and begin to go through the files. From time to time I look up and stare out over the city. It feels as if I am trapped in a tower high above the world, a spectator without power or presence.

IV

I WORK THROUGH MOST OF THE NIGHT, GOING HOME ONLY AT FOUR fifteen for a shower and a change of clothes. When I arrive back Kay is already busying herself about her desk.

"There's a message for you from Mrs. Buckles," she says stiffly. "You'll find it on your chair."

I take my coffee mug and walk to the break room, but on the way back I see Mrs. Buckles heading toward me down the passage, striding in her official, bow-legged way as if she has not a moment to lose. A Stepford Wife whom I have not seen before is trailing her. Just the sight of them makes me irritable.

"Didn't you get my message?" she asks.

"There was a note on my chair. I'll read it when I need to sit down," I say.

"Do you have a moment now?" she insists, and then, before I can answer, both Mrs. Buckles and the Wife follow me back to my office. Mrs. Buckles closes the door behind us. I decide to try a conciliatory gesture.

"What can I do to help?" I ask, but I know that I sound insincere. There is nothing I can do about it. I am being insincere.

"This is Shannon Bertucci," Mrs. Buckles says. "She's our new Assistant Move Coordinator, and this is her first day with us."

"Welcome," I say.

"Later in the day a memo will be distributed describing her background and her duties," Mrs. Buckles adds. "I expect she will get your and your secretary's full cooperation."

"Of course," I say, and addressing the new woman I add, "You're with us temporarily, are you?"

"After the move," Mrs. Buckles cuts in, "Miss Bertucci is going to be the head of our new Administrative Coordination Department."

"Our what?"

"Our Administrative Coordination Department," she says, and though for an instant I anticipate she is about to tell me what that is, she stops short.

There is a brief silence. If I am to find out more, I will have to ask. I will not.

"Oh," I say instead. I mean, I do know what the words mean. It's just that strung together they suggest a particular kind of meaninglessness.

"Her assignment now, however, is to take charge of moving you and your secretary to Triumph Plaza out of sequence."

"Who else is going now?" I ask.

"We will be adjusting the out-of-sequencing schedule this morning," the new woman says, eager to show that she can take charge. "Mr. Olwine, yourself, and perhaps three others in the first phase."

"What we are again appealing to you for," Mrs. Buckles interjects, "is the cooperation of yourself and your secretary."

"What specifically is it you want us to do?" I ask warily. I have had two hours sleep. I will agree to anything to get these people to go away.

"We can arrange to move your entire office on Saturday," the new woman says, "if you will confirm that the packers can box your office on Friday."

"Fine," I say. "At some point before I move I would like to see these new offices of ours."

"Union rules don't allow non-scheduled personnel on the floors without a special permit," Mrs. Buckles says, and is about to continue when I cut her off.

"Forget I asked," I say.

• • •

"Well," Kay says when she hears. "I like that. No notice, no 'by your leave.' Just orders."

"Please, Kay," I beg. "Let's just give up and do it their way."

"It's very easy for you to say that," she replies. "You're professional staff. You're insulated from them. I'm the one who's going to have to worry about making copies and getting the mail out and finding things that the movers have lost after they've destroyed my systems."

"Kay, please," I say again.

She lifts papers from my out tray and begins to leave the office.

"I trust that at some point you'll explain to me what all these folders on the floor are," she says, and then closes the door.

Kay is a creature of habit, more than a creature of habit. She arrives at the same time each morning and one can set one's watch by her routine. Immediately after she takes off her coat and gloves, and before she makes herself a cup of tea, she comes in here and straightens up my desk. 'Work in Progress' is stacked in the center, files requiring attention on the top left, files with which I am finished on the top right. If she has any doubts about where one belongs she attaches a little yellow sticker with whatever question she has: "Mr. Dover: May I return this to the file room?" And underneath that: "Kay Parsons," as if it could be anyone else, let alone any other Kay.

Kay shares an apartment, an ancient, immaculately tidy little place I am sure, with a Miss Silversmith and has done so for a number of years. Kay is vague about Miss Silversmith, but she has said that she works at M.I.T. and is something more than an administrator and something less than a teacher. I am sure that whatever Miss Silversmith does she does efficiently, tidily, and completely. Kay could not possibly live with anyone who did not. Each morning they come into the city in the back seat of the same taxi driven by a man called Tom, and each afternoon Tom picks them up at five o' clock sharp and drives them home.

On weekends, so I understand, the two of them go on "little adventures," or so Kay describes them, outings like a bus trip to see the foliage or a walking tour of the historic houses on Beacon Hill. Faithfully each Monday she gives me her report. It is part of our routine that I listen and appear interested.

"Malta was good," she might say of a food festival. "But I don't see how they eat so much of that okra in West Africa. Miss Silversmith was quite unsettled by it."

"I think they're lesbians," I once said to Maria.

"I don't think anybody's ever been more wrong about anything in the history of the United States, perhaps in the history of the world itself," she replied.

This morning I notice that there are no yellow stickers on my desk. It is exactly the way I left it when I went home. There is something disappointing about this.

The door opens and Lioce walks in.

"What's this I hear about your leaving us?" he asks. "There are all sorts of rumors flying about. And what's with your secretary? I just passed her slamming things down on her desk. It's like Kay's evil sister out there, not Kay."

"She's mad about something," I say. "I don't really blame her. This new crowd doesn't treat people very well."

"So what else is new?" Lioce says. "But is it true? Are you going?"

"Yes," I say. "On Monday Tony Olwine and I will be sitting cheek by jowl over in our new offices at Palace in the Sky."

"You realize of course," Lioce says, "that you're the first civilian to see the inside of that place. Perhaps you ought to prepare yourself in some way."

Before I can answer the door flies open. It is Maria.

"I just found out what this is all about," she says excitedly.

"Hey, we were talking over here," Lioce says. "You just barge in like it's your own office. We could have been doing something important."

"There's not much chance of that," Maria replies, pushing him aside. "Listen. I just found out the real scoop on why Olwine's so mad."

"Why?" Lioce asks.

"Because the trial's in three months time, Margaret Kelly has already diaried over a million dollars worth of time to the file doing God knows what, and the case is nowhere near ready to be tried," she says. "The families are threatening to sue us for malpractice if we don't sort this out, and all Margaret can do is blame the firm for not standing behind her, whatever that means."

"Who told you this?" I ask.

"Margaret's secretary told mine," she says simply. "She ought to know."

"Guess who'll take the blame if you fail to save the day," Lioce says.

"And guess who'll take the credit if you do," Maria adds.

"She just barges in like it's her own office," Lioce mumbles.

· · ·

"Did you tell him about us?" Maria asks after Lioce has left.

"I tell him everything," I say.

"You're like a sieve," she says. "Do you know how many people in the office must know?"

"Know what?" I say.

"How late were you here last night?" she asks, changing the subject.

"Four something," I say. "I didn't even make a dent in what I have to do to sound half-way intelligent when I report to Olwine."

"You'll do fine," she says, and then asks: "Is it as bad as it sounds?"

"It seems as if Margaret Kelly's gotten into arguments about everything in this case except what's important," I say. "Scheduling, deadlines, who goes first. They wrote complicated briefs arguing about whether Massachusetts or New Hampshire Island law applies because the factory is in Massachusetts and some of the houses are in New Hampshire, until the judge pointed out that the relevant law is the same in both states. Lined up against that wall," I say, pointing to the files, "is a million dollars worth of rubbish."

She looks across at the files. They are four deep, the usual worn-looking brown files in which Nibble & Kuhn stores its papers.

She shrugs.

"Better you than me," she says. "I'd quit if I had to go through all this stuff."

"Oh?" I say. "And then what would you do?"

"I'd exercise until I was in great shape," she says. "Then I'd go to Spain for a while."

"And then?" I ask.

"Then I'd come back and get a job in a law firm," she says.

"And then?"

She looks at me skeptically.

"Why are you asking these dumb questions?" she says. "I'm not on the case so it's all academic. And as much as you bitch about it, it's in your blood to do a good job. You don't know how not to."

"I think you intend that as some sort of criticism," I say. "From anyone else it would be a compliment."

"In any event, it's just a job," she says. "Are we having lunch or aren't we?"

"Didn't you hear what I just told you," I ask incredulously. "How can I go out?"

"You're never going to read that lot in time anyway," she says. "Do what you can and wing the rest. That's what lawyers are supposed to do."

We make a time to meet, and she leaves.

"Gotta go catch a billable moment," she says as she closes the door.

• • •

There are some days when it is much harder to practice law than others. Outside it is a clear summer's day. Cars on the expressway beneath my window flicker as they move unevenly past the Custom House Tower, around the bend, out of sight. A fireboat goes through its drills, spraying water in wide arcs into the air. On the far side of the harbor planes take off and land at the airport, and I watch one as it hovers steadily lower and lower, past the smokestacks, over South Boston, Pier Four, the water, and then down onto a runway. I wish I could be somewhere else, on one of the planes headed who knows where, in a car going out of town over the Tobin Bridge, on the Martha's Vineyard ferry waiting to begin its passage off through the Cape Cod Canal.

A great lethargy descends on me.

I look down at the files. I have tried to start with the ones that will tell me most efficiently what is going on, but I found out quickly enough that there is no order to them. And Margaret Kelly was unpleasant when I called to ask her some questions.

"I have to leave for a meeting," she said, "and I won't be back today. Perhaps some time next week."

I am taken aback. I mean, it is her file, and she isn't a judge yet, but she has suddenly acquired a haughty edge that catches me off guard.

"Most of the file is self evident," she adds. "Maybe you could get me your questions in a written list."

"I'm just asking you to tell me how these files are arranged so that I can read them in some logical sequence," I plead.

"Everything's been moved around since I last had them," she insists. "I can no longer take any responsibility for them. I'm sorry."

I fantasize about showing up at her confirmation hearing and letting the panel know a thing or two about her demeanor. It is just a fantasy.

• • •

I am learning more than I had ever wanted to know about the company we have sued. It makes gadgets, things one sees advertised on late-night television with only a post office box to order from.

"Would you believe," I ask, striding into Lioce's office waving a document, "that Morganic Continental makes nose hair clippers?"

"Of course they do," Lioce says off-handedly. "They also make rubber Mounties for sale at Niagara Falls and disposable hair curlers. That's why they're called a conglomerate. What's the big deal?"

"They make the most useless stuff in the world," I say. "How can anyone take them seriously?"

"That's easy to answer," Lioce says. "Go on the Web and you'll see. They have revenue of several billion dollars a year, and when they went public four years ago the stock market went crazy precisely because of what it makes, the sort of useless junk that every person in America buys and forgets how useless it is and then buys again. Nose hair clippers isn't the best of it. They have factories in China that make those crappy cigarette lighters and key chains and squeezable bunnies you see on the counters of drug stores. They have factories in Burma that make cheap knock-off grills and those chintzy rotisseries you see advertised at three a.m. Every time you see a baseball cap or a wrist watch or a bar of soap with some corporate logo on it, think Morganic. Everyone takes them very seriously."

Lioce is right, though given my situation in life at this moment I don't see much to laugh about. There is a division that makes seventy million dollars worth of costume jewelry every year, another that makes novelty shower heads and picture frames, a place in Iowa where they make commemorative medallions, a plant in Texas that makes chrome desk sets. I can't get too worked up about it, though. I've worked with companies whose sole activity is to make stuffed animals in pin-striped suits, or the molds for toilet plungers, or the casings for sausage. At Nibble & Kuhn it all seems so serious and elegant, negotiating deals with teams of lawyers from New York and Chicago, participating in ponderous conference calls, fighting over the rights to software that keeps track of what is being bought and sold in real time, whereas in reality none of it is grander than the sink cleaners and the staplers themselves, the pizza franchises and the glow-in-the-dark telephones, a new brand of cookie.

For the most part I am used to it, even used to the rambling litigation process to which these giants of industry turn when they decide to duke it out. Then something like this file reminds me of how vast all this activity is, how enormous and inept the machine we are a part of, how creaky and inefficient and smelly. It moves like a behemoth with four hundred million people on board, chopping down forests, distilling chemicals, paving grass, emitting smoke, leaving in its wake nothing grander than chrome pencil sets and fake jewelry to be worn out and forgotten long before the chemicals that were used to make them are absorbed back into the earth.

But when all is said and done what right do I have to complain? I am as much a part of it as anyone else, here at my shining desk, in my well-cut suit, my new shoes, my fifty dollar haircut. I have my own office with a beautiful view, my potted plant grown from a twig, all this and Maria too down the hall, Lioce next door, Kay out front zealously protecting me. Indeed, it is as comfortable as any person has a right to expect a job to be. Sometimes in the winter, watching men being buffeted by the wind on scaffolds hundreds of feet above the sidewalk for a fraction of what I earn, I wonder whether I have a right to feel any dissatisfaction at all.

Both of my parents had at least pretended to be amazed by my decision to go to law school.

"Why would you want to do a thing like that?" my father asked.

"The boys I went to college with who went to law school were uniformly dull," my mother added.

My mother, to be truthful, has something of a drinking problem. Not a major one, but by ten o'clock on most evenings she is quite definitely tipsy. She has also, lately, begun to revise her memories of her youth so that instead of being the rather serious and straight-laced girl I suspect she was, her stories suggest unmentionably daring escapades I am convinced she did not have.

"I don't like business," I said. "You buy a bar of soap for ten cents, you sell it for eleven. That's fine. But it's not what I want to do."

"Listen to him," my mother said. "He doesn't realize that everything works that way. Even law."

"He'll see," my father said directly to my mother, as if I was not even in the room. "Everything that does not cater to the senses is pretense."

Sometimes I have a feeling of imminence, as if I am constantly waiting for something to begin.

• • •

The afternoon sun streams in through the window, warming my neck. I have had my sushi with Maria and now I can procrastinate reporting to Olwine no longer. What's the worst the man can do to me anyway?

This is a singularly bungled file, there are no two ways about it, and in talking about it here I have to be careful not to violate the Dover-Lioce cardinal rule, that is, not to bore others to death with stories of the cases we happen to be handling. I mean, I'll deal with it and spare everyone else the minutiae. But here's the problem. Once you start to immerse yourself in something like this file, it does, in its own odd way, begin to acquire a certain kind of interest. It has to, or you'd stab yourself with a letter opener. I suppose if you look hard enough just about any story has at least a glimmer of human interest. At least I find, as I go through the process of dismangling what Margaret has mangled, that this is true of these files.

It all starts out simply enough. A couple of years ago someone who sat on the board of some charity, of which Margaret was the chairman, mentioned to her that several of his neighbors' children had become ill and mentioned his suspicion that the illnesses were linked to runoff from a Morganic factory not far from their homes. I suppose—and I'm adding a layer of comment here—that if you aren't a lawyer and know very little about the system, Margaret may seem to be someone you would go to with a problem like that. I mean, if lawyering skill were somehow a function of how many panels you sit on and how many charities you support, Margaret would be at the front of the line.

There are a bunch of letters in the file from which it is relatively easy to retrace what happened next (introductions, reports of meetings in living rooms, doctors' letters, scheduling). To cut a long story short, it all culminated in a meeting in a Nibble & Kuhn conference room attended by seven sets of parents of children with various kinds of cancers, at which the parents signed a contingent fee agreement with the firm. The agreement provides, in short, that Nibble & Kuhn will sue Morganic Continental on the parents' behalf, will carry all the costs of bringing the case to trial, and will receive forty percent of whatever amounts it recovers.

Simple enough. I don't want to be glib here, but just because someone has cancer, and because there's a factory nearby, that does not mean that what went on in the factory has anything to do with the cancer regardless of how smelly or unappetizing the factory may be. And for the claim to get anywhere in court, one needs to persuade a judge that there is, in fact, some real science to support it. And that's where poor Margaret gets out of her depth.

For about a half an inch there is order in the files, and then they fall apart. The firm was fronting all the bills, and so while it kept track of Margaret's time nobody was actually paying for anything and so nobody seems to have paid any attention at all to matters such as efficiency and cost effectiveness. It was as if Margaret had been given a cart of money and had no experience shopping. It takes hours even to sort into piles the reports she has commissioned: Reports on the kinds of processes that may have been used in the factory, on the federal, state, and local regulations that govern waste disposal, on ground water flow patterns, on cancer in young boys. They have taken soil samples and analyzed them, re-analyzed them, crushed rocks, built computer models, rebuilt computer models, written reports and then written more reports analyzing the earlier reports of others. In the end, at least two of her experts flatly contradict each other, reaching so hard for their three hundred and fifty bucks an hour that their conclusions look like transcripts of a high school debate.

Worst of all, if what Margaret wanted was an honest exploration of her case, the kind of hacks whose reports litter her files are the last people one would turn to. I can see straight off that she has made no attempt to distinguish between the real experts and the made-for-litigation charlatans. In truth, they do look pretty much the same. What lawyers are prepared to pay for testimony is handsome enough to attract some credible-looking characters. Instead of grinding away in a lab somewhere and sweating it out for federal grants, or worrying about students, testifying gives scientific bit players the liberty to say whatever they darn please and for an hourly rate that approaches that charged by lawyers.

To prepare the case I will have to find out two things: What toxic chemicals actually escaped from the factory, and whether these can cause cancer in anyone, let alone whether they did in the seven boys. It doesn't take a genius to figure out that unless the boys' illnesses can be linked in some tangible way to something that happened at the factory, I, and the families, and the law firm, are in trouble up to our hoo hoos.

Margaret Kelly's contribution on these issues, as opposed to a host of others, is zero.

"I haven't told you the best part either," I say to Stan. "Guess who the factory has hired as its lead expert witness, the person who will tell the jury that Morganic Continental is as clean as a whistle?"

"Search me," Stan says. "Mother Theresa?"

"Almost," I say. "Endicott Wigworth."

"You mean the former Dean of the Harvard School of Public Health?" Stan says, for a moment sufficiently taken aback so as to forget to be sarcastic.

"Not only that," I say. "M.D. Ph.D. Margaret took his deposition and spent the whole time arguing about whether he'd brought his file with him, and then having him read aloud every paper in his briefcase. I know nothing about what he's going to testify."

"Oh you'll do fine," Stan says, his zeal returning. "Just push him around a little."

"Thank you," I say.

Out of interest I have pulled the billing folder to see what Margaret has told the firm she was doing as she flailed about in her rain forest of papers. If discussions with other lawyers in the office alone could have readied the case for trial, she would be in the Supreme Court already. She and Marvin Babbet, a *real estate* lawyer, have each diaried an average of ten hours a week "brainstorming issues." (Do the math. At $460 an hour each, that is almost two hundred and twenty-five thousand dollars.) Hell, there is even an entry describing a discussion she supposedly had with me, with *me,* in which I am alleged to have given advice about something or other. I have no recollection of the "Consultation with Dover" for which she diaried well over an hour. Maybe that's why Olwine thought of me for this delight. I have already consulted on it.

There are advantages to the chaos in the file, of course. For one thing, I won't have to try and figure out what is useable and what is not. Nothing is.

• • •

Olwine wants to see me at three, and it is almost time. I put on my jacket and tell Kay where I am going, and then I stop off in the men's room. I find Babbet, the same Marvin Babbet who has contributed so significantly to my case, combing his beard in the mirror. I think for a moment to ask him about it, but decide not to.

"You look beautiful, Marvin," I say instead.

Babbet, though a partner, is a breed apart. He is no more than five feet tall, almost unbearably earnest, incredibly literal.

"Nice day, Marvin," one might say.

"Yes, but I hear there's a forty percent chance of precipitation in the P.M.," he will reply.

Babbet also seems incapable of not speaking in clichés. "When the rubber meets the road," is a favorite. He always wants to be "kept in the loop," and seems to have a number of hats for different occasions. "Wearing my real estate developer's hat," he might preface a remark, or: "Wearing my Legal Personnel Committee hat." He is, of course, perfectly harmless, even as a partner.

"I've been thinking of shaving it off," he says.

"How long have you had it?" I ask.

"Since college."

"Be daring," I say.

"My wife says she'll leave me if I shave it off," he says thoughtfully.

"Oh, you'll find someone else," I tell him.

• • •

Olwine is sitting in his red armchair, silver half-glasses perched on his nose, reading from a case book. He scarcely looks up as I walk in, gestures me to a chair across the room.

I sit, watch for a moment as Olwine continues to read.

"Do you have a plan?" he asks, closing the book at last.

I will expect nothing of human dimension from this man, I think. Not a word about the size of the task, about nights spent in the office, about this unfathomable tangle.

"I think so," I say.

"And what is it?" Olwine asks calmly.

I haven't had much time to rehearse this, but it's obvious Olwine needs to be given some sobering news. If this case is to get to a jury within the next three months—I don't mean get to trial only; I mean be good enough that a judge won't throw it out before it goes anywhere near a jury—I not only need to do a whole bunch of work myself, but I will need assistance from other lawyers in the office, perhaps three or four. I will also need, and here is where Olwine is in for a shock, a rather large budget to hire actual experts to do the things I need to accomplish. Real experts, the sort we hire for our big corporate clients, university professor types who can examine the boys, their medical charts, the epidemiology of this whole thing, and then try and correlate it with whatever is done at the factory.

I tell this to Olwine. He is holding a pad, occasionally makes a few notes, remains inscrutable.

"In short," I say, "in order to try this case we are going to need to do a lot of work and I'm afraid we're also going to have to spend a lot of money."

I begin describing to him what sorts of expert witnesses I have in mind, several names I have found on the Internet and in the library. All the while he is watching me, a strange and serene look on his face.

"No," he says at last with a solemn finality. "I find it difficult to believe—I do not accept, in fact—that in order to try this case you need to reinvent the wheel in this manner. Perhaps it is your relative inexperience in a courtroom, perhaps something else, but the firm will not countenance your spending money to redo work that Margaret Kelly has already done."

"It hasn't been done," I say, and he raises his hand.

"The answer is no," he says. "You will have to take yourself in hand and try this case based on the significant work product already available to you. The firm anticipates that experts will be needed at the trial, and you will select these from among the well-qualified men who have already been consulted, done the work, and written the reports. I will not authorize the retention of anyone beyond that."

"That is not possible, Tony," I say. "No judge will allow the soft stuff we have in the file to go to a jury."

"Now listen here," Olwine says, standing. "I wouldn't be quite so confident if I were you in prognosticating what 'no' judge will or won't do. Cases have been won with far less resources than have already been spent on this one."

I think about this for a moment, how I might respond, and then I decide to leave it. He is not going to budge. There is nothing I can do. How can a mere mortal move a mountain, especially a glacial, impervious, reptilian mountain.

"May I have some help," I say meekly. "This is a huge file and one way or another there is a lot still to be done."

"How much help will you need?" Olwine asks.

"Perhaps two senior associates," I suggest, scaling back my expectations *sua sponte*, as we say.

"Continue to master the file," Olwine says at last. "I'll think about it and let you know."

• • •

"That Miss Bertucci was just here," Kay tells me when I return, deflated and defeated, to my office. "She wanted to put those sticker things on everything all over again."

"Oh, for Christ's sake," I mutter. "They already did that."

"Miss Bertucci says that because you're moving to the new building early, they have to do it again," Kay says simply.

"Did she perhaps tell you why?" I ask.

"She says it's because they're using a different company to move the out-of-sequence people, of which species we are apparently two," Kay says. "Don't ask me these questions. Ask her."

"Look Kay," I say. "You know that I don't often take this approach, but there's simply too much going on to try and reason with them even if I had any hope of getting anywhere if I did, which I don't. They're like a juggernaut and they'll roll over us if we resist. So let's just let them do what they want. When we're in the new building we can get on with our lives."

"You know I would do nothing to prejudice you and the regard in which you're held," Kay says. "I'm not even surprised that some of the senior people here would let the firm take the turn it has, though I must say I am surprised that someone as sensible as Mr. Cabot is allowing it."

"It's not Cabot, I don't think," I say. "It's Olwine and Shein-burg. They have this bizarre vision and they're doing every-thing they can to see it realized. The reality of things out there doesn't seem to faze them. They're like a pair of Walter Mittys."

"But money is still money," Kay says. "And whatever your vision, you don't treat people like this."

"Believe me," I say, "the scale of money made and spent around here is quite different from the scale you and I are used to, the kind of money that buys tuna fish and Kleenex."

Kay likes it when I discuss office matters with her. She softens, nods earnestly, lifts a blonded curl off her forehead and tucks it into her hair.

"Well I'll be pleased when it's over," she says, moving some papers on her desk.

• • •

I have just sat down when there is a knock on my door, two quick little knocks, and Miss Bertucci comes in. She is carrying a briefcase in one hand, and, of course, a clipboard in the other.

"I have to go over to Triumph Plaza to take some measure-ments," she says. "If you're at all interested, and have thirty min-utes, you can come over with me and look at the office we've given you. I'm sure no one will object, especially if they don't know."

She is being conspiratorial, quite gutsy if you think about it, for someone new on the job.

"Sure," I say. "I could use some fresh air."

As we walk, she makes an effort to endear herself to me. She describes in some detail how the moving company operates, how many men will be assigned to the task, how they will go about it, how she, and only she, will be there each weekend until the move is quite over. She even tries to explain the importance of the stickers, and I find it difficult to retain any antagonism under the circumstances. She is really a bit player in a far larger saga.

"How do you train for a job like yours?" I ask.

"Oh, these are pretty standard corporate move sequencing procedures," she says. "It's a matter of strategical planning, objectivization, interfacing with vendors. Mrs. Buckles is well known for her expertise. I expect more and more law firms are going to be adopting her systems in the future."

I say nothing, and am then surprised to hear Miss Bertucci asking me about my own work, what kind of law I practice, how long I have been with the firm. She even asks me about the case that is so disrupting their sequencing and I am half tempted to confide in her, to vent some of my desperation because it is desperation I feel, and then I decide against it. You can never be sure when you're simply talking, and when you're providing ammunition to a potential adversary. I answer her questions non-committally, make small talk, notice that she is huffing along beside me, her obviously heavy briefcase weighing her down. I know that I am being malicious in not offering to help her with it. By the time we reach Triumph Plaza she looks exhausted.

I have never stood as close to the place as we do now, though I have passed it many times as it rose slowly up into the skyline. Across the mud and slabs of concrete stacked on the sidewalk I see that the foyer looks impossibly lavish. There is a patterned marble inlay on the walls and at least three varieties of stone pillar. I half expect to see statues of saints or plaster reproductions of little boys pouring from urns into giant clam shells.

"This doesn't much look like a Nibble & Kuhn kind of place," I say.

"Everyone about to commence a move says things like that at first," Miss Bertucci replies. "You'll see how quickly the atmosphere of this building grafts itself onto the firm."

This is not a comforting thought. I feel suddenly quite solicitous of Cabot's stuffed fish which is going to look quite out of water in a place like this, even of Olwine's plaster seagulls which are going to look like they migrated to the wrong continent.

Marvin Babbet's mounted collection of baseball cards, which look odd enough where they are, even Sheinburg's inflatable flamingo, are going to look perfectly strange in offices with vaulted ceilings and diamond shaped windows.

Miss Bertucci goes into the foreman's shed and comes out with a man carrying two plastic hard hats, one for me and the other for her. Even as I put the little plastic shell on my head I wonder what kind of debris, if any, it could stop. I am prepared to bet that head protection on a construction site is required by some meddlesome jerk from OSHA, and that these pathetic beanies are the bare minimum the contractor can come up with and still meet the standard.

We follow the foreman into the mausoleum of a lobby and I see that from up close the effect of all the marble is even more overwhelming than it has seemed from the street. In addition to the medley of marble there are travertine balustrades, oversized wrought iron fixtures hanging from the ceiling, a cacophony of excess that looks staggeringly expensive and yet is completely without beauty.

"One wonders what clients are going to think about all of this," I say. "Paying customers may do some math; so much for lawyers, so much for marble. If it were me, I'm not sure I wouldn't want a little more lawyer and a little less marble."

Miss Bertucci does not respond and we ride up in an elevator cab with walls of, well, marble. When we reach what is apparently to be my floor the foreman tells us that he will return in thirty minutes and leaves. With a floor plan in hand, Miss Bertucci and I set out to find my office, and when we do I see that it overlooks the water and is at least twice the size of my present one.

Miss Bertucci walks in first, checking off items on her pad as she goes. She checks to see that the light switch works, and marks it down, and then that there are two outlets, vent covers, window shades.

"Isn't it wonderful?" she asks.

I don't know about that. Really I don't. It is big, and it does have an expansive view, but isn't it also sort of pretentious? I mean, what does a person who works in a place this grand have to do to justify himself? And, above all, though it is not my business, *what is all this costing?*

"I don't know about wonderful," I say. "It's nice and sunny, and much bigger than the one I have now."

"They all are," Miss Bertucci says. "And all of us have windows too."

"Us," I think.

Maybe I am being unkind, or elitist, or something. Who knows anymore?

Miss Bertucci fishes from her briefcase a measuring tape and starts to take some measurements, and then she shows me a carefully drawn scale map of my present office, showing, I am surprised to see, the exact location of everything in it, including my potted plant and my telephone stand. Someone has taken the time to draw this to scale, quite well, too.

When she is done with her examination of the office she puts away her measuring tape and we walk slowly around the perimeter of the floor, looking into the rooms and checking the views from the various windows.

"I love the feel of empty buildings," she says.

"It does feel quite removed up here," I say. "Like we're on another planet."

"Very removed," Miss Bertucci says. "One could get up to no end of mischief. It's a perk of the job."

I look across at her in her yellow beanie, damp patches under her arms, what could only be a suggestive smile on her face. So that's what this unexpected invitation is all about. I wish Maria were here to share the moment.

"No doubt," I say, and walk quickly, steadily but quickly, back to the elevator bank.

• • •

There is a memorandum from Olwine on my desk when I return. Kay says that his secretary hand-delivered it just minutes before. It reads:

Re: Toxic Tort Litigation
To: D. Dover
cc: Ms. Kelly

You will assume, immediately, responsibility for the prepara-tion of this case, and for its trial. I will entertain the suggestion of assigning one additional junior associate to assist you once you have outlined in detail what tasks there are on which you require assistance.

You will submit to me for approval all proposed expenditures in excess of $100.

A. Olwine

V

I CALL THE LAWYER WHO REPRESENTS THE COMPANY, PETER HILL, to introduce myself and in the hope that I can begin to repair some of the interpersonal damage Margaret Kelly has done. I am, after all, just a lawyer, just a lawyer doing his job. This is not a civil war.

He is wary, and rightly so.

"Are you sure you don't want to just drop this whole thing?" he asks. "I mean, there's nothing there."

"That's not a possibility," I say. "We have very sympathetic plaintiffs and a factory that does appear to produce carcinogens. I believe I can connect the two."

"I believe you can't," Hill says, on the edge of becoming testy.

"Let's leave it for the jury to decide, then," I say. "If we didn't disagree we wouldn't be doing our jobs."

"That's not necessarily true at all," Hill says. "If I represented a client and brought a case in good faith, and then saw that there was no merit to it, I don't believe I would press on irregardless."

I'm about to tell him that *irregardless* isn't a word, but of course I don't.

"You can always settle," I tell him.

"I offered Margaret Kelly $25,000 a family," he says. That's $175,000 for a case I don't think will ever see the light of a jury room. She dismissed it out of hand. You'd do well to reconsider it. The offer won't stay on the table forever."

Oh, to settle and get rid of this all. The problem is that the firm's in it so deep that unless I can get him to do far better than that it's a non-starter.

"You make it easy for me to say no," I say. "We have seven boys who were made terribly ill."

"We didn't make them ill," he snaps, and I see that it is useless. Oh, to settle and get rid of all this.

• • •

I picture the scene at the depositions I am reading, those pre-trial skirmishes in which supposedly you're learning what a witness has to say, but trying at the same time to snag a damaging sound bite or two for use at trial. I have done enough of these to last a lifetime. One lawyer asks questions, the witness answers, the other lawyers listen as if every word has to be weighed for its importance. The court reporter tap-taps away. Usually everyone is at least outwardly civil.

The depositions Peter Hill has taken of the families are relatively short. He has seen the boys' medical records, knows what he has to do, and it is easy to see what he is after—where they have lived, what other diseases the boys have had, whether they may have been exposed to other chemicals at some point in their lives. I am not pleased to see the warts on my supposedly sympathetic plaintiffs. We have two fathers with whom one hopes a jury will sympathize even though they are in trouble for failing to pay child support, two children with lots of other cancers in their families, one boy who does have something, though whether it is actually cancer is not so clear.

"And what is your present address, please?" Hill asks one of the fathers.

"Must I answer that?" the transcript shows the father saying.

"Yes you must," Hill says. "It's not a complicated question."

"Do you mind if I counsel my own client?" Margaret snaps.

"What's the problem with that question?" Hill asks. "If he can't answer that, we're not going to have a very productive day."

"My client tells me," Margaret says, "that he is in immediate apprehension for his safety and the safety of his family if he divulges his new address to counsel. Morganic Continental has already inflicted enough damage on this family and the witness insists on his privacy as far as that company is concerned and will not give his address."

"Margaret," Hill asks, "are you suggesting I'm going to make some sort of improper use of that information?"

"Are you threatening me?" Margaret demands. "If you are, we can take it up with the judge."

"Am I threatening you?" Hill muses. "How would I do that?"

"Can we go on with the deposition?" Margaret demands, ignoring him.

The transcripts of Margaret's depositions are another story. Here's one where she is supposedly questioning the factory's comptroller. Its comptroller! What could he possible know?

"These innocent little boys have died painful deaths," she says on the record. "And because of corporate America."

"Dry up, Margaret," Hill says, and on the record too. What would a judge say if ever he got to review all of this? "Corporate America, whatever that may be, has nothing to do with this. No one's happy the boys got cancer. Our job is to finish discovery and to present evidence on two simple questions: Did any chemicals leak from the factory into the groundwater and, if so, did they cause your clients' cancer? Can we get to those subjects at some point?"

"That's easy for you to say," Margaret replies.

I can see her sitting there at a conference table, breathing heavily, overwrought.

"I know Morganic is responsible for these children's cancers, and you know it too. And I suspect Morganic is hiding the evidence that would enable us to prove it."

"Oh, get a life," Hill says, his patience long since lost. "There's no hidden evidence in this case. There's not even relevant discovery in this case."

"There's no discovery in this case because you have obstructed me at every turn."

"Look," Hill says, and what a record this is, how classically useless this is, page after page of expensive transcript that all looks like this. "If you ask pointless questions you get pointless answers. If you seek to take depositions from corporate executives who I've told you a dozen times have no relevant knowledge, you are going to end up wasting everyone's time. But it's your dime, your deposition. Go ahead, please."

"It's not pointless," Margaret says. *(Won't you stop, please, I want to shout as I read.)* "Who did what in the past is very significant."

"What good will it do to argue about it here?" Hill says. "What we have to do is to complete preparation, try the case, and whatever happens will happen. Don't you at least agree with me on that."

"Of course not," she says. "Seven innocent little boys are deathly ill. Some of them will die, Peter. They're going to die. It's not just another lawsuit."

"Oh, puhleeze," Hill says, and I suppose one can read anything into why the stenographer has chosen to transcribe it just like that. "Puhleeze. Every injury lawsuit is sad. Don't you think we have to retain just a little distance."

That's waving meat in front of a lion. Courageous man.

"Speak for yourself," Margaret snaps. "You represent big and rich corporations. For us these things are a matter of life and death."

For us these things are a matter of life and death. I want to laugh out loud. That's all Nibble & Kuhn does, or would like to do, represent big and rich corporations. It's all Margaret does, this one tortured, sad, bankrupting expedition of hers aside. If she feels so strongly she can always forfeit the forty cents on every dollar that will go to her if, in the highly unlikely event, if elephants fly and the moon really is made of cheese, Margaret actually wins this thing.

Not Margaret. Me.

• • •

In the old building, the offices were crammed in no particular order on either side of narrow passages, but at Triumph Plaza the floors don't have passages and each office is set against a single diamond-shaped window overlooking either the harbor or some part of the city. Kay has her own canopied hutch of granite and cherry wood, and the hutch, in turn, is set apart from the lawyers' offices by an expanse of carpeted boulevard the width of a small apartment.

Let me describe this in greater detail because it really is quite spectacular and also deeply disheartening for a variety of reasons, mostly economic but some aesthetic, too. As you step from the elevator you find yourself on a broad corridor lined with columns, art deco light fixtures, and specially commissioned artworks depicting the firm's long history. On the main floor there are portraits of Alfred Nibble and Lionel Kuhn, each framed with ornate gilded paneling and illuminated in its own dark alcove (one doesn't know at first whether to laugh or to light incense, honestly), and a painting of the first building in which the firm did business, long since demolished but reconstructed from old photographs by an artist on commission. There is a picture of Alfred Nibble's son, Arthur, who headed the firm when both Nibble & Kuhn were dead, and then one of Peter Knickerbocker Bittlenood, IV (I'm not making this up. Believe me, I couldn't) who came after him and tyrannized the firm for close to half

a century. Finally, near the end of the boulevard are pictures
of Harry Cabot (informal, more than informal, surprised to be
there), of Tony Olwine, so rigid the painting looks like a portrait
of a portrait rather than of a man, and of the final member of the
triumvirate, the pint-sized David Sheinburg, recently escaped
from a pogrom, or so one would think from the triumphant
look on his face which is wreathed in a halo of thin curls as he
sits complacently behind his garish chrome desk.

Forgive me for that. My grandfather, as it happens, is Jewish.
But it's what I think when I see the picture.

• • •

Sharing an empty hallway with Tony Olwine is like living
with an apparition. There are just four of us on the floor for
now, Kay and I at one end of the boulevard, Olwine and Cindy
at the other. Between us there is an array of objects and shapes,
unused hutches, shadows, stretches of carpet, but nothing that
moves or appears alive. And yet when Olwine passes my door—
from the elevator when he arrives each morning, to the elevator
when he leaves promptly each day at four—he does so without
any glimmer of recognition. On a few occasions when I look up
from my desk and see the edge of his suit as he passes, or when
occasionally I come out of my office and catch a glimpse of him
moving into his, he seems encased in an almost ghostly detachment. Not once does Olwine acknowledge the hours I am working or ask for information. Having made the assignment he has
become perfectly indifferent.

"I swear," I say to Stan. "The man's from another dimension."

• • •

Olwine's office is separated from the public areas by a vesti-
bule all his own. It is, of course, in the corner, overlooks the

harbor from one set of windows and Faneuil Hall and Charles-town from another. There is nothing from his old office in the new except the Navy flag and some of the photographs, and the cracked leather sofa and seagulls are nowhere to be seen. Instead he has apparently had a decorator re-create, in minute detail and with astonishing accuracy, if the feel of the room is any measure, an antique barrister's chambers. It comes com-plete with heavy mahogany paneling, burnished wood floors and, most eye catching of all, a spiral staircase leading up to a gallery lined with bookshelves, which was intended to be the office above and which has required the contractor to break through the ceiling. Even amid the disorder elsewhere in the uncompleted building there are thick Persian carpets on the floor, an old, waist high globe in the corner, and an enormous black chair behind his new launching pad of a desk.

Every day at noon Olwine's lunch is delivered by a messen-ger from the Bostonian Hotel. I hear a rattle and then, almost immediately, a boy in uniform pushing a cart draped with a linen cloth passes the door. Then I hear them rattling off into the distance and am left to imagine the boy wheeling the cart into Olwine's office and slowly setting the silver tureens on a round table at the window. An hour later the boy returns, and then I hear the rattling coming from the other direction as the boy sets off to the hotel with the dishes. What a production.

Once, I walk beside the boy for a few yards just to see what it is that Olwine eats with such ceremony and am surprised to see nothing that tempts me. For all the show, the man's lunch consists of things like grapefruit and cottage cheese, thin soups, pinched slices of turkey.

● ● ●

There are, in the file, several old bills that really do need to be paid. I take them to Olwine's office, ask to see him, to my surprise am waved in by Cindy. He is sitting in his chair reading the *Wall Street Journal*. I tell him why I am there.

"Were these bills approved?" he asks.

"I don't know," I say. "They came in before I became involved."

"Then what is it you require of me?"

"They are expenses that exceed $100," I say.

"They are existing obligations of this firm," Olwine says, "and obviously will be paid."

"Shall I leave them with you then?" I ask.

"Anything you please," Olwine says impatiently, and raising the *Wall Street Journal* in front of his face makes it clear that I have outstayed my welcome.

• • •

Others begin to move into Triumph Plaza, three associates, all quite junior to me, a few secretaries, two paralegals. Because of their lack of seniority they are closeted on the far side of the floor in offices that face another building and so receive only a few hours of sunlight a day. Try though I do to warm to them, to exchange pleasantries, to inject a personal element into my dealings with them, I find myself keeping my distance. The truth is that beyond being overworked and preoccupied, my head filled with Margaret Kelly and Peter Hill and this whole absurd morass, I harbor these niggling grudges, dislike them for reasons they could never guess.

It annoys me, for instance, that the three young lawyers all wear bow ties, little silk affairs with small paisley patterns, and that one of them wears matching suspenders as well. They mince about like a colony of worker ants, or like astronauts single-mindedly conducting experiments in a rubble-strewn landscape.

Perhaps I was once like that.

"Never," Maria, who is in the same class as two of them, insists. "You can't imagine what they're like as people."

"What *are* they like?" I ask.

"They're so ruthless it's scary," she says.

"Ruthless about what?" I ask.

"About succeeding here," she says. "About living in the right part of town. About certain places being okay to have a drink at after work, and others not. About being rowdy at ball games, chugging beer and hollering and pretending to be drunker than they are and then snapping back the next morning as if nothing had happened. It's like they're programmed to behave in patterns. Mostly they're just prissy, and dry, and label conscious, and boring. If they came to Spain we'd throw fruit at them."

"I know Stan was never like that," I say. "I can't remember how I felt back then."

"I think things were different," she says. "Or at least it seems that way. Sometimes this place feels like a money-making machine with practicing law as a pretext, so you can either be cynical and pretend to care but not give a darn, or you can set your sights on being a partner and catching the gravy train yourself. You're seeing the worst of it because only the overachievers were taken to Palace in the Sky early. I think it's supposed to be some sort of reward. For the rest of us, let's face it, you do your work and you get a paycheck. This is hardly the sort of place you get to feel loyal to."

"It's as if I don't exist for them," Kay says. "In the morning they go past without looking at me. Didn't their mothers teach them manners?"

To me they are unfailingly courteous, if without discernible personality.

• • •

It troubles me how little of Maria I am seeing. Triumph Plaza is closed to the rest of the firm, and if she hadn't persuaded a

messenger to lend her his building pass whenever she asks for it
I probably wouldn't see her at all. As it is, I have to be satisfied
with her dropping in from time to time. In the old building,
Kay treated her visits with a mix of suspicion and impatience,
but now she seems resigned to them, indeed almost welcomes
a friendly face.

We have also become more daring, Maria and I, touch each
other right in my office with Kay there outside, have dropped
the pretense of carrying on legitimate conversations and allow
her to hear what must seem like long stretches of a pregnant
silence or traces of a whisper.

To make matters worse, I sense that Maria is almost relieved
by our separation.

"I've got more work done in the last week than in any week
since I arrived here," she says.

"Me too," I say. "It's a bad state of affairs."

"I'm not sorry to be giving practicing law a serious try," she
says. "This thing with you and me has hijacked my career. I
could have been a little superstar like you if I hadn't been so
distracted by you since my first day."

"You sound as if you prefer it the way it is," I say.

"Well at least I don't spend the whole day hoping you're going
to stop by, or wondering whether it's too soon to visit you without annoying Kay," she answers.

"I didn't realize it was all such a burden," I say sullenly.

"Oh come on," she insists. "You can't look me in the face and
tell me that this doesn't simplify things."

"This doesn't simplify things," I say without looking up. "I
can't imagine how you would think that it might."

• • •

"I believe it has become essential that I have assistance with
this," I say to Olwine.

The idea descends on me as I walk home. I think about it overnight, weigh the consequences, wonder whether it will stand up
to the scrutiny of morning.

Somehow it has. I walk to work thinking it through, and now,
standing in Olwine's office, I am awed by my own nerve. Of
course Maria will see it differently, but I have also decided that I
will not even try to justify what I am doing. It is hardly a secret
that in some respects this affair with her is a campaign. I didn't
invent the notion that all is fair in love and war.

"And why is it again that you need assistance?" Olwine asks
before I can continue. "We have already discussed, have we not,
your notion that much of the work Margaret Kelly has already
completed needs to be redone?"

I have tried to come up with approaches that will take the
edge off Olwine, things like imagining him sitting with his family over dinner, which he must do. The man must once have
been young, loosened up, God forbid transgressed.

"This case is not ready for trial," I say. "None of the required
pre-trial motions has been written, no draft jury instructions,
no required disclosures, to say nothing of the fact that we are
going to need to spend some time with Margaret's experts. I still
don't know whether we're going to get plausible testimony out
of any of them, but I'll try. Either way, it's not going to be easy.
You had said that you would entertain a request for assistance,
and I'm making one."

Olwine mulls it over. I stand there, just stand there, as he
mulls.

"Without accepting for an instant your characterization of
the caliber of scientist already retained," he says at last, "and on
your representations that assistance is essential, I will make an
assignment."

"I have discussed the case with Maria Parma," I volunteer.
"She writes well and could get what we need done efficiently."

God alone knows how Olwine will take it if he ever finds out.

"I'll consider it," he says, and to my great surprise, he adds: "You appear to have the matter in hand."

"Thank you," I say, my spirits suddenly lifted.

It amazes and irritates me how much I allow such skimpy praise to affect me. If I were to tell Stan he would say I was suffering from Stockholm Syndrome.

• • •

The shoe has not fallen by the end of the day—Maria knows nothing of my intrigue—so I go ahead, as I had planned, out of curiosity, to the thirteenth floor lobby of the old building to hear what has been billed in one of Mrs. Buckles's lime green memoranda as the first in a series of informational meetings about the move.

Olwine stands stiffly at the podium.

"The atmosphere in our new offices," he is saying, "will indeed be somewhat different from that which exists in the present building. But we have matured as a firm, are far beyond the kind of practice Alfred Nibble and Lionel Kuhn may have envisaged when they founded us over a hundred years ago."

"More's the pity," Lioce, who is standing next to me, whispers.

"Shabby offices do not befit a firm of our stature," Olwine continues. "If we show confidence in the future, an unrestrained self-confidence befitting a major Boston institution, others will place their confidence in us."

Across the room I see Maria, standing on tiptoes, listening expressionlessly to the speech.

"Mrs. Buckles will now describe to you some of the features of Triumph Plaza," Olwine says. "Kindly attend closely on her remarks."

Several lawyers exchange glances as Mrs. Buckles struts to the podium, shuffles her notes, adjusts her glasses on her nose. Her poodle hair has obviously been freshly set for her address to the nation, but even before she starts talking people begin to move around, to pour drinks, to gather in groups. At first it is only a quiet murmur, but then it becomes louder and louder until eventually Mrs. Buckles realizes that the features of the new phones, the new system of color-coding she has devised for our filing, are not holding anyone's attention.

"I'll be happy to answer your questions informally," she concludes uncomfortably, and, almost unnoticed, steps away from the podium. I am pleased to note that she looks very rattled.

"That's what you call charisma," Lioce says.

"What a bunch of piffle," someone standing behind us says.

I turn and see that it is Richard Havens. I have always liked Richard Havens. He became a partner when I was in my second or third year here but there has always been something in his manner that suggests none of it has gone to his head.

"Dream on, Tony."

"You're not happy about the move?" I ask, surprised to hear a partner break ranks on a decision of such importance.

I note that Havens has been standing at the refreshment table and that he is carrying an empty bottle of beer in his left hand and a full one in his right.

"Self-important bullshit," he says without looking at me.

He takes a slug from his beer.

"One of these days I've a good mind to drop in on you to see how you're doing with that new case of yours," he says.

I wasn't aware that he knew about it, or that he had any interest in it.

"You're breaking new ground, my friend," he says.

"Why is that?" I ask, but instead of answering he raises an eyebrow, then a bottle, and moves off.

I edge away and cross the room to Maria. She is talking with a paralegal, but pulls my arm and holds me at her side by my sleeve.

"Don't call him," she is saying. "Don't. Do you hear me?"

"What was that all about?" I ask when the paralegal has moved away.

"Boyfriend stuff," Maria answers. "Sometimes I think that if I could stand in her shoes for just ten minutes I'd straighten her whole life out."

"Yes," I say. "And you do such a good job with your own."

She looks at me quizzically and then decides not to respond.

"Do you still have work to do?" she asks.

"Nothing that can't wait until tomorrow," I say. "Things are so bad I'm not sure anything I can do will make any difference."

"Let's get out of Dodge," she says.

I look around.

"You go first," I say. "I'll meet you in the parking lot."

• • •

She has to be home for dinner, so she says, but she calls and tells her mother she will be late. God help us, that's progress. The little tidbit feels like a victory.

We drive to Chestnut Hill and walk around the reservoir and then up into the estate area. We stop at Frederick Law Olmsted's house and walk through the garden, and then climb a hill and wander past a little monastery and then a church, which for some reason we have not noticed before.

"Let's go on in and get married," I suggest.

"Don't say things like that," she says.

"I mean it," I say. "Let's go in and find a priest and just do it."

"If you knew I could say yes," Maria says, "you wouldn't be so quick to ask."

"Try me," I say, and I begin to walk to the side of the church toward what looks like a residence.

She runs after me, takes my hand, and drags me away from the building. As we go down some stone stairs, me in front and she behind, she stops, puts her arms around me, pulls me close to her.

"I love you more than I can describe," she says.

I feel her legs pressed against my back, the flatness of her lap, her breath on my neck. I reach behind me and hold her, close my eyes, wait.

"This has got to end soon," I say.

"I know," she agrees.

• • •

It is dusk. We have long since stopped speaking, walk hand in hand beside the stone walls and trees of the sprawling estates.

"Doesn't Sheinburg live in Chestnut Hill?" Maria asks suddenly.

After thinking for a moment, I nod.

"Why are you asking?" I say. "Do you want to pay him a visit?"

"We can't visit him," she says. "He's not home."

"How on earth do you know that?" I ask.

"He's out walking his dog," she replies.

I look at her sideways.

"What are you talking about?" I say.

"Look," she says, and points.

In the distance I see Sheinburg holding a leash and coming toward us. There must be a dog at the end of it, but it is so small that it looks as if the leash is walking itself. Maria grabs my arm and pulls me behind a tree. Sheinburg's short little figure, his scrappy walk and wreath of curly hair, is unmistakable.

"Fuck," I mutter, and looking about see that we are now in a garden, almost blackened by shadows, with hedges and furrows and large, moss-covered trees.

"I'll go around the back and meet you at the car," I say, but she has already pulled away from me and in a moment is out of sight.

Sheinburg has, in fact, not seen us. He would have kept walking, trying to keep his eyes on his dog lost somewhere in the grass, if I hadn't spoken first.

"Hello, David," I say respectfully, trying to sound relaxed.

"Why, Derek Dover," Sheinburg says, noticing me at last. "You don't live around here, do you?"

"No, but I like to walk here in the evenings," I say. "It's beautiful."

"That it is," Sheinburg agrees. "I've lived here for close to twenty years and everything else in the city has changed a lot. But things haven't changed much here, thankfully."

"It's beautiful," I say again.

"Talking about what's beautiful," Sheinburg says, "they tell me you're part of the crew that's already moved into Triumph Plaza. What do you think of it?"

I weigh my words.

"It's rather different from the offices we're leaving," I say carefully.

"And don't be apologetic about it either," Sheinburg says quickly. "A successful business must present the face of success to the world. A law firm that is prosperous must appear to be prosperous. Prosperity is nothing to be ashamed of."

"Tony Olwine said much the same thing at the firm meeting this afternoon," I say, and am about to make a remark about a "talking points" memo but think better of it.

"You must remember where we came from," Sheinburg says. "Not long ago we were a minor firm in the city. My practice for years consisted of picking crumbs off the tables of the larger and more established firms. But that's all in the past now. The stock market will be on its way back up soon, a new real estate boom will come, and we're poised to be a real player in all of it. We have the presence, the aura, the air of prosperity. I can just smell it."

"I hope so," I say, trying to be tactful. I am thinking about Maria now walking alone through a grove of trees in the dark.

"You can count on it," Sheinburg says, pulling on the leash as the dog at last appears and runs yipping around his trouser leg. "Don't ever stop thinking big, using leverage, taking risks. That's what business is."

He looks down. The dog is urinating on his shoe.

"No, Mitzi," he says. "Bad, bad girl."

• • •

"It's amazing," I say.

She is standing next to the car waiting, starts laughing when she sees me.

"This should happen all the time. Boston isn't such a big city that we can walk around indefinitely without being spotted by people from the firm."

"My guess is that we've been seen by people who we haven't seen," she says. "Alfonso has lots of friends here. I'd be dead meat if one of them saw us."

"If one of them saw us and did what?" I ask. "Told whom? Alfonso? Your family? I wish someone would."

For a moment she is silent.

"That's a selfish thing to say," she says.

"So it is," I reply, and we drive the rest of the way in silence.

• • •

We enter her neighborhood and I drive very slowly. We will be on her block in a minute or two at the most.

"I suppose no time would be better or worse to tell you this," she says at last, "but Alfonso called last night. He's coming home in ten days for a visit."

"And?"

"I can't see you while he's here."

"How long will he be here?" I ask tonelessly.

"He's interviewing for jobs. Not long. Until he gets one."

"Are you pleased he's coming?"

She is silent for a while and then, again clenching and unclenching her hands, she says, "He makes me nervous."

"I can see why," I say.

"Not only for the obvious reasons," she adds. "I didn't tell you this because you don't like me to talk about him, but when we were in Barcelona he bugged me."

"What do you mean by 'bugged you?'" I ask.

"Little things," she says. "Like the way he swings his arms when he walks, with his hands dangling on the ends like little rags. Or the way he eats his cereal in the morning, picking out the raisins first and then the nuts before he eats the cereal. It bugged me."

I look across at her in astonishment.

"With all that's going on between you and me, and you and Alfonso, what bugs you is that he picks the raisins out of his cereal first, and swings his hands funny when he walks."

"You know that's not what it means," she says. "If you were in the same room with him for five minutes you'd understand everything I'm saying, and I obviously can't explain it. But I've always respected him so much and it kills me what I find myself thinking when I'm with him. This was not supposed to happen. I can keep saying it. This was not supposed to happen."

"I doubt I'll ever be in any room with Alfonso," I say. "I can't think of any place I'd rather be less."

"Of course you think that," she says without emotion. "But you'd like him despite yourself. I can't remember a time in my life when he wasn't around, like an older brother when we were kids. Everything Alfonso did was always exactly right. We clamored for his attention, drank in everything he said. I look back on the summers we all used to spend in Spain together as if they were a dream, and when it got to be understood that I would marry Alfonso it seemed that something magical would continue forever. And now, despite that, I find his mannerisms annoying me, and when I'm with him I want to be alone. I know what it means. I'm not stupid. But it's still sad."

"What are you going to do then when he's in town?" I ask.

"For one thing he's staying with us," she says. "It was my mother's idea. I wasn't even asked if I thought it was a good idea."

"And you don't?"

"I don't know what I think."

We are on the same stretch of sidewalk outside her house. Perhaps the end is near, the strange months of waiting almost over. And then I am jolted back to the reality of it.

"Christ," she shouts, starting forward in her seat. "My parents are out walking."

Without more, and for the second time that evening, she jumps away from me and rushes from the car. I wait for a few moments, see a pleasant looking elderly couple walking up the street, the man in a cloth cap and carrying a stick, the woman in a sweatsuit and sneakers. As they pass the car they look down at me, the man nods, and then they are gone.

Maria's parents.

I take some satisfaction in the knowledge that I am somehow related to them and that they know nothing at all of it. God, what a scrap to have to celebrate. Then the old frustration returns. I start my car, turn around so as not to have to drive past them.

In my rear view mirror I watch as they walk briskly up the road, turn into their forbidden driveway, and disappear from sight.

VI

"Are you the Anti-Christ?" she demands, storming into my office. "Did you put that venomous creep up to this?"

Well maybe I did, maybe I did, but the need to temporize appears strong.

"Up to what?" I ask.

For a moment she is disarmed, and then I am distressed to see that she is on the verge of tears. You don't see this side of Maria often, I don't imagine. I certainly never have.

"I've been assigned to work with you on this fuck of a case," she says. "Why me? What could have made him think of me?"

I don't answer, look down at my desk with my lips pursed, hold tightly onto my pen.

"I swear Derek," she says quietly, "if you did this it would cross all boundaries. I would be truly pissed."

I want to deny my involvement, but I find it impossible to lie to her.

"It's not so terrible," I say and now she looks at me incredulously. "In the end it's just another lawsuit. Just more of the same."

"Working on this sinkhole," she exclaims. "You've been complaining about it for weeks and now you say that it's just another lawsuit."

"You'll be working with me," I say, trying to turn things around. "The case has its redeeming features."

"Did you put him up to this?" she asks again, and then says, suddenly almost subdued and before I can say anything, "I guess you have the right to remain silent."

It must be noon. From the hall comes a rattle that grows steadily louder and Maria turns just in time to see first the cart and then the waiter passing outside the door.

"What in hell is that?" she asks.

"It's Olwine's lunch," I say. "Didn't I tell you about this little ritual?"

"His lunch?" she says and goes out the door.

She stands for a moment with her back to me, watching as the tray tinkles off into the distance.

"*Hola*," she calls down the hall and the tinkling stops. Then she disappears and I follow her through the door and stand at Kay's desk as Maria goes after the trolley. Even Kay stops typing and watches. Maria says something to the waiter, in English and then in Spanish, laughs, takes him by the lapel and gestures, and then he smiles broadly and lifts a silver cover from the tray. She reaches underneath it, pauses, returns carrying a strawberry.

"Olwine was having five of these," she says. "Now he's having four."

"I'm not sure that's a good idea," I say.

"He won't miss it," Kay says and goes back to work.

"Do you have a death wish?" I ask when we are back in my office.

She bites off half the strawberry, offers me the other half and when I refuse, plops it down in the middle of my daily billing sheet. It leaves a crooked red stain.

"I'll tell you one thing," she says. "I'm not knocking myself out for this stupid case. I didn't ask for it, I don't even want to know how I got into it, but it has the look and feel of a black hole."

"There's stuff that has to be done," I say. "And whatever else you say about it, it'll all be over in less than three months."

"Let's get one thing straight, bucko," she says. "Perhaps you're going to get a higher perch in heaven than I am for killing yourself to do things well even when you know they're worthless. But I'm not interested in that. My goal is just to slide by, to score more points in the 'Had Fun' column than in the 'Applies Herself' one."

I say nothing. If any other young associate had said this me, or if I had ever said anything remotely like it to a partr would have meant the end of a career. I know she think things—hell, I do too a growing percentage of the tir her saying them now, and in this context, presents a Perhaps it wasn't such a great idea to drag her int Someone has to do the work and if it isn't going to h have to be me. Perhaps she is now even with me, poetic justice, but whatever it is, for the first tir ing me.

"Look," I say, "they may be assholes but th salary and you're taking it, and this is work

"Don't you be getting all didactic with m was perfectly happy with my cases befor I'm expected to pass them all to someo fortable office, to move into this crypt help on a case you've told me a hu and you have the nerve to say I hav my goose."

She stands and walks angril am, my back to her, looking (particular. Something catch Olwine standing in the d long for my liking, he ju is caught off guard.

"I assume," he says

"Yes," I say, and then there is another long silence as he looks first at me, then at Maria, then again at me.

He nods slightly, turns, and walks away. I look up at Maria and her face has changed entirely, emptied of truculence, is filled with anxiety.

"I'm sorry," she says softly. "It's not your fault." And then again, "I'm sorry."

"It's okay," I say.

Although it really isn't, some part of me is almost beyond caring.

VII

BACK TO THE CASE. I IMAGINE MYSELF STANDING IN A GROUP IN THE
thirteenth floor elevator lobby as I do this. I will keep it to a
minimum.

I have to do two things to get this case into the jury room.
Once it's there, in front of the jury, I am hoping, child support
delinquencies and an actual juvenile delinquency aside, the
emotional appeal of the sick boys and their families will carry
me to a large verdict. But, as I keep saying, first I have to persuade the judge that there is enough evidence of two things:
one, that there *were* chemicals from the factory in the ground
water and the swimming hole, and two, that these chemicals
caused the boys' cancers.

This is not going to be as easy as it sounds. Professor Endicott
Wigworth, Morganic's expert and former Dean of the Harvard
School of Public Health, no lightweight however you cut it, says
pshaw in no uncertain terms. He has supplied a written opinion
that actually scoffs at the idea that trace amounts of the chemicals we're talking about can cause cancer in anyone or anything.
He has won so many awards for academic excellence, written so
many papers on the subject of cancer, that it is difficult to find
a subject on which he isn't an acknowledged expert. For some

reason this does not seem to have deflected Margaret from her chosen path.

Arrayed against him I have selected from among Margaret's chorus of has-beens and never-weres, her potential expert witnesses, in other words, two men who offend one's sensibilities the least. One of them is an oncologist originally from India, Dr. Vijayananda Krishnapatnaram, God help me with that in front of a Massachusetts jury, who has been continuously located, since immigrating from Jaipur in 1982, in Beverly Hills, Mississippi. Without casting aspersions on a place which I have never visited though I am sure it is a regular garden spot, my bet would be that Beverly Hills, Mississippi is not now, and never has been, a plum venue for the practice of sophisticated medicine. But the papers reveal that he is prepared to, and more to the point can, make the thinnest of thin cases that some of the trace elements found in both the factory runoff and the swimming hole are associated with cancer.

I'll take it. He's eventually going to have say to the jury that he believes these trace elements *caused* the boys' cancer, which is a very different thing, but from his letters to Margaret I get the sense that for enough money he'll do just about anything. I don't mean to be unfair to Dr. Krishnapatnaram, but his letters suggest that he is very keen on getting his monthly bills paid on time, and indeed in advance if at all possible. And he has found, to his credit, a couple of very obscure medical articles that seem, if held upside down and read in a certain light, to support his opinions. It's the best I can do and it's going to have to be enough.

The second expert, who will supposedly explain ground water patterns to the jury and retrace for them the path of the chemicals from the factory to the swimming hole, is a little more problematic. Dr. Maxwell Finkbiner is both a chemical engineer and a geologist, a two-fer, and from Boston too, and he is the best of several Margaret has come up with and already paid considerable amounts of money. What he has going against him, well it's my problem as much as it is his, is the complex topography of the site, or put another way, that water doesn't usually flow uphill. It would have to if it were to reach the swimming hole and the aquifers that supply water to the neighborhood.

Leaving that aside for a moment, a second problem is that he stutters, and terribly.

"You know," Stan Lioce says when I describe to him a telephone conversation I have just had with Dr. Finkbiner, "this could work to your advantage."

"And why is that?" I ask.

"If your witness talks rubbish, but does it incomprehensibly, you may actually come out ahead," he says.

"As I told your colleague," Dr. Finkbiner intones, and it takes him a little while to say 'colleague,' "this does not present as great an obstacle as it may seem. Hydraulics is not such a simple matter. Water can, under some circumstances, indeed flow uphill."

He is being paid $400 an hour for this kind of insight. The firm is out of pocket $38,000 on account of Dr. Finkbiner.

• • •

A visit to the Morganic factory has been in the works for months, since long before I became involved. Margaret and Peter Hill have been to court four times about it already, arguing first about how many people would be allowed to examine the site on behalf of the plaintiffs ("One Lawyer. One Engineer," the court has ruled), how long we could be there ("Three Hours,") and how many soil samples we would be allowed to take ("As many as the plaintiff's expert can fit in a wheelbarrow.") One more trip to court was required to get the definition of wheelbarrow.

"Are the parties truly incapable of sorting these things out without the intervention of the court?" the judge has written on his Order.

I meet Dr. Finkbiner in the parking lot outside the factory. He drives an aging black Lexus and looks older than he sounds. He is wearing overalls, carrying several rolls of paper under his shoulders, has a series of plastic buckets. No wheelbarrow. We greet each other and I ask him what the rolled bundles of paper are.

"Several site plans and engineers' reports Ms. Kelly commissioned," he says. "They may come in handy."

Peter Hill has already told me the ground rules for this visit. We will not be allowed to speak to any Morganic employees, we will not be allowed to touch anything other than the soil outside of the factory, and each soil sample we take his own engineer will duplicate for parallel testing. It all sounds a little formidable, but I can't quarrel with any of it. I ask Finkbiner to tell me, quietly, what we are looking at as we walk through the building. Given his speech challenges, I wonder whether this will be possible.

The reception area is efficient and Spartan. On the walls are laminated copies of articles about the company and framed covers of *Fortune* and *Business Week* with pictures of one or other of the founders, long since bought out by Morganic. One of the articles trumpets someone called McCafferty as "Tycoon for the '90's." I certainly never heard of him.

Peter Hill with his chipmunk cheeks, jutting jaw, perpetual razor burn, is waiting for us in the reception area, and when the formalities are done he makes a phone call and soon enough a small phalanx of men and one woman filter into the room. I am not, of course, allowed to talk to any of them. There are no introductions, no pleasantries, rather a twilight zone of silence, as if we are all mourners or mutes.

"At least we're not putting anything to a vote," I say to Hill before we set out, and he looks at me as if I have just sneezed, or worse.

He says nothing.

"This way, please," the woman, who is quite attractive and wearing a white lab coat, says.

It's rather like one of those James Bond movies where the villain's pretty sidekick leads the hero off to a lavish imprisonment, but with impeccable politeness. We all follow the woman from the building and across a courtyard, and then up some stairs and into another building that is both windowless and spotlessly white. Through a glass panel I can see rows of tubs stretching into the distance, each one manned by a person in rubber gear and goggles. Conveyor belts run slowly overhead, dip things into the tubs, lift, and then dip again. I draw my breath sharply in the acrid air.

The woman leads us to a small room across the floor and opens a cupboard. She hands each of us a rubber outfit and goggles and we suit up without discussion. Given the court order, and Hill's response to my early attempt at levity, I remain silent. There is a surreal edge to the whole affair.

"What are they making in there?" I ask Finkbiner when we get back to the glass panel.

"From the papers they've turned over, and my own research," Finkbiner says, "I believe this is the largest facility for plating on plastic in the world. They make more coated plastic products than their next three competitors combined."

"What kind of products?" I ask, curious about the shapes being moved from tub to tub.

"Anything from aerosol caps to pen covers to auto moldings," he says. "They don't make these things here, of course. The processes we're seeing are all cosmetic."

This exchange—need I say it; the man has a speech challenge—takes quite a long time and anyone watching from a distance must wonder what is going on. As he stutters Finkbiner twitches, straightens his collar, rolls his eyes. I'm not making light of this. I'm simply wondering what happens when he testifies.

We leave the room and walk onto the floor, and I make notes of what I'm seeing, but without much understanding of what it all means.

"I think," Finkbiner whispers, gesturing at the first row of tubs, "that what happens here is that the products are immersed in some sort of etch, probably heated chrome sulfur. It creates microscopic anchors in the plastic to which later plating adheres. It's a very dangerous solution."

I look into the tub. A thick, brownish liquid roils about in it. We walk down the line and Finkbiner nods knowingly.

"See there," he points. "The plastic is taken through a series of rinse cycles," and he gestures to a conveyor taking various objects through sprays of water and immersing them in other tubs. "The plastic is then placed in a chrome neutralizer to remove all traces of the first chrome bath."

He points to a new line of tubs.

"And then the products are immersed in a solution that creates a conductive surface that hooks into the microscopic anchors left by the chrome sulfuric etch."

Holy smoke. I don't think of these things much, but are human beings suicidal? What a process to make something shiny. I can't help wondering, and I don't want to jump the gun here, what happens to all this liquid crap when they are done with it. Maybe we do have a case.

Our minders keep us moving, and each time Finkbiner and I pause they all stop and look back at us with strange, pregnant postures, as if we have brought an entire city to its knees by our slowness.

"See here," Finkbiner says. "The wash must then be removed with another acid solution, primarily to remove all traces of tin."

We are reaching the end of the line and Finkbiner nods again, takes a few notes, gestures.

"Here," he says, "the plastic part is placed in a copper solution, washed again, and immersed in an acid copper strike."

I look into the tub and see chunks of copper, some partially eroded, attached to its wall.

"The plastic is given layers of this material in the acid copper plating bath, and then in an electrolytic nickel plating bath until it is fully plated," Finkbiner says.

Now he is quite worked up, excited even.

"And look down there," he says. "The finished product. Let's see what it is."

A worker is holding something in a long pincer.

"What is it?" I ask.

It is a shiny disc, not readily identifiable.

"What is it?" Finkbiner asks, turning to the Morganic group.

One of the men in the group is about to say something when Hill steps in, takes his arm, looks angrily at me.

"You know the rules," he says.

"You're not allowed to ask them questions," I say to Dr. Finkbiner.

He looks perplexed, shrugs.

"My guess is" he says, lowering his glasses and peering through the window, "is that it's the base of something, maybe of a toy."

"How do you know?" I ask.

"It's the base of something," he says. "This is all a cosmetic process. Routine, very routine indeed. No surprises here."

Maybe that's how he feels, but I feel as if something in how I see the world has changed. I certainly won't look at a shining toy quite the same way again.

• • •

It is a muggy day but the air smells clean, at least it does when compared to the dank fumes we have left behind. It may be my imagination but even my yellow pad seems to have wilted, become more absorbent. Finkbiner has spent an hour now pointing to different places on the ground outside the building from which he wants to take soil samples, and each time he does one or other of the white suited people follow him and take exactly the same amount of soil from an area inches away. Peter Hill, it seems, is watching especially closely to make sure we don't get beyond the one wheelbarrow level, whatever that may be.

"Are you expecting to find any traces of the chemicals used inside?" I ask.

"One never knows," Finkbiner says. "The federal and state environmental agencies have a book filled with regulations about how the chemicals they use have to be barreled and shipped to special dump sites. I doubt they're disposed of here."

"But then how do we prove that any of these ever got into the ground water?" I ask.

"Well," he says, and it's all so matter of fact, vague, detached, "they have to rinse things off. There's always a little spill here and there."

"How do you know it?" I ask.

"I worked in a place just like this for years," he says. "No disposal system is perfect."

"And then how would it get up there?" I ask, pointing in the direction of the boys' homes and the swimming hole.

"That's the question, isn't it?" he says.

Yes, I want to say. It is. And if I had your $38,000 I'd be a little more concerned that I didn't have the beginnings of an answer. Of course I say nothing of the sort.

"I need to do some work on this," he says, "take apart these samples, re-analyze the data. We can prove some of this in time."

"We don't have a lot of time to do it," I say. "And before you do any further work I need to get the expense approved by the firm."

"Right ho," Finkbiner says.

In some way the visit has energized me. I mean, it does look horrible and we are, aren't we, custodians of the earth? Don't we have to be at least a little bit careful? Maybe I'm too caught up in the moment, but what I've seen has convinced me that we do have something here, that if I can get this to a jury their instincts will tell them that while there may be a hole here and a hole there in my theory, on balance it's not possible to have an assembly line of poison like the one I've just seen and not have some effect on the people and earth around you.

· · ·

There is a lot of traffic and I don't make it back to Boston before five. I show my card at Triumph Tower's security desk and run the gauntlet through the half-finished lobby to the elevator. I have perspired a great deal and my clothes have taken on the bitter odors of the fumes to which I have been exposed, toxic or not. I need a shower, I am worried about the case, there are a heap of papers on my desk that require my attention. My hand, when I hold it to my nose, doesn't smell quite right. Olwine and Kay will have gone already, though the bow ties will still be grinding away. I need to sit quietly in my office and digest what I have learned, what I need to do.

I find, however, on my chair, a folded piece of paper and my name in what I recognize as Olwine's handwriting.

"See me on your return," it says.

I keep on my jacket, walk to the end of the hall, and find that his light is still on. This is unusual. I knock and walk inside.

"I just returned from the Morganic plant," I say. "Quite a toxic little operation they have there."

He does not respond, rises from his chair and walks to stand behind his desk.

"I am constrained out of an excess of caution to raise a matter of some severity," he says.

"What is that?" I ask, startled.

In case I haven't made it clear enough, I don't like the guy, but I am up for partner in a few months time and have tried to keep my nose clean, Maria aside. He pauses, focuses what I'm sure he sees as a laser-like stare on me, clears his throat as if he has been recently bereaved.

"I have noticed," he says, "a certain absence of professional decorum in the interactions between yourself and a young woman attorney employed by this firm."

I miss the point for just a moment. When I get it I feel as if someone had swung at me from behind.

"I'm not sure what you're referring to," I say, trying to delay the inevitable, casting about for some adequate response.

"Come now," he says impatiently. "It has not escaped my notice that you specifically requested that she be assigned to this file. I cannot help but wonder at your motives, but whatever they may have been, she spends an inordinate amount of time in your office and I suggest you wean her of the habit. The firm does not tolerate such distractions in its associates' practices."

"If you mean Maria Parma," I say, "she has done fine work for me on other cases and will doubtless do likewise on this case too."

"Be that as it may," he says, "one expects from senior associates in this firm an adherence to certain standards and one is surprised by a departure from them."

"Her manner is breezy," I insist, "but she is conscientious."

"That," Olwine says as he turns a page on a book before him, "is for others to decide. I shall be keeping an eye on this situation. I regret that this discussion is even necessary."

There is no rebuttal possible, only mild, distracted protest. It is better, for now, just to let it be.

At least he seems to be preparing to leave for the day.

•••

"We're doomed," I tell Maria on the phone as soon as I return to my office. "Olwine not only heard something of our little discussion yesterday, but he seems to suspect that something's going on as well. You wouldn't believe how hostile he is."

"I'm being moved over there tomorrow, you know," Maria says. "If you don't stay as far away from me as the floor plan allows we could both end up in the soup."

I detect an undercurrent of relief in her voice.

"Terrific," I say. "A perfect end to a perfect day."

"Let's go for a walk and forget this place exists," she suggests.

"I can't," I say. "I'll be here until past midnight as it is."

"So what happened today?" she asks.

"Maria," I say, a spike of energy returning. "You wouldn't believe the garbage they generate at that place."

"What kind of garbage?" she asks.

"They use the foulest, the most horrible, the most corrosive chemicals in the world to plate children's toys for no good reason," I say, "and when they're done, my gut tells me even though I can't yet prove it, they leave it places where it ends up in the ground water."

"How are you going to prove it if nobody's been able to yet?" she asks.

"I don't know," I say. "It's brown with blue bubbles and pieces of dissolving copper, and then people drink it when they're done with it."

"That's nice," she says. "What time can you go for a walk?"

"I can't," I say. "And frankly you've got a stack of papers to read as well."

"Well then I'm going home," she says, pointedly ignoring me. "It probably isn't a good time to tell you this since you're being so grumpy, but Alfonso's going to be in town on the day of the firm Prom."

She's referring, of course, to a perfectly horrible event the firm grandly calls its Annual Dinner and Dance. Every right-think-ing associate calls it "the Prom," and you don't go, of course, unless for some reason you think you have to. New lawyers at the firm seem to think they have to. When you're up for partner, I've been thinking, you go as well.

"Excuse me a moment, please," I say, trying to sound as if I am on a business call as Olwine walks into my office.

"I have received and do not approve your request for further research by your experts in the Morganic case," he says. "Margaret Kelly confirms that the expert work that needs to be done has been done."

"That's not true," I say. "And even if it were, we have to pay our experts for the time they'll be spending at trial."

"At trial, yes," Olwine says. "Until then, not another dime."

He stands for a moment at the door, buttons his jacket, and walks away.

"You wouldn't have thought the day could get any worse," I say to Maria when I am sure he is out of earshot. "I can't talk any more now."

"Time's up anyway," she says. "Since you're being such a stick in the mud, I'm going home. I have to leave now or I'll miss the six-twenty chooch."

"I'm not ready to say goodbye yet," I say.

"Later honey," she insists, and then asks, "You're not mad now are you?"

"Oh, go home," I say. "But if stupid Alfonso comes to the Prom, don't expect me to be civil."

"Anything you say," she agrees, humoring me.

The office is quiet. Through my window I can see that it is hazy outside, noisy, dusty. Someone has to do the work I am doing, and even if the system isn't the most efficient in the world, it has its advantages. Down below, men in hard hats pull jack hammers around for a quarter of my salary. Across the street some poor character has been walking a tightrope across a steel beam so high it makes me dizzy.

I am steadily sinking into the feel of the place, the isolated floors, the spot-lit marble, the long, shadowy hallways. With

Maria here soon the old building will be part of the distant past. It's like that urban myth about frogs, how they won't jump out of a pot if you heat the water very slowly. One can get used to anything, it seems.

VIII

Maria's new office is with the bow ties on the other side of the building, two doors from the corner that has been earmarked as Sheinburg's. What is most distinctive about it is the large pillar in the middle of her window. To look out the window you have to peer either to its right or to its left.

"This pillar is Mrs. Fuckles's revenge," she says when she sees it. "It's like working in San Quentin."

"You're the only associate with two windows though," I say. "Admittedly they're only three inches across, but they're five feet high."

"The other thing that makes me sick about this office," she says, "is that I'm close enough to Sheinburg to be within one yell every time one of his marginal clients dreams up some new get rich quick scheme and he needs an associate to try and figure out why it's not illegal."

"That is a problem," I say.

"I once heard him tell a client that borrowing money for a real estate deal was like getting a gift from the bank," she says. "He said that you get all the money you want and all they get is a signature on what he called 'a *fahrkakte* piece of paper.'"

"In some twisted way I suppose that's accurate," I say.

"Well, then help me figure out a reason why they have to move me to another office," she says. We can't, of course, and the office quickly begins to bear her imprint. There is her mirror hanging crookedly behind the door, her photographs of Spain, the tiny set of lithographs Emma has made for her, somewhere not quite out of sight, her collection of shoes. Tommy II, the successor to Tommy, the goldfish I gave her months before, swims around his bowl on her credenza. Within an hour of her moving in the room is every bit as untidy as the old one was, yellow pages with her spidery handwriting scattered about her desk, files on the floor.

She does not, however, have a bookshelf. I vaguely remember a green memo from Mrs. Buckles asking how many "feet" of books each lawyer had and warning that those who didn't respond would be deemed not to need bookshelves after the move.

Maria apparently did not respond.

• • •

I have asked her to do some of the technical research that needs to be done, and more than once have left articles on her desk and then returned to find them exactly where I put them, ostentatiously untouched.

There is a certain irony in how she takes my requests, too—with distance, almost as if she is not registering the content of whatever it is I have said, as if she barely understands me. I have to let it go. If she won't work, under the circumstances there is very little I can do to make her. It has reached a point, in any event, where I know much of the testimony by heart. I can't think of any other way to prepare for this thing other than to know whatever is in the file and to be ready to be creative when the trial starts.

Olwine has now disapproved my requests for money three

times, the latest for Dr. Finkbiner to test more of his soil samples, those taken from higher up the incline that separates the factory from the swimming hole. I dream of this case, of hospital beds with dying boys in my office, of Maria and me standing in a great wasteland of sludge.

I am pessimistic but not resigned, if that makes sense.

"People who win windfall court judgments spend the money in record time and usually end up worse off anyway," Lioce says, trying, I think, to console me. "What would those families do with that kind of money anyway? Drive expensive cars? Tell their bosses to go to hell? Ain't nothing gonna bring little Johnny back."

"Nice," I say. "Very nice and compassionate."

"Hey," Stan says, shrugging his shoulders. "If I don't tell it to you like it is, who will? Ms. Parma?"

• • •

Cindy knocks softly on my door and comes into my office carrying some papers from Olwine. She walks straight past me to the window and peers down into the street below.

"There's been an accident on the expressway, but you can't see it from here," she says.

I turn and watch her, marvel again at her perfect figure. She is wearing a satin blouse with puffed shoulders, a short skirt, white nylons. As she leans on the window, her hands pressed against the glass, her bracelets fall back against her forearms with a soft jingle and her wrists look smooth and fragile.

I suspect she is doing all this on purpose.

"Where can you see it from?" I ask.

"Mr. Olwine's office," she says. "He was watching it through his binoculars."

"Observing destruction is probably relaxing for him," I say.

"He's not so bad," she says. "He treats me well."

She continues to search the scene below for another moment or two, and then she turns to face me.

"I'm supposed to give you these," she said, and hands me some papers.

"What are they?" I ask.

"Nothing important," she says. "I think expense reports for the case you're handling. I felt like taking a walk. I felt like coming to see you."

"It's nice to see you out of your little alcove there between Olwine and the wall," I say.

"I hate it," she says. "None of my friends is anywhere near me, and all I have to look at are the walls and that stupid painting they've hung right in front of my desk."

"It'll be better when the rest of the firm moves over here," I say.

"I suppose so," she agrees.

There is a silence during which she does not take her eyes from my face and I watch her closely in return. Something about her is very appealing. She is uncomplicated, unspoiled, optimistic, available. She wants me too, and in a way uncluttered with Alfonsos and parents and shady driveways into which she always disappears.

Yet I am not interested.

"Are you ever going to call me again?" she asks at last, a tremor in her voice, her eyes on the carpet.

She is now leaning against the window.

"It's difficult," I say and then add, vaguely, "It's not the right thing to do. There are complications."

"Is one of them that you're going out with that new lawyer Maria?" she asks.

"No," I say, trying to sound surprised. "What makes you think that?"

"A lot of people think you are," she says.

"We're good friends," I say. "And she's engaged."

"Engaged?" Cindy asks. She sounds relieved, happy almost.

"Then I don't see what's complicated," she adds. "I had fun with you. I wish you wanted to see me."

This is ironic, I think. I recognize in her face an emotion that is no stranger to me, a peculiar loneliness born of being held at bay.

"It's something I just can't do now," I say. "But I do think you're terrific."

She waits for me to say more, but I have no more to say.

• • •

I have become used to the isolation, to having almost the entire law office to myself, but the relative solitude, the peace and quiet of it, is now eroding daily. "M Day," as the green memoranda calls the move, is steadily approaching, and we are seeing more and more of Mrs. Buckles and her Wives. A skeleton staff of administrators has even moved into their new offices to oversee deliveries and installations, and they have begun infesting the new place just as they did the old, busily pointing at things, scribbling on clipboards, poking their frosted heads in my door at will.

The deliveries are constant; huge marble tables slowly carried into conference rooms, granite floor tiles installed and polished, great alabaster flower pots placed alongside the pillars in each of the elevator lobbies. All the paintings are up now and illuminated, a gallery of faces which, though newly painted, have been given an almost ancient luminescence. Most of the reception stations, even on floors that are still totally empty, are manned, and above each of them hang light fixtures that throw uneven lights across the carpets and wrap diamond-shaped shadows around the columns. The entire place, in short, has come alive with activity of every sort, administrators, delivery men, craftsmen, messengers, and whatever lawyering that may be going on is overwhelmed by an atmosphere of unremitting industry.

Every so often I go up an extra floor or two just to see how far along things are, and as the place begins to look more and more complete so does my dread of the day the rest of the firm will move in. It's funny, really, how proprietary one can become about something in which one has no ownership at all, but soon I'll be intruded on by Cabot in his green fishing hat, Babbet and his Wizard of Oz beard, Phil O'Malley with a story just longer than the time the elevator doors are open, and the rest of them.

Only Olwine, buried there in his office, appears oblivious to the approaching move. Except that it seems hardly a move at all. Everything is brand new. It is as if there has been a plague in the old place and nothing that has been contaminated over there can be allowed to cross over.

• • •

"Are we having lunch?" Stan asks.

He has walked across from the old building and is now leaning over my desk, moving papers around, reading those that catch his eye. With his baggy, poorly fitting suit, his crooked tie, his disheveled hair, he is truly a comforting sight.

"I'd better stay in," I say. "This kiss of death trial is just a few weeks away. There's still a lot to do."

"What's going on anyway?" he demands. "It's just a court case. Not a calling."

I try and explain, briefly, very briefly, what is going on, how little there is of value in the file, how unhelpful, obstructive even, Olwine is being.

"I'm going to try it," I say, "on what they call where I come from a wing and a prayer."

"Hey listen," Stan says. "That's how the world outside of Nibble & Kuhn tries cases. Only in big firms do cases get prepared to death. You may actually have to think on your feet."

"Margaret deposed just about every person who ever worked for the town of Asheville," I say, "every inspector including one who's eighty-seven and stone deaf, every engineer, even a garbage man who says he used to smell something funny every time he went near the factory. She deposed every neighbor, consulted with every doctor who saw these boys, every member of the boys' families, and we still have nothing. I mean, it's hard to believe I haven't been able to find something to hang my hat on. Does that explain why I'm a tad concerned?"

"Are you saying you can't have lunch?" Lioce asks.

"I was going to, but to hell with it," I say. "Let's go."

• • •

"Did you ever wonder whether you actually wanted this at all?" he asks.

We are eating lunch at a deli that may have another name but that we've both called Cholesterol Palace for so long I have no idea what it is. Somehow we always end up here. The food is marginal. I expect the explanation is that we are creatures of habit.

"I don't have the energy for that kind of metaphysics today," I say. "There'd be similar bullshit in any job."

"I wouldn't be so sure," Lioce says. "There's something about this profession that brings out the worst in people."

"Oh, I don't know," I say. "If you want to moralize, moralize after the partnership vote."

"Moralize?" Stan exclaims. "Hell, I'm in no position to pass judgment. I even accepted an assignment from Sheinburg today. He has a client who's being sued by a bank for money he owes, and he's countersuing the bank and saying it's the bank's fault for lending him the money in the first place. Negligent lending, in other words, that led to the client being able to build a luxury apartment building in a run-down neighborhood over a Chinese restaurant. It would be funny if I were just reading about it rather than alleging it. The poor soul didn't sell a single apartment, not one, and now Sheinburg wants me to argue that it's all the bank's fault. The *they should have known I was an idiot* defense."

"Maybe it'll work," I say. "Maybe they should have."

"Don't be droll with me," Stan says. "I have to wash my face every time I get off the phone with the client."

"So don't speak to him."

"Have you considered the possibility that they might not only not make us partners," he says, "but that they might actually chuck us out? The partnership vote's only eleven weeks away."

"I try not to think about it," I say. "Perhaps this trial's a blessing; there's no room for another set of worries. Sometimes I wake up in the middle of the night and find myself sitting bolt upright."

"That must please Miss Parma," he says.

"You really don't believe me about that, do you?" I say.

"Are you still expecting me to believe that because she's a good Spanish girl she won't make a break with some moron in Europe her parents have chosen for her?" he asks. "It's rubbish. I should know how southern Europeans behave. My sisters are good Italian girls. Between them they've slept with every white person in the Bronx."

"I don't want to talk about it," I say.

"All right," Stan agrees. "We'll talk about something pleasant. What are you going to do if you don't make it?"

"Scramble," I say. "Try and find a job with a corporation, or with a smaller law firm. That, or jump off a bridge. And you?"

"Things always work out in the end," he says. "Trust me. I'm thinking of buying a time-share in Stowe. There's this girl who lives downstairs from me, she's really great, and somehow I just can't seem to make the grade with her. She's buying the same time slot in the unit next door."

"You're going to buy a time-share on some half-baked notion that you'll end up with the girl who's buying one next door, and who already lives downstairs from you as it is?" I ask.

"It's fully baked," he says. "And if they pass me over, one time-share or another isn't going to make much difference. We will land on our feet even if it doesn't seem so at the time."

The most distasteful possibility Stan and I face is that one of us might make it and the other not. Until my recent run-ins with Olwine it has always seemed as if it is Stan who is more at risk. No one questions his abilities, but his manner, the way he affects an offbeat jauntiness, must cause some partners to dismiss him as unpolished, someone who would be better off defending minor criminals or doing paperwork for barbershops and ethnic restaurants. He has these mannerisms—who knows where he acquired them—that really do suggest he would be more comfortable haggling about bail in Malden District Court than discussing the Noerr-Pennington doctrine before a federal judge. Some of the firm's real estate developer clients, back in the days when there were real estate deals being done and fought over, would allow no one but Lioce to try to save them when they got into difficulty. But he is not asked to work on more genteel matters, sensitive lawsuits for the old money trusts and patrician ladies with portfolios, or for the preppy start-up companies where the founders wear tweed jackets and drive Volvos. Yet by every measure except Nibble's, Stan is more cultured than almost everyone else in the firm, *than* everyone else in the firm. He knows ancient Greek, reads the classics, is conversant with Gibbon and Toynbee, once told me that an argument I'd made was "proleptic" and I had to look it up and still wasn't sure what he meant. But I don't think the partners have his measure, or, if they do, that it makes any difference to them. It's just not currency at Nibble & Kuhn, being decent and civilized, without something else, something tangible and commercially quantifiable.

Earlier in our careers we might have followed different tracks, climbed a corporate ladder somewhere, tried to make it at a less competitive firm but now the die is cast. It's Nibble & Kuhn or ignominy. Occasionally, on the street or in other law offices, I run into people who have been passed over for partnership at

Nibble & Kuhn. There is always an unspoken consolation, a momentary lowered eyelid, a whiff of humiliation.

I don't like them, if that isn't already clear enough, but I can't countenance the prospect of being rejected by them. I just don't have Stan's kind of confidence, I suppose, the sense that things always work out.

• • •

I make the mistake, as we walk back to the office, of describing Cindy's visit. Stan is merciless.

"And you call my escapades half-baked," he says. "Sooner or later yours are going to catch up with you. There's probably a special section in the report on your prospects for partnership, coauthored by Olwine's nymphet, Parma, and that little co-op student from Northeastern who used to work in the mail room. It won't be a pretty sight."

"The statute of limitations has long since run on the co-op student," I say.

"It's a longer statute of limitations when the party in question is a foreign student from Venezuela who comes to work with flowers in her hair and bright pink lipstick," he says.

"I don't know why I tell you these things," I say. "You're no help at all at the time, you remember them for far too long, and you always bring them up when it serves no useful purpose. Besides which, your own romantic judgment is so bad that you couldn't possibly offer constructive advice."

"Do you want my honest opinion?" he asks, suddenly serious.

"I'm not sure," I say.

"You're crazy," he says. "Maria aside, you're playing fast and loose with Olwine's secretary. Is it too far-fetched to imagine the following. She comes to work looking tragic. Black rings under her eyes. Mournful look. Olwine asks her what's wrong. She sniffs and says nothing. He asks again. She sniffs again and says nothing. He asks a third time. It all comes pouring out.

Ba-boom. Dover finds a job prosecuting welfare fraud for the Department of Social Services."

"Nothing happened," I shout. "You don't need to believe me but it's true."

"You'd have your own little office, of course," he goes on. "With a nice linoleum pattern on the floor and a perfectly serviceable metal desk. And the cut in pay wouldn't matter that much given the perks, like a government-issue Chevette and your own desk fan."

"Oh, stop," I say, but I can't help laughing.

"You asked," he says.

"No I didn't," I say. "And in any event, it's too late to change anything."

"Given your record," he says, "I would be prepared to bet that you will do something—I'm not sure what, but something—between now and the partnership vote that will make what's already happened look tame."

"How much?" I ask.

"Ten bucks," he says.

We shake hands on it.

• • •

"It's ridiculous," Maria says.

"It's not ridiculous at all," I say, holding the receiver away from my ear, narrowing my eyes, looking out my window over the city.

"It's like you died and got buried under a pyramid of paper," she says. "Olwine's spooked you so that you barely acknowledge me inside of the crypt, and every night now you're too busy to leave when I do. What's a girl to do?"

"Someone has to do the work," I say. "And you're not being much help."

"Don't even think of starting down that road," she says. "And in any event what specifically is it you're so concerned about?

Writing long briefs that some judge is barely going to read? Memorizing how much sludge flowed through pipes that no longer exist? It's a beautiful evening. In three hours it'll be gone forever."

"Maria," I say slowly. "I've told you what's going on. I'll be out of here tonight at nine or ten o'clock and if you didn't hustle off to be with Mummy and Daddy we could get together."

"Don't make fun of my parents," she says, and her tone is flat, even a little unfriendly. "What's ridiculous is that you think this whole thing's balanced on a hair, but you're devoting your life to it anyway. The facts are the facts. There's nothing more you can do. Strength of character can't win a losing case. If the firm won't give you the resources you need, pushing extra hard on yourself isn't going to remedy things."

"Show a little responsibility, will you," I say. "This is my career. I work here to eat and pay the rent. I'm up for partner. Olwine's breathing down my neck and seems to hate me anyway. And now you're mad because I won't leave work early and go for a walk."

"You think the legal system's a Ponzi scheme," she says.

"That's irrelevant," I say. "It's my job to get this dead duck up and dressed. I just don't get what you're demanding I do."

"I'm demanding nothing," she snaps. "But you seem to have forgotten that Alfonso arrives in three days."

A well of rage surges up within me. To hell with Alfonso, with Maria, with her childish uncertainty and petulance. But then I picture her at her desk in the other building, her goldfish darting around in its bowl, her pictures of Spain on the wall, and soften, though not completely.

"Alfonso's arrival is as much your problem as mine," I say. "You're going to have to watch him pick the raisins out of his cereal and swing his arms when he walks. In the end it's all your choice."

"That's disgusting of you," she says.

This is beginning to take shape as an argument and yet I somehow feel as if I have it coming, as if it does not really matter. Anything is better than this, anything that has some small chance of blowing out the cobwebs. When I was a boy and sad I would turn the radio on as loud as it would go, as if the throbbing in my eardrums could somehow wash away, neutralize, all other feelings.

"It's really unfair to take something I told you and use it to belittle him," she adds.

"I don't apologize for belittling Alfonso," I say. "But I'm sorry for distorting what you said."

"It's okay," she says at last, and gently. "I know you're under a lot of pressure."

There is a moment of silence.

"Well, if you're not coming, I'm going to catch the train," she says.

"When does he get here?" I ask.

"Sunday lunchtime," she says.

"Look," I say, aware that somehow every word, every nuance, counts. "This is Mrs. Buckles's big move weekend, so even though I'm finally meeting with the families I supposedly represent on Monday, I can't work even if I want to. If I plan the next two days carefully and work Sunday, I could take Saturday off. Will you spend it with me?"

"The day?" she asks.

We have not been together on a weekend, or in the day except when, in the old days, we cut out from work or dawdled on our way to or from lunch.

"The day. In the sunlight. For twelve consecutive hours," I say.

"You know I can't do that," she says, but I catch something in her tone, an even newer, deeper, ambiguity than usual.

"I don't at all know that," I say. "You've spent Saturdays in the office before. Tell your parents that's where you are. We'll go out of town. We'll drive to the Cape. We'll have that unheard of luxury, a few hours without Nibble & Kuhn, Fonzie, or Mummy and Daddy."

"Alfonso," she says, "and don't make fun of my parents."

But this time there is humor in her voice.

"All day?" she says again, and I know I have persuaded her.

"The whole day," I say. "We'll go to the Cape, walk on the beach, eat lobsters, drink Bloody Marys, hold hands, kiss in the shade."

I say nothing else, wait. She waits too, wants me to add something, to persuade her, to make further arguments for her to reject. I do not.

"Okay," she says finally, her voice very low, her manner timid. "Pick me up at ten o'clock. And don't be late."

• • •

Another ragged evening approaches, more Styrofoam boxes filled with Chinese food from Weylus or from the deli downstairs. The bow ties order off elaborate menus available on the Internet and each night there are deliveries from some of the city's best restaurants. I was never like that, for better or for worse. How good can ornate food taste when you eat it in a Nibble & Kuhn conference room? Get the task of nourishment over with, I say. Perhaps that is a feature of whatever character flaw in me makes me take it and take it and take it.

Kay is gone. The office is quiet. The same crew rustles about in the corridors; ambitious young men, the Sandinistas, a secretary ticking away at her screen in between spoonfuls of something brown in a Tupperware bowl. With Maria gone the building loses its juice, or at least it seems so to me. I live with a sense of imminent change that is somehow also attached to a conviction that no real change is possible. I see myself, years in the future, still eating lunch, with or without Lioce, at Cholesterol Palace, still vaguely disconsolate, still without any real respect for my partners, or for the pasty prima donnas who sit as judges, or for the firm's clients. For some reason I picture Marvin Babbet combing his silly beard in the men's room and wondering whether to shave it off or not.

Success at law, it seems, makes men prissy, feebly narcissistic, women as alluring as barbed wire. And failure is worse. At times I have a premonition of an onset of the kind of restlessness I have seen in some men as they approach middle age.

• • •

I could call my parents in Toronto.

"You don't call, son," my father once said, "when things are bad down there in Boston. You call when everything's fine. We're always happy to hear from you, but we'd be just as happy if your calling pattern were reversed."

I have not spoken to them for weeks already. At this time, I know, they will be preparing dinner. I picture my father, doubtless in his beret, stirring some fragile sauce on the burner, a glass of wine by his side, and my mother, into her third Kahlua and milk—we laugh at her for this; she may be becoming a drunk, but her taste in alcohol remains teenage—cutting and dicing, preparing the ingredients for whatever it is they are making. They will be in their slippers, my father in a loose silk shirt, my mother in a caftan, chattering away about nothing in particular. They have few friends, are still, after all these years, absorbed by each other.

By some measures we have been quite poor at times and they are still far from wealthy, but they lack nothing at all. I know that I earn more than three times what my father ever has.

"There are some things," my father said once, "that no one can be told, that each person just has to learn for himself."

"Like what, Dad?" I asked, a touch of condescension in my tone.

Occasionally my father says something truly sensible. Most

often, though, the great conclusions he has drawn from life seem quite inconsequential.

"One of them, young hot shot," my father says, "is that only the simple things can make you happy."

I think for a moment of calling them, and then decide against it.

• • •

I begin to work, taking papers from the endless piles that Kay has sorted so fastidiously. The air conditioning is less effective than it was in the old building, after hours blows a cool but rancid mist through the vents that leaves a taste of mildew and concealed dust. Maria is on the train home by now, sitting against a window, staring out at the passing suburbs. Her hands will be in her lap, her handbag on the floor beside her, her thoughts, I hope, of me and of the argument we have almost had. Of Alfonso too, no doubt. In a few miles she will disembark, disappear into a dark house filled with people who mean everything to her and to whom I mean nothing. So much lies between things as they are and things as I hope they will one day be.

And in the meanwhile, life is passing me by.

IX

As I approach the spot where I always leave her, I am not sure where we are supposed to meet. She has said nothing that leads me to believe that this time I should simply go up the driveway and onto the grounds. But then I have never taken her from this house before.

I stop the car and wait in the street until I am five minutes late. It is extraordinary that, at my age, I should feel trepidation picking up a girl at her parents' house.

After I have been waiting for almost fifteen minutes, I call her on her cell phone.

"Are you coming?" I ask.

"Are you?" she says.

"Are you saying you want me to come in?" I ask, surprised.

"Of course, Magellan," she says. "I'm sitting here waiting for you."

I close the phone and start the engine, and then I see her coming down the driveway and beckoning to me. She turns and begins to walk back up, and I follow her, around a slight curve, up into territory as distant as the moon.

• • •

How do I put this without hyperbole? I had no idea, none whatsoever, one would not have seen the dimensions of it driving by, that the house, this house, was here. One doesn't need to describe it really other than to say that it is Newport in Boston. It is very large indeed with perhaps six or seven chimneys, four stories, and curving dormer windows in the roof. To its right is a neatly groomed tea garden complete with stone walls and the remains of a maze. Behind it one glimpses stretches of lawn. It is, in short, astonishingly affluent. Maria has said nothing of any of this, has allowed me to live with whatever assumptions I have chosen to make on the subject of her background.

As I approach the house, see the driveway curve off and then circle back around a huge oak tree, I am relieved to see that there are no other cars. I pull up and turn off the motor.

Maria runs up to me. She is breathless, takes me in her arms and holds me tightly.

"What's the matter?" I ask when I have kissed her repeatedly.

"I'm nervous," she says. "Having you at my house makes me feel funny."

"Where is everyone?" I ask.

"Away."

"Where?" I ask.

"In Rhode Island," she says quickly.

"With Alfonso's family," I add.

"Yes," she says, and when I stiffen adds, "Don't be acting surprised. I've told you. His father and mine are like brothers."

"You don't mind staying alone here?" I ask, brushing off her explanation. "This house is enormous. You said nothing about any of this. You said nothing about living in a Stately Homes of England catalog."

"No," she says. "I don't."

We enter the foyer, walk through a hallway with black and white marble tiles on the floor and lined with paintings. At the far end is a set of double doors and to either side openings into other rooms that are equally grand.

"How long have you lived here?" I ask.

"Since I was eight," she says. "I love this house but I can't remember the last time I brought anyone here. Would you like to see it?"

"Of course," I say.

She crosses the hall and opens a pair of double doors into a room which is the size of a hotel ballroom. On the floor are richly embroidered oriental carpets, it is furnished with chairs with carved arms and velvet cushions, shining tables, and long, high backed couches covered with brocade. Several chandeliers hang in the center of the room and, as in the hallway, the walls are covered with paintings which came to light under tiny overhead lamps when Maria turns a switch.

Two paintings beside a piano look familiar and I walk over to look at them.

Determined not to show the astonishment I feel, I say, "Your parents own work by Toulouse-Lautrec?"

"My grandfather gave us those," she says. "He collects art."

"Where does he live again?" I ask.

"In Madrid," she says.

"What does he do?" I ask.

"Why do you want to know?" she asks and then she says, "He owns buildings."

"Whenever you mentioned your grandfather in Spain," I say, "I pictured a little old man playing bocce in the town square. I guess that doesn't describe him."

"No," she says, "it doesn't."

The show of wealth is a new dimension to her and I am having difficulty reconciling it with everything else about her, her simplicity, how painfully genuine she is, how unaffected, how unimpressed by wealth or possessions in others. It does not add up.

She takes my hand as she goes around the room turning off lights.

"Come. I'll show you the rest."

The rest of the house is what one would expect once one has come to terms with the public rooms. Her parents sleep on a canopied bed in a room filled with oversized chairs and polished tables and Maria's room on the far side of the house is equally ornate. It adjoins a much larger room which belongs to Emma, who is in Spain.

"It feels empty without her," she says as we look in.

"This place would feel empty if the Vienna Boys Choir were staying here," I say, and because it seems as if everything about Maria and her family is acquiring a new dimension I ask, though she has told me before, "What is Emma doing in Spain?"

"She's at the university," she says. "So's Alfonso's brother. I think they're going to get married. Very soon. In Spain."

"Why not here?" I ask.

"My grandfather wants it there," she says. "There's a chapel attached to his house where everyone in my family gets married. I told you that already."

"The chapel, maybe," I say. "Not the bit about everyone getting married there."

She stops walking, shakes her head, sits on the edge of a bench. The feeling that I am out of my depth, on a hopeless quest, has never been stronger.

"Don't be fixing to make a fuss," she says. "My family is different. They're very traditional and though it probably seems like a contradiction to you, I like it."

"You have a beautiful house," I say, simply but with a touch of resignation.

"I tidied my room especially for you," she says.

"How long did it take?" I ask.

"Over an hour," she says.

"What could get messy in here?"

"Lots of things," she says. "Do you want to see?"

I say I do and she opens the door to a closet, just for a moment, and I catch a glimpse of a great jumble—clothes, hangers, boxes, papers—all piled together inside. It returns things to normal, places Maria squarely in the room for the first time, makes me smile.

"That was on the floor," she says, struggling to close the closet door.

I put my arm around her and begin to kiss her, but she resists.

"Not here," she says.

"Yes, here," I say.

"This is my bedroom. If my father knew I had a boy up here he'd have an aneurysm."

"But your father's in Providence."

"It still weirds me out," she insists.

She runs her hands through my hair and kisses me on the forehead and then pulls me from the room.

"Which room is Fonzie's?" I ask.

"It's a closet in the cellar," she says. "You don't want to see it."

"I do," I say.

She leads me down the passage and opens a door.

"I lied," she says. "It's this one."

I don't go in but from the doorway I can see that it is, like the others, large and comfortably appointed. It has its own canopied bed, a writing table, its share of sofas and chairs. An elaborate mirror hangs on the wall.

"Have you made up the little bed and cleaned out a place for his booties in the closet?" I ask.

"If you must know," she answers, "I did make the bed for him last night and it made me so sad I felt like throwing up. I don't know how I'm going to do this."

I soften. I imagine her making the bed, folding the linen, and I feel, suddenly, almost invincible.

"I've seen enough," I say.

We leave the bedroom and I follow her down the wide stairway until we are back in the entrance hall.

"I'm ready to go," I say. "Still coming?"

She pauses, stands at the bottom on the stairs, and watches
me closely.

"There is something you should know that you don't," she
says finally. "Something you never would have guessed and that
I don't generally tell people. At least not here, not in Boston. In
Spain, everyone knows."

"What is it?" I ask. "It's going to be big, isn't it?"

"Yes and no," she says and she is suddenly now so bashful,
so reserved, I'm not quite sure what to make of it. "My father
insists that this is just one part of who we are and he's worked
hard not to let it dominate everything else in our lives. So have I.
I have cousins who have let it define them and it hasn't brought
them any happiness."

"What cousins have let what define them how?" I ask.

"For one thing," she says, "you may as well know that my
name isn't exactly Maria Parma."

"No?" I say.

"It's Maria Teresa Sofia de Bourbon Parma," she says.

"And?" I say, though something in this does ring a bell.

"I don't want to spend the rest of the day going into it," she
says, "and if you go and get all pissy I'll regret telling you anything at all, but my family's quite old in Spain. If you go back a
bit it intersects with the Spanish royal family."

"You're not serious."

"As serious as the plague. I'll tell you one other thing, ducky.
You get to ask one question per day about this, and that's it. My
parents have worked hard to strike a balance between what was
and what is and I think they did a good job."

"I can see that," I say, gesturing at our surroundings.

"Don't be dumb," she says. "Half the houses on this street are
like this except that my parents think it's a point of preserva-

tionist honor to keep the plumbing the house was built with. In the end who my great-great-grandfather was makes very little difference today but it's something that's always present in my life. It's up to me to keep the balance my parents struck, and I thought, until you came along, that I had."

"I do have today's question," I say.

"And?"

"What are you doing at Nibble & Kuhn, Countess de Bourbon?" I ask, and suddenly it seems funny, for whatever reason, very funny indeed.

"What do you want me to do?" she asks. "Stay home and eat bonbons? That's your quota. Let's go."

"One more?" I say. "Tomorrow's question today."

"Okay," she says.

"Alfonso?"

"De Bourbon. Actually Two Sicilies," she says. "His grandfather and mine opposed Franco together and that's what we're doing in America in the first place. And don't go jumping to all sorts of conclusions. There's nothing dynastic about this."

She purses her lips, nods, gathers her things.

"It's still exactly what it's always been."

"Can you imagine the look on Olwine's face?" I say, and now Maria becomes deadly earnest, almost urgently so.

"It'll never happen," she says. "Never."

X

THERE IS A LINE AT THE MARTHA'S VINEYARD FERRY OFFICE, AND even though I have reserved the tickets, we have to wait to collect them. I sense, as we stand there among the small crowd, most in T-shirts and sunglasses and carrying hampers, that Maria is becoming jumpy and distracted. It has happened before. She answers my questions in monosyllables, keeps looking around, when a kid behind her drops his satchel she jumps as if hit by shrapnel.

"You're not going to do that to me again?" I say.

"Do what?" she asks, barely listening.

I take her by the shoulders, shake her, bring her face to within an inch of mine so that her eyes seem improbably close together, especially large and childlike. She remains totally passive. A few people around us are watching.

"Become all freaked out like you did once before, that night we went to the North End," I say. "You're not. Right?"

She shrugs.

"It feels funny to be going away with you like this," she says.

"What does 'funny' mean?" I ask. "'Funny' is not an adult word. Are you having fun? Does being with me make you feel sick? What is funny about any of it?"

"Don't be funny," she says, and shrugs my hands off her shoulders. "I'm not used to this."

"Used to what?" I shout, and now there is no one in the line who is not watching us. "At twenty seven you're not used to being on a date with a boy?"

"Not one who isn't Alfonso," she says softly. "Not one who everyone doesn't know and understand and approve of. Surely you get it."

There are tears in her eyes.

• • •

The argument, if it is an argument, does change her mood. I put my arm around her waist and pull her toward me, and then we stand side-by-side in the line until we reach the window. When the man in the booth hands us our tickets, Maria reaches into the pocket of her shorts and pulls out two crumpled twenty dollar bills.

"Here," she says.

"Don't be silly," I say.

"I'm not going to let some boy pay for me to do something," she says.

She is insistent and so I take one of the bills and hand it up to the window.

"You really are an amazing set of contradictions," I say.

We walk along the wharf and then down the gangplank and onto the ferry. It is a perfect day, bright and clear, breezy and with the smell of seawater and mud flats in the air. The ferry is a giant catamaran, swift and sharp, able to reach the Vineyard in under three hours. In the galley there are chairs and tables, a bar, a counter with snacks. We take a corner booth and spread out our things on the benches.

"I like the way you look out of work clothes," I say.

"And I like how you look," she says. "Did you buy these clothes on your own or did a girl help you?"

"Different girls helped me buy different things," I say.

She takes my hands in her lap and strokes my fingers. My palms rest on her warm thighs and then move down her leg, over her knees and calves.

"You're bold," she says. "Every other time, if we'd been seen, there would have been an innocent explanation for what we were doing no matter how far-fetched it may have seemed. But if we get seen now there is absolutely nothing we could be doing other than what we absolutely are doing."

"What are we doing?" I ask.

"What do you think?" she replies, and looks out the window at a boat roaring toward us.

"Do you care?" I ask.

"Of course I care," she says. "My parents' friends show up in the oddest places, to say nothing of Alfonso's."

I had thought she was talking about being seen by someone from Nibble & Kuhn. Until the ferry's engines start up and the vessel moves with a shudder away from the wharf, I remain silent.

• • •

Once we are clear of the pier the boat picks up speed and begins to move at such a rapid clip that it leaves a speedboat's wake in the water.

"Let's go up top," Maria suggests, and we stand and put on our windbreakers. As we walk through the cabin Maria reaches for my hand and we walk as a couple through a room filled with people. I hang back, watch her as she walks ahead, her long, slender legs, her glossy hair tousled by the wind, her fragile waist. I know that I could be so absorbed by her that nothing would remain.

It is as we near the end of the second flight of steps, the ones that lead onto the deck, that she rears back as if struck, turns with a look of terror on her face, begins to hustle me down into the cabin.

"It's Alfonso's Harvard roommate," she says, her voice frantic. "I think he saw me."

"For Christ's sake," I say. "Is this going to be the theme of the day?"

"I don't know," she says meekly. "Let's go hide."

"You can't hide on a boat this size," I say. "And in any event, I don't see why we should. If he doesn't like seeing you, that's his problem."

"I shouldn't have come," she says.

"Maria," I say, again turning her to me, again bringing her face to within an inch of mine. "If you say that one more time I'm simply going to ignore you until we get there, and then I'm going to take the first boat back."

"I shouldn't have come," she says, and then as I let go of her and turn away she pulls me back and kisses me on the mouth, a long, firm kiss.

"I scoped this thing out when we came on board," she says, her spirits returning. "There's a small deck out front of the pilot's cabin. We'll go there if they don't chuck us off and we'll stay there. If what's-his-name sees us, I'm cooked, but I did everything I could."

"Do you promise that's how you'll be?" I ask.

"Yes," she answers. "Yes. This isn't fair to you."

We sail the rest of the way on a deck of our own, on a ledge beneath the pilot's cabin, in each other's arms.

• • •

At the landing we hire a moped and crash helmets, and after we've practiced by taking a few turns around the parking lot we set off for Edgartown, creeping along at the edge of the highway and wobbling nervously each time a car passes.

"These shouldn't be legal," I say. "This is dangerous."

"It's fun," she says, "although if you go any slower I could get off and walk alongside you."

"Do you want to drive?" I ask.

"Yes," she says.

I stop the moped and she climbs in front. After one stall we take off in a hail of gravel and soon are cruising down the road.

"We're going to die for sure," I shout.

"Not today," she says into the wind and accelerates.

We follow the signs to Edgartown, and then beyond, past Menemsha and the little beaches, and then double back and soon we are in Edgartown again. It has become overcast and as we walk through the town the cool air feels like a fine mist on our faces. We hold hands, talk, behave as unremarkably as any other lovers. It is an adventure beyond description. I am happier than I have ever been.

We stop for lunch at a restaurant on the edge of town, all pastels and outsize drawings of petals, and then walk again until we find ourselves back at the moped. This time I drive, and when we find a stretch of beach that seems isolated I pull up and wheel the moped off the road and onto the sand. Lying beside her, the sun beating down on us, her arm in mine, I feel a fullness and an exhilaration that makes all the waiting, each time I have watched her walk into the shadows, worth it. We swim, fall asleep, wake up, and eat apples from my hamper.

"This shouldn't be such a treat," she says as we sit at the edge of the water and watch the ripples brush our feet. "Sometimes it seems that it really isn't so complicated."

There are many things I could say in response, but all I say is, "It is nice, isn't it?"

She nods, draws patterns in the wet sand.

• • •

"I don't know if I will ever feel this free again," she says as we stand at the rail heading back to town.

She runs her hands through my hair, watches me intently.

"It's your choice," I say, and turn away from her, back to the island.

"Perhaps it is," she says at last.

When I think that at this time tomorrow she will again be isolated in her parents' formidable home, immersed once again in routines wholly alien to me but open to Alfonso, a great sense of foreboding descends.

My day with her will be nothing more than a slip of light on a canvas already almost completed.

• • •

It is eight o'clock when we disembark at Commonwealth Pier. The size of the city, its great buildings and tiers of lights, the rush of its traffic, is jarring after the tranquil pace of the day. We walk to my car and when we are there sit in silence.

"I could take you home, but I'd rather not," I say.

"Me too," she says.

"Would you like to see where I live?" I ask.

She sits without moving in her seat, looks into my face and then down again.

"In the Back Bay?" she asks.

"I haven't moved."

"Just see it?" she asks.

"What else would you do with it?" I say.

"Okay," she says. "But my parents will be back at midnight."

"And?"

"I plan to be home before then," she says.

Through the city, past the Common, up Commonwealth Avenue, and soon we are pulling into my parking space behind the building.

"I've tried to picture where this was, how it looks," she says.

We leave the car and she waits as I unlock the door. We stand in silence as we ride the elevator.

"I like the way this smells," she says. "Of linseed oil and old plaster."

I open the door and step in ahead of her to turn on the lights. I have hoped that this moment would come, have prepared for it, but as she enters my apartment I am apprehensive. She walks around the room slowly, touches my possessions, runs her hands along the back of my sofa.

"That drawing used to be in your office," she says, pointing.

"It did," I say, waiting in the center of the room.

"It's funny to see it here now," she says.

"It's funny," I say.

"It's exactly what I would have pictured," she says. "Everything in its place. Nothing excessive. All in good taste."

"I'm pleased you like it," I say.

We turn to face each other, again shy, and then, standing in the middle of the room, we hold each other for a long time.

"I can't do this any more," she says. "It's too much too ask."

I do not respond, stand waiting, hold her very firmly. When she sees that I will do nothing, she takes my shirt sleeve between her fingers and, slowly, pulls me into my unlit bedroom.

By Monday morning no hint of the euphoria remains. It has gone, wafted away with the scent she left on the pillow and which now refuses to return even as I lie quite still, my face buried deeply in it. The radio pops on. I open my eyes. Light streams in through the shutters. I stay where I am for as long as I can. I am dreading this day. Today is the day I finally meet my clients.

Margaret, of course, has met with them many times. I know this from confirmation letters in the file, not from any notes she may have kept describing whatever it is they have told her. I have gleaned some of the background from medical records and reports but there is a lot I do not know. It is sobering that I am meeting them for the first time so shortly before their trial is scheduled to begin.

"Where is Margaret Kelly?" has been the first question each of them has asked when I call and suggest a pre-trial meeting.

"She's been appointed a judge," I say to each of them. "Great news for her, and of course I'm really happy to now have the opportunity to represent you."

This declaration of happiness has been met, almost without exception, by a spell of silence. Some of them have asked questions about me, my background, my experience trying cases. Others have become completely passive, resigned to whatever has been decided for them. On balance, whatever Margaret Kelly's shortcomings may have been, they seem to like her and are not happy to hear that she is being replaced.

The traffic on Storrow Drive is unusually light and before long I am on the bridge over the channel, paying the attendant, and walking across the lot to Triumph Plaza. In front of me, the garish building sticks into the sky like a giant phallus. The air is chilly, hints of summer's end. I am late for work but the office is quiet. For whatever reason Kay does not seem to be in yet. I welcome the unexpected respite.

Respite isn't in the cards. In the center of my desk is a lime green coffee cup inscribed with the words "Moving to Triumph—Nibble & Kuhn," and beside it a small stack of Mrs. Buckles's lime green memoranda. The one on the top announces that the mug is a memento for all personnel, pronounces the move a great success, and invites everyone in the office to a welcoming breakfast. Well that's where everyone is, at least. I can't bring myself to read the other papers just yet.

I walk back to the elevators and ride up to the cafeteria. For the past few weeks it has been deserted, smelled strongly of new carpeting and fresh paint and was dark except for the colored lights shining from a row of vending machine. Now as I enter the room the carpet smells are mixed with the aromas of food and coffee and there are a number of people, mostly secretaries and administrators, standing around in small groups. Several partners are clustered together in the center of the room, gathered, I see, tightly about the little trinity of Olwine, Sheinburg, and Cabot. I notice a pod of title examiners huddled by the vending machines and then, to my relief, Stan Lioce and a handful of associates standing by the window.

I choose a pastry—the plate has been fairly well picked over and it isn't easy—and then walk across to them. Lioce has a cup in one hand and two pastries held at strange angles in the other. I watch as he takes alternating bites, first from one then from the other.

"Free nibbles at Nibble," Lioce says.

"Say it louder," I say. "One or two partners may not have heard you."

"Nobody heard," he says, suddenly somber. "Are you saying you haven't seen the memo?"

"What memo," I say, and there are a couple of snickers at my elbow.

"Nibbles is big," Stan says.

"I don't know what you're talking about," I say.

It isn't as if you can't make fun of the firm's name, of course. It's a free country. It's more that the senior people around here find any attempt at its humorous use spectacularly unfunny, unfunnier than it could possibly be. It's as if when you become a partner you somehow lose the frame of reference entirely, as if by magic.

"The new 'Branding Campaign,'" he prompts.

"Why does a law firm need branding?" I say. "We are what we are. Perhaps they're going to number us on the arm so we can't get lost?"

"No," Stan says. "They're shortening the name of the firm. It's the rage now, or so the consultants say. Long archaic names are out. Short punchy ones are in. On stationery, in an avalanche of advertising, even how the receptionists answer the phone. Apparently our new name is more catchy and thus will bring in a slew of new business."

"Shorten it how?" I ask.

"Guess."

"Please," I say. "I'm in a hurry. How could they possibly shorten the firm's name?"

"We're going to be 'Nibbles,'" Stan says.

"No."

"Yes. May the Lord strike me dead if I lie."

"Nibbles?"

"Nibbles. And that's not all. We have a new slogan too: 'Nibbles Knows.'"

"You're a liar."

"Nibbles Knows. There's a memo in your in box somewhere that explains it all," Stan says. "And by the way, where's your sidekick?"

"She's in her office," Jennifer, one of Maria's friends, says. "She didn't want to come."

"Something you did?" Lioce asks casually, looking at me and raising an eyebrow.

• • •

Kay is at her station when I return, and though I note something terse in her manner I let it be and walk into the office. I start to collect the files I will need when the families arrive. They should be here any minute. As I start to organize my thoughts, Kay knocks on the closed door and comes in before I can answer. She sits down across from me.

"You've read the material on your desk, I would imagine?" she says.

"Actually no," I tell her. "I have a meeting with the families of the boys in a few minutes. I can't imagine there's anything in there that can bring joy."

Kay sits in stony silence for a moment.

"Do they think we're in grade school?" she suddenly demands. "Do they set out to insult us?"

"Who?" I ask, suddenly very weary though the day hasn't even begun.

"You know who," she says, and sinks into a another pregnant silence.

"Can we do this later?" I ask, trying to sound moderate, receptive. "I have this meeting in a few minutes and there are things I need to go over."

Inside Kay there is clearly a battle, her professional instincts which urge her to stand up and leave the room and whatever makes her human that requires her to stay.

"Please," I say, and tip the balance.

Kay stands, straightens her perfectly straight collar, and leaves.

"We can talk later, I promise," I say as she disappears.

• • •

They shuffle together, the twelve of them, as if I am moving them through a museum. My first impression is that they look like the sort of people you might encounter in a subway car, some of the men in jackets and ties, others in colored shirts, the women all in dresses of one sort or another. They are standing in a group when I arrive in the reception area to greet them, shake my hand, one by one, with a certain solemnity.

"Let's go this way," I say. "I've reserved a conference room."

I should have scouted this all out in advance, I suppose, because things don't get off to an auspicious start when I get lost on my way to the Alfred Nibble Conference Center. I know what floor it's on, but things tend to get a little confusing in their sameness floor to floor, especially on the conference center floor because for whatever reason, security probably, there are doors that only open one way. I lead them in one direction to a grand set of doors, and then they don't open.

"I'm sorry," I say, trying to prompt the herd into a U-turn. "I think we need to go that way."

As I say, this doesn't seem to inspire confidence.

"How long have your worked here?" one of the men asks.

He is probably in his fifties, wearing a plaid jacket, blue flood pants, a college ring rubbed smooth by age. His hands are gnarled.

"The whole firm just moved over today, as a matter of fact," I say, and he is reassured, though only partially.

"Nice place," he says.

I can't deny a vague feeling of proprietorship. I do belong here, after all.

• • •

They listen politely as I describe the trial process, what our evidence will be, what a jury may find persuasive, but as I proceed I have the undeniable sense that there is something else going on. Finally it emerges. They have had their own meeting over the weekend, it seems, and are less than confident that Nibble & Kuhn is doing the right thing by them. Someone apparently has consulted with one of the better known plaintiffs' law firms and has a list of questions for me.

They are the obvious.

How many plaintiff's cases like this one have the firm's lawyers tried?

The answer to that, all fudging aside and I get the sense that if I do not gild this lily they will walk straight out, is none.

There is a knock on the door. It is Shannon Bertucci, clipboard in hand, and three men in overalls.

"Can you come back?" I ask.

"This will take less than a minute," she says, and the men file into the room, fiddle with a dial somewhere on the wall, gesture to her that all is in order, and leave.

How many cases have I actually tried to verdict in front of a jury?

The answer to that, all fudging aside, and I fudge here too, is three.

"We have lots of experience trying toxic tort cases in this firm," I say. "Admittedly we're not often on the plaintiff's side, but that has its positives too because we know how corporations defend these things, and we have the resources and the skills to prosecute a claim like this properly."

Is my nose growing yet?

There is, so help me, another knock on the door. This time it is Mrs. Buckles herself.

"Please," I say. "Can you come back?"

She glares at me. She needs to count electrical outlets. I can't guess why, but it has to be done now. She circles the room, counting, checking, making notes on her clipboard. We all watch her as if she is doing something entirely entertaining. When she leaves I write Do Not Disturb For Any Reason on a sheet of paper and tape it to the door. In case anyone misses it, one would be justified in concluding that I am a person who does not have much clout within my own law firm.

I continue talking to them though it is all very disjointed. I will pretend that I am in the thirteen floor elevator lobby, among friends. The short version, then. They have decided, it is clear, and far from unanimously, to go ahead with Nibble & Kuhn, to go ahead with me, but there is an undercurrent of doubt that is less than heartening. I go around the table, have each of them update me on how their boy is doing. There are five couples and two single parents. Most of them are working people, three are college graduates. Four of the boys seem to be in remission, two, it seems, will die, and one has already died. As the parents talk they tear up, Kleenexes are passed around, backs are patted. This has been going on for a long time now and I think I understand, for the first time really, that Margaret Kelly, Nibble ogress though she may be, has actually been a source of comfort to them. I can easily imagine her crying with them and expressing an entirely genuine empathy.

I am not a callous person and to see parents in pain is difficult, but it is important as well to balance this awareness with other things, that whatever the outcome this lawsuit will not restore

their sons' health, that I have come to doubt that the factory
has anything to do with their colossal misfortune, that they ask
more questions about the money they stand to win than about
any other subject. One other thing is as clear as daylight, and
that is that if this case goes off the rails they will be fixing to sue
the firm, and me, in a heartbeat. Not that I'm supposed to be
distracted from my task, mind you. I am not a callous person, as
I say, or at least I hope I am not, but I am not sure, other than the
money, what it is we are doing here. I had thought there might
be talk about the principles that may be involved, about holding
the factory accountable, but there is very little of that.

At a construction site across the way the skeleton of a building is quiet, half-shrouded, shadowy. The days are becoming
shorter. In the distance I can see a boat sliding into a berth alongside Commonwealth Pier and it is the Vineyard ferry. Her legs
are slim and dark. I dropped her off at ten minutes to twelve,
watched her walk off into the shadows. For a brief moment the
shadows did not seem as dark as usual, her leaving not as bleak,
our separation not as definitive. That all changed, of course, as
soon as she was out of sight. Outside the sky has turned very
bright, as clear and blue as it gets at the end of summer when the
humidity is gone, before the warmth disappears.

Across the expressway a man sits on a girder as it is lifted by
a crane, his safety belt looped down into the emptiness beneath
him. He is bare chested, in jeans, boots, wearing a helmet. I
watch a girder as it swings upwards, then as it swings around,
then as it comes to rest.

• • •

I see Maria coming down the broad corridor lined with pictures and urns, walking alone, reading something as she goes. I
see her first, slow down, wait for her to reach me.

"Hi," I say.

"Hi," she answers and continues walking. Just as she passes me she stops and half turns.

"Hi," she says again.

"Hi," I say.

"How are you?" she asks.

Her face is filled with concern, is sadder than I have ever seen it.

"I'm okay. And you?"

"Okay."

Again we are silent.

"I gotta go," I say.

"Me too," she answers.

"Gotta see a lawyer about a case," I say.

"Me too," she says.

"Meeting," I say.

"Me too," she says.

It doesn't make sense, of course, but why should it?

• • •

I sit back in my chair and begin to open the mail. Lioce comes in without knocking.

"You may be fooling somebody that you're busy when you close the door like that," he says. "But I know better."

I say nothing and he walks to my desk, leans over, and examines some of the papers.

"Well?" he says.

"Please feel free to read my mail," I say. "I've just been savaged by seven sets of parents, and now I have to deal with you and your pregnant pauses."

"You could save yourself the pregnant pauses if you just came out with it and told me what happened on Saturday," he says.

"I knew I would regret telling you," I say.

"I could drag it out of you," he says. "But why not just be efficient and volunteer." He stops, slicks back his hair. "I mean, get real."

"I can't compress this into a headline," I say.

"So?" he says. "Who said to limit yourself to a headline?"

"Saturday was fine," I say. "And you wouldn't believe the quarters the Parma clan inhabits."

"Oh, come on," Stan says. "Did you get a load of the duds on that broad? If you paid any attention to things like that you'd have been under no illusion that her father was a house cleaner or whatever insane notion you may have had."

"He's a history professor," I say. "So who knew?"

"Just how exactly do you think a person gets to be so casual about the whole thing of earning a living?" Stan asks. "I could tell there was money there from a mile off. You're blinded to everything except certain features I needn't go into."

"We had a fine time," I say. "What isn't fine is that Alfonso arrived yesterday."

"Why would that make her miss a free breakfast?" he asks.

"Maybe she wasn't hungry."

"She doesn't miss a chance to socialize when she should be working," he says. "How long is this Alfonso character going to be lurking around?"

"Long enough," I say. "She's even bringing him to the firm Prom."

"Well at least we won't have to see him, then," he says.

"Yes we will," I correct him.

Stan gets up.

"You're not going to that stupid thing, are you?" he demands.

"Keep your voice down," I say. "I can hear everything that's said in the next office even when they don't shout."

"Of course you're not going," he insists. "The better element never goes to those things."

"They do when they're up for partner," I say. "Unless they want to earn demerits for lack of firm spirit."

"I haven't been since my first year," he says. "I swore I'd never go again."

"I remember," I say. "We ended up at a table of probate lawyers."

He grimaces.

"Where is it anyway?"

"Don't you read your memos?" I say. "In the Grand Ballroom at the Taj. It was at the Harvard Club last year, but it's not quite grand enough for the new Nibble & Kuhn, apparently. Also, only spouses and "significant others" are invited, so you and I go stag unless you want to certify some girl you barely know as "significant.""

He laughs.

"Look who's talking," he says. "You're playing out a sordid little melodrama right under the noses of the people who write your paycheck, and yet somehow you think it appropriate to comment on my personal life."

"Would you please go away," I say.

"I'm sorry I ever came in," he replies.

• • •

Less than a minute after he leaves Kay knocks. It is clear that she is bursting with some new annoyance. She picks a piece of non-existent lint from her sleeves and pauses. What will it take to be left alone?

"Have you read the latest insult from on high?" she asks.

"If you mean these jolly green memos," I say, "I haven't had a chance," and then, because she obviously needs to vent I ask, "Why?"

"I know you've taken a light-hearted approach to this," Kay says, "but to tell you the truth I don't know how much more I can take."

"More of what?" I ask. I have not seen her quite so agitated before.

"Shall I start with the twenty-five percent mark-up on phone calls, even personal ones," she says. "I don't make non-business phone calls during the day so I'm not affected by their attempt to make a profit off employees, whatever my personal views on the subject may be. I am, though, affected by the software they've installed in their new computer system."

"Is something wrong with it?" I ask.

"You could say that," she says. "The secretaries were just informed by Mrs. Buckles that the firm plans to monitor our work, how fast we type and how many corrections we make and how long it has taken us to type any document we create. They will be evaluating from it how efficient we are. It is spying, pure and simple."

Her face is now red. She has become scarcely articulate.

"This goes beyond *stickerization*," she says. "We may only be secretaries, but we are professionals too and there is no need to humiliate us in this manner. It's just . . ." She waves her hand weakly in the air and gives up on finishing the sentence.

It is insidious, but what to do? What can a person do?

"You're right, of course," I say.

Kay shifts in her chair impatiently.

"It's an affront," she says.

"It is," I say. "But Mrs. Buckles has Mr. Olwine's ear and keeps threatening to involve him if she believes you and I are not cooperating. You know what the consequences of Mr. Olwine's disapproval could be."

"Oh, dear," Kay says, her whole manner suddenly changed. "Would they hold my belligerence against you?"

"You're hardly belligerent and it doesn't matter," I say. "But I think we should both just lie low for the next three months."

"You're so highly regarded," she adds. "I would never do anything to damage your reputation."

She pauses.

"By the way," she says. "Mrs. Buckles was here. She's livid."

"Why?"

"Something about access to a conference room," she says. "I couldn't quite make it out, but it seems that you obstructed the wiring of the entire Alfred Nibble Conference Center."

I inherited Kay from a probate partner who retired. She had been with me for over a year before she allowed me to find out that she was a graduate of Vassar College.

"Young people didn't have so many choices back then," she told me over lunch one Secretary's Day. "Especially not young women."

"What would you have done if you could have chosen?" I asked.

"Heavens, I don't think of those things," she answered. "What purpose would it serve?"

She leaves my office and closes the door behind her. There is, somehow, a feeling of finality in how she does it, slowly, carefully, completely. I stand and look out the window for the umpteenth time since I have moved into this office, as if the act of staring through the glass and down onto the city will provide me with answers to questions I haven't yet asked.

A plane is approaching the airport, hovering over the smokestacks. The air is dirty. I turn and lift a memorandum from my box, a new one that was not here this morning.

I see that it is from Olwine:

The Executive Committee is not unaware that the name "Nibbles," on its own and out of context, may have associations in the minds of some that are inconsistent with the image of this firm.

We are confident, however, that our reputation for professional excellence, and our long history in this city, will overwhelm any such associations, and that our re-branding campaign will successfully position the firm for many years to come

Well at least someone said something to somebody.

· · ·

The day is over. Most people have left.

If Maria would just walk past my door it would go a long way to redeeming things. I long to visit her, to pretend I am casually strolling by her office, but I will not.

XII

It has been one hundred and ten years since Alfred Nibble and Lionel Kuhn started their law partnership in a bleak little office near the federal courthouse. The firm they started has grown into something that would be unrecognizable to them. The new lease at Triumph Plaza is being reported in the newspapers as the largest ever signed in Boston.

The firm's annual dinner and dance, carefully scheduled this year for the first weekend after the move, is planned as an event of extraordinary elegance. People will say that it was a defining moment, that it marked the crest of an era of explosive growth and seemingly unbounded optimism. A few may wonder quietly whether the show of opulence, under the circumstances, isn't, oddly enough, quite inappropriate. They will say it, of course, only much later.

• • •

Lioce has still not decided whether he is going, even with the affair only a few hours away. When I call him on Saturday morning, an answering machine takes my call.

"Listen here," I say to it. "Either you're home and you're screening your calls, in which case pick the darn thing up, or you're out renting a tuxedo. In either event, pay close attention. My engraved invitation says that cocktails are at six thirty, which means we can't get there much after that."

"Hold on, hold on," I hear him say, and then a series of clicks. "This is going to be septic," he says.

I agree. "Just looking at my tux makes me queasy," I say.

There is a long silence.

"What's that you said?" he asks.

"You don't have a tuxedo, do you?" I say.

"I had one for my sister's first and second weddings," he says, "but I haven't worn it for seven years and in any event it's at my parents' house in New York."

"You could rent one, I suppose, if you hurried," I suggest. "Or you could wear a dark suit with a red bow tie. That sort of passes."

He mulls it over.

"I have a dark suit," he says. "It needs to be dry-cleaned."

"Why don't you just iron it and you'll be fine," I say, trying to sound reassuring.

"I don't have an iron," he tells me.

• • •

We meet at the Eliot Lounge for a drink before the ordeal begins. Stan looks surprisingly dapper.

"You're not going to believe what happened," he says.

"What?" I ask.

"On the way out to buy an iron I passed this girl I've mentioned to you before who lives on my floor," he said. "I don't really know her, of course, but I was desperate and desperation is the mother-in-law of invention, don't you know. So I asked her if she had an iron and she said yes."

"And?"

"I'm taking her out for breakfast tomorrow," he says. "We started talking and I could have stayed in her apartment all night, but I felt sorry for you. Also, she had a date she couldn't blow off."

"Who is she?" I ask.

"Her name's Farida." Stan says. "She's from Morocco and I swear I'm in love."

"Watch out for her brothers Hamid and Abdul," I say. "Touch her and they will de-man you with their scimitars. It is their custom."

"Very nice," he says. "Very multi-cultural. In any event I was only there long enough for her to iron my stuff."

"She ironed your clothes?" I ask in amazement.

"Yes. And when I was dressed I went back down and she tied my bow tie. I haven't a clue how one of these damn things gets tied. Even if this Prom is a total bust, it will have been worth it."

We order our drinks and calculate how long it will take us to walk to the Taj.

"At this moment," Stan says, "a gaggle of pudgy partner wives are probably tailgating in a field somewhere as a warm up. It's what Wasps do, isn't it?"

"If you'd gone to this thing even once in the last six years you'd know that most of them aren't pudgy," I say. "They're sort of leathery from too much exposure to the sun."

"I can't imagine Olwine making small talk," Stan says. "Or him with a wife."

"We met the first Mrs. Olwine years ago at the Harvard Club," I say. "I didn't think to look at her too carefully, though I'm fairly sure she was one of the brown, wrinkly ones. He divorced her and who knows what he's come up with this time."

"And your fickle little love interest," he says. "She's still going?"

I haven't thought of Maria all day.

"She'll be there," I say.

"It's a quarter to seven," Stan says looking at his watch. "We still have three minutes to sit here."

• • •

It takes us longer than we had thought to get to the hotel and we are both perspiring when we walk into the lobby. We have also drunk more than we should have and I feel a vague but distinct sense of elation that I know is inappropriate.

Stan does too.

"I think the last time I drank too much I threw up without warning," he says, as we reach the landing and see familiar people in the distance.

In the early days, invitations to the Dinner Dance, as it was formally known, had been restricted to partners and their wives. Not too long ago the partners apparently decided there was mileage in including associates and their spouses, and when someone pointed out that many of the associates weren't married, the invitation was extended to include "significant others."

Sheinburg, in one of his periodic and supposedly amusing memoranda to the entire office, had attempted to define, using legal terminology, what a "Significant Other" was.

"A Significant Other," he had written, "is an asset or encumbrance, real or personal, who or which, if disposed of in an arm's-length transaction, would qualify for long-term capital gains (or loss) treatment under the Internal Revenue Code."

He must have an interesting marriage.

• • •

I look about for Maria but she is nowhere to be seen. I want to be sure that I see her first, that I have time to look at her from a distance. Before I am placed in a position where I may be forced to talk to her or to shake hands with Alfonso, I need to experience how it feels to be in the same room with them, to see her at his side. I'm not technically a cuckold, I suppose, but it certainly doesn't feel that way.

The reception hall is filled with vases of flowers, each on a table draped in linen, and every so often a waitress passes with a tray of hors d'oeuvres or a salver with glasses. I take a glass of wine, am suddenly irritated to see Mrs. Buckles at my elbow with her beaten down Jack Spratt of a husband. She is talking about—what else?—The Move to one of the partner's wives and the woman is trying to appear interested. The effort makes her look as if, at midnight, someone will have to cart her back to Madame Tussaud's. Distracted, I almost bump into Olwine and am astonished and more than a measure annoyed to see that his wife is considerably younger than he is, my age in fact, and not unattractive in a horse ridey, Manchester-by-the-Sea, kind of way. I avoid them just in time, see her take Olwine's hand and hold it.

Stan walks by and looks at me sourly.

"In case I forget to mention it later," he says, "thank you again for a lovely evening."

"It's not so bad if you take it in the right spirit," I say.

"We're relying on the spirits," Stan says.

We approach the bar, Stan and I, and then, out of the corner of my eye, I see Maria. She looks tall and impossibly elegant, her thick hair in a French braid down her back, her dress long and full. She is wearing lipstick, a little eye shadow perhaps, looks older, sophisticated, beautiful. I see Alfonso too, of course, and am surprised at how unlike my expectations he is. His hair is blond, where I have assumed it would be dark, straight and long, swept back and curling onto his collar, and his suit is unlike any other in the room, formal but somehow looser, tapered at the waist, very European. If I have ever thought I could face them with equanimity, I know in this instant that it is impossible. He looks, or maybe it is only in my imagination, like royalty. I see him shaking someone's hand, saying something, smiling. I look away.

Stan sees them too. He puts his arm on my shoulder, shakes his head.

"I can't believe she actually had the balls to bring Euro-creep," he says. "Until the moment I saw them I thought she was kidding."

Soft music begins to drift in from the ballroom.

"I always knew she wasn't," I say.

"It's time to drop her," Stan says.

"He doesn't look like I thought he would," I say.

"Who cares how he looks?" Stan says. "This is ridiculous. She can have him. Find someone who deserves you."

We enter the ballroom and see that whoever has decorated it has gone to extraordinary lengths. At the far side, eleven men are playing instruments on a bandstand and the room is filled with tables spaced in a wide arc around a dance floor. On each table stands a large arrangement of lime green flowers, silver bowls, a forest of crystal. On the head table is a great silver candelabra, ablaze with lights. The air smells of flowers and fresh perfume.

Stan looks around with his mouth open.

"Is this a law firm or is this a law firm?" he says.

"A few hundred dollars an hour here," I say. "A few hundred dollars an hour there. It adds up."

There is a group of isolated tables in the shadows beneath a balcony and we pick our way across the room in their direction. As we reach them, I look back and see Maria entering the ballroom with Alfonso at her side. They are in a crowd, talking, gesturing, occasionally laughing. As Maria talks I can see that she is looking around and I know that she is looking for me. I step into a shadow and make sure I am out of her line of vision.

• • •

Stan and I stake out our turf in a far corner at a table behind
a pillar. I should be glad-handing, my future may depend on
it, but I can't. I just can't. Our table is almost empty except for
an Asian real estate associate and his palpably terrified, possibly
mute, wife. Siberia, in other words.

"Are these two seats taken?" I hear someone behind me ask.

I turn and see that it is Richard Havens. His wife is with him.

"A civilized table, too," he adds.

"Completely un-Nibbled," Stan says, and Havens laughs and
pulls out a chair for his wife.

"This is the young fellow who'll be trying that cancer case,"
Havens tells his wife and gestures at me. "See how tired he
looks."

"The sick boys?" his wife asks him. "The one they wanted you
to take?"

This is news to me, that Havens was asked and refused to take
the case that has become my albatross, and to Stan, too. We
exchange a glance, he and I, but I suppose in the end it shouldn't
be a surprise. No one with clout would have agreed to take
responsibility for Margaret Kelly's train wreck, and Havens is a
partner. I, of course, am not, and whether or not I ever become
one hangs in the balance every moment.

Havens's wife sits next to me and I like her immediately. She
is serious and yet gentle, trusting even. I see how, without reacting, she watches her husband as he calls a waiter and orders a
double whiskey, how she looks carefully at his face as if analyzing his condition. The whiskey arrives and Havens drinks it,
calls the waiter over and orders another. Having introduced his
wife he makes no further effort to communicate and sits instead
with his eyes fixed on the centerpiece.

"Do you suppose," I ask, trying to engage him, a vote is a vote after all, "that the flowers are lime green because that's the color of the move?"

He laughs. He has already drunk too much, that much is obvious, but if his motor functions are impaired this is not unambiguously noticeable. He is not drunk, not clumsy, just studied in his movements, slower than usual. His speech is deliberate.

"It wouldn't surprise me," he says. "It wouldn't surprise me if Mrs. Buckles's underwear were lime green either."

There is a moment of awkwardness. This is not funny, but rather somehow vulgar. He calls the waiter over to order another drink and I see his wife put her hand on his. He withdraws his arm and drops it into his lap.

"She's a poet, you know," he says without looking up.

"You are?" I say.

"I've had a little volume published," she says. "It's not a big deal."

"Can a person buy it?" I ask.

"I'll send you a copy," she says. "It's the kind of book you borrow."

The band plays on, waiters open wine bottles and serve meals. As he eats, Havens orders and drinks a series of whiskies, his eyes begin to redden, and he retreats into a blurred world all his own. He spears his food carefully but not messily, seems to be in the midst of some private argument into which no intrusion is welcome, mumbles only when he knocks over a glass of water. I pick it up quickly but there is still a stream of water which trickles off the table and onto my trousers. Havens's wife apologizes but I dismiss the incident as trivial. As Havens continues to ignore her she begins to look increasingly fragile, and I sense something heartbreaking in it. I am beginning to find it difficult to say anything at all to her, and she to him, and so we sit in silence.

The evening is turning out to be even worse than I had imagined, seems to be stretching on forever. Occasionally too, through everything else, I hear strains of laughter from the direction of Maria's table. I imagine that some of it comes from Alfonso and picture his face and then Maria's across from it.

She looked peaceful, perhaps a little anxious but not uneasy, when I saw her.

• • •

A clink of knives on crystal starts at the head table and spreads and soon the din is silenced and all heads turn to where Olwine, standing now behind the candelabra, awaits the room's attention.

"Sweet Jesus," Havens mutters. "Is it speech time already?"

Olwine adjusts the microphone and touches his tie. He clears his throat, puts on his reading glasses, and apparently begins to talk. Back in the shadow of the balcony we see that his lips are moving but we cannot hear a word of it.

"Thank you, Sweet Jesus, for this technological miracle," Havens says too loudly, and all except his wife laugh. She again places her hand on his and he again withdraws it.

Whatever it is that Olwine is saying few people, even among those who can hear, are listening. They pick at their desserts, motion to waiters, look around. Others begin to talk quietly among themselves, but if Olwine senses that he has lost his audience he does nothing about it. He continues to talk as the murmur rises, occasionally gestures, refers to his notes, and I watch the spectacle with fascination, Olwine bobbing about behind the flames like a puppet, mouthing off about some future and some past into a microphone that may or may not be working, a fact that nobody seems inclined to share with him.

"The Living Legend of Nibble & Kuhn," mumbles Havens.

• • •

After the plates are gone, while the coffee is being poured, the band begins to play again. This time it plays dance music and to my consternation people begin moving onto the floor. The first on are the Cabots, Harry and his stubby wife, her dress far too short, clasping each other like two muppets as they step across the parquet. Soon others follow.

"That's it," Stan leans across and says. "I've done my duty. Good night to one and all."

He stands, folds his napkin and turns to leave, but as he does Richard Havens stands up as well, grasps his hand, and shakes it as he begins an incoherent monologue of praise.

"I always said," he is saying, "that you were the best, the very best, of the young lawyers."

He goes on in this vein for a while and then, swaying, reaches for his wife.

"Let's dance," he says.

She looks at him, tries to reason.

"Richie," she says, "maybe we should go outside for a while."

"Nonsense," he says, and loudly.

People at a neighboring table look over, but fortunately quite a few couples are now standing and making their way to the dance floor. No damage has been done yet.

"Hey, Richard," I say. "Maybe this isn't a great idea. Why don't we take a bit of a walk first."

"What you mean?" he says, his words slurred, and he moves forward and is about to fall but Stan and I catch him and help him into his seat.

"I seem to have had one too many," he says.

"One or two," I say. "But come, let's go outside for a stroll. There are a few things I want to ask you anyway. Outside would be better."

I have no idea what it is I want to ask him, but it just seems that this is something that might work, and indeed it does.

"Sure," he says. "Why not?"

We all stand now, Havens and his wife, Stan, and I, leaving the young real estate guy and his wife alone at the table. Slowly, with Stan on one side and me on the other, we make our way, shielding him, to the door. Nobody pays any attention to us.

"Can we see you to your car?" I ask, and his wife gratefully accepts.

When they are both packed in, Stan says he's going home and I realize that I have left my jacket at the table.

"I'll be out in a sec," I say, and Stan nods.

Most people are dancing, leaving at the tables only the lame and the afflicted. I notice that the table at which Maria has been sitting is empty, and then I spot her on the dance floor, just a glimpse before she disappears into the crowd. Her arm is draped over Alfonso's shoulder and she is moving gracefully. Alfonso is smiling down at her.

I leave the room.

• • •

Stan is waiting somewhere in the hotel lobby and I try to look, as I make my way back out of the ballroom, as if I am going someplace specific, with intent, am somehow in a hurry rather than simply making my escape. The quicker I walk, the farther away the sweet fresh air of the street begins to seem.

I do not see, as I leave, that Maria has left the dance floor and is following me, running in fact, down the hallway. I do not see her at all until I reach the top of the stairs and hear her call out.

"Wait," she says.

I stop, look back up at her.

"I've been looking for you all evening," she says.

"Don't do that," I say, and continue down the steps.

"Will you just wait, please," she says.

"What for?"

"Why are you being so unkind?" she asks.

"I'm being unkind," I say.

"Yes," she says.

"I'm being unkind," I say again.

"You are," she says.

"What did you expect I would do?" I ask, incredulous.

I am about to go on, but I check myself.

"I didn't expect you'd be hostile," she says, shrugging her shoulders.

"You didn't expect I'd be hostile," I repeat.

"Don't mimic me either," she says. "People can't have a conversation if one person just repeats what the other person says."

Sometimes we do act like children. I say nothing.

"Poor Alfonso is going frantic with uncertainty about what's possessed me," she says. "I've been so rude to him all evening he says it's like being out with a Harpy."

"Poor Alfonso," I say softly.

"Don't do that," she says again. "I mean it."

She looks at me, two steps down from where she is standing, her face filled with concern. For a moment I almost pity her. Maria is incorruptible, always the same, unable to change.

"Can I ask you something?" she says.

"What?"

"Can I introduce you to him?" she says. "I need you to know each other even if he doesn't know why and you do."

I try to picture this, the pivotal moment where Maria introduces her cuckold to her cuckold.

"I can't help talking about you," she adds. "He'd think it strange if you were the one person here he didn't meet."

I pause.

"Let me get this straight," I say. "You want me to meet the king of bloody Spain or whatever he is because if I don't he may be upset."

For a moment she glares at me, and then her face softens.

"It's not like that," she says. "I feel schizophrenic sitting in the same room with both of you on different sides like enemies. You're two parts of my life."

"What planet do you come from, Maria?" I ask, my face burning. "I mean, where do you get your ideas about life?"

There is a long pause. She looks down, brushes the carpet with her shoe.

"Incredible as this may sound to you," I say slowly, "Alfonso is not now my friend, nor could he ever be. Nor is he my problem. You've made your choice, so grow up and make the most of it. Or better yet, I give up, so you don't have to choose anything. But now you are going to have to stay well clear of me. You owe me that much, and I expect it of you."

I turn and walk down the stairway. I hear her call me, once, twice, but I do not slow down. I reach the lobby, cross the foyer, step into the street. I listen to the sounds behind me, wait and hope that, as I go, I will hear her footsteps, her calling once more, her breath on my cheek. But there is nothing.

Some part of me feels strangely free.

XIII

FROM THE MOMENT I WAKE IN THE MORNING, ONCE CONSCIOUSNESS sets in, I am plunged into a trough out of which only she, or so it seems, could lift me. I try not to think of her. If my mind drifts to thoughts of her I hurry to stifle them, get up out of bed, up from behind my desk, take a walk, devise ploys to distract myself. When I pass her in the office I nod, purse my lips in some form of greeting, but mostly I do all that I can to avoid her. I run into her in the copy room. She is copying something as I walk in, freezes when she sees me.

"I can copy your stuff for you," she says with a slight smile.

"Don't start, Maria," I say, and leave the room.

I hope that it will become easier as time passes. I hope that the sense of loss will be so constant that in time I will scarcely notice it, that it will be like that kind of noise that grows on you and grows on you and then comes to seem quite silent.

• • •

There are a few evenings that smell of fall, and then days so steamy it seems as if cooler weather will never arrive. My parents come from Toronto for a long weekend and I insist that they stay with me rather in a hotel I know they can scarcely afford. I regret this, of course, numerous times while they are here, but I know I will do the same thing next visit. They take my bed, and I sleep on the couch.

I try only once to explain to them what has happened with Maria, but am unable to convey to them how everything I have done made sense at the time.

"If she were engaged, dear," my mother says, "I don't see what basis you ever had for optimism."

"She didn't tell me she was engaged until it was way too late," I say.

"One doesn't want to be indelicate about this," my father says thoughtfully, "but if the young lady worked for you as your junior, there is some chance that she felt inhibited from saying what she really wanted all along. Have you thought of that?"

"It wasn't like that," is all I can say, and then the subject is dropped.

• • •

Olwine summons me and I walk to his office and knock on the door. When I receive no answer I stand wondering whether to knock again or simply to open it.

"He's having lunch," Cindy chirps.

"You just told me he wants to see me," I say. "Should I go in or what?"

"He's expecting you, isn't he?" she says.

"So's St. Peter," I mutter. "That doesn't mean this is a good time."

"He didn't say what to do when you came," she says. "His lunch arrived just after I put the phone down."

I hadn't seen the messenger. It is different now that there are people about, new sounds, different activities.

"I thought lunch was sort of a sacrament," I say.

"What?"

"Does anybody disturb him during lunch?" I ask. "I mean, are there standards to gauge how important your message has to be?"

"I wouldn't go in if the building was on fire," she says. "But that's me. And there are lots of things I would do that you wouldn't, so who can tell?"

I stand at her desk and look carefully at her. She smiles up at me, wrinkles her brow, offers me a peppermint from a jar on her desk.

"Well he did call me," I say.

I knock on the door, wait and then knock again a little louder. I turn the handle and open the door a few inches, peer into the room. Olwine is sitting at his table next to the window, a white table cloth draped over it, silver serving dishes arranged before him. A book is propped on the table and Olwine holds it with one hand as he eats.

He turns in my direction, looks over his glasses, and says coolly, "What is it please?"

"I understood you wanted to see me," I say.

"Didn't my secretary tell you I was not to be disturbed?" he asks.

"She wasn't sure what I should do, frankly," I say.

Suddenly I feel more annoyance than anything else, see something fragile in Tony Olwine sitting there eating his miserable, mingy salad at a table by the window.

"I could come back," I volunteer.

"Why don't you do that," he says.

I understand that I have been dismissed and turn to leave. I see that Olwine is reading Rimbaud.

● ● ●

"I don't know what you've done to the great Parma," Stan

says as he strolls into my office for the third time in under an hour. "She's actually in the library as we speak. And working too, believe it or not. She claims to be working on something for you."

"I'll believe that when I see something useful out of her," I say.

"You can hardly blame her if she refuses to play along with your little contrivance, Prince Machiavelli," Stan remarks. "She's taken a lot from you lying down, so to speak. Why should she take this too?"

"Don't you have anything better to do?"

"You have to admit, in the light of day," he says, "that you have created an almost perfect predicament. Olwine gives you one body, so to speak, to assist you in this foul mess of yours. You nominate Parma for perfectly unsavory reasons, and then because of your persistent sexual harassment, you can't do a darn thing about it when she refuses to work. Now that you want to pretend she doesn't exist, she is determined not to burrow out from under your skin. The perfect storm," he adds. "It's like watching drama, right here at Nibbles. To say nothing of the fact that Olwine's watching you both like a cannibal. God, do you guys all deserve each other."

"I don't want to talk about it," I say.

"What's with her anyway, for Christ's sake," he demands. "She needs to grow up, and I'm sick of her doing it on my time."

"It's hardly your time," I point out. "And in any event it's more complicated than it seems."

"What's more complicated," he asks. "Either she wants him or she wants you. This isn't Utah. She has to pick."

"She already has," I say resignedly. "It's over."

"Oh no, boykie boy," Stan replies. "Not by a long shot. If you think so you're being as naive as she is."

"Don't you have anything better to do?" I ask again.

"Are you kidding?" he says. "The whole firm's slow. It feels like a great machine that's run out of oil. Everything's just grinding to a stop. Cases finish, projects end, and nothing comes in to replace them. It's like we have this dance hall and no band. The Corporate Department is asleep with its head on the desk. With the exception of work for Sheinburg's awful clients who don't pay their bills anyway, nothing new has come in for weeks."

"That's good news," I say. "They're sure to be clamoring for new partners when there isn't enough to keep the existing ones busy."

"There isn't even enough for them to pretend to be busy," he adds. "We're on the cusp of something here, I'm sure of it. I overheard Sheinburg talking about some of the assumptions they made about how fast this firm was going to grow when they took this space. Maybe this new Nibbles campaign will actually pull it off, but for law firms to grow like this one would have to for their projections to work, every man, woman, and child in the United States would have to be a lawyer by the year 2020."

"I don't like them any more than you do," I say, "but I still find it hard to believe that Olwine and Sheinburg are the fools you think they are."

"Believe it," Stan says. "I never saw anything like what's going on in this place. They assumed the preposterous and when it didn't happen they have no Plan B. None. So here we sit with our marble and our fake statues and we wait for something to happen. And I'm Italian, mind you. I like marble and fake statues."

"There are some smart people in this firm," I say. "They don't all not know what they're doing."

"Can you spell hubris?" Stan says. "And one other thing. I've worked with Sheinburg on deals for his clients. Two out of every four of his ideas are smart. The other two are deluded. And he's a dishonest fuck into the bargain. If some black kid in Dorchester stole as much in a month as Sheinburg does each time he sends a bill, the poor kid would spend the rest of his life in a penitentiary. These people are as subtle as finger-paint."

Kay sees on another secretary's desk a request for nominations to the partnership to be considered at a meeting in six weeks time. Maria and I are ignoring each other in the hallway. I receive a final trial call from the court. Things are, one way or another, like it or not, coming to a head. And good for it.

• • •

I am sitting in my office at the end of another day when I look up and see Richard Havens standing in the doorway. His tie is undone, his jacket is slung over his shoulder, and a sheaf of papers is tucked crookedly under his arm. For a moment I think he may be drunk, but when he begins to speak it is clear that he is not.

"I owe you a spot of gratitude," he says. "My wife tells me that once again I was on the verge of doing something I may have regretted."

"Forget it," I say. "Sometimes I wonder how I stay sober at things like that."

"She wanted me to give you this," he says, handing me a slim blue book. It is called *Landing Lights Along the Shore*, and it's author is Melissa Havens.

"Thank you," I say. "I look forward to reading it."

"She liked you a lot," Havens, says sitting down. "And that's something. She doesn't have much time for most of the people she's met around here."

"They're an odd bunch, aren't they?" I say, and although we are supposedly now confiding, I do have to remain vigilant. Whatever else he is or isn't, Havens is a partner. My future depends in part on what he thinks.

"You know," he says, "Tony Olwine had just become a partner when I joined the firm. Peter Bittlenood was running the place then and he was doing it as if it the firm was his own private fiefdom. If he had to buy his wife a new Mercedes, there might be a large distribution of profits, and if he didn't feel like it, nothing was handed out. It was Tony who led the coup, so I'm told, and everyone rallied around him. At the time it didn't seem that a little benign despotism was such a bad thing."

"You don't think he's done a good job?" I ask.

"He was fine for a few years. Things evened out, Bittlenood was given some fancy title and retreated into a corner office to sulk himself into a coronary. But at some point poor Tony got ahead of himself. Perhaps you saw Mrs. Olwine, Version III. I think she places rather stringent demands on the old turnip, but either way he's become insufferable. He seems to have the world's strangest ideas about who he actually is."

"Not a charming man," I say.

"No," Havens agrees.

For a moment he appears to be lost in thought.

"There is something else I want to tell you," he says. "I was pondering doing this regardless, but my wife insists."

"What?" I ask, curious.

"It has to do with this case you're killing yourself over," he says. "A certain lack of candor about its history."

"I'm not sure I know what you mean," I say.

"I'm not quite sure where to start," he says. "You may have noticed that the firm is not devoting a great deal of resources to this enterprise."

"Olwine refuses to approve anything that costs more than $100," I say. "This promises to be a somewhat makeshift presentation."

"Look, you poor sap," Havens says. "I can't stand this. A couple of years ago, at one of those interminable firm retreats, after we'd committed to this new place and were trying to figure out how to find new business to pay for it, several of the trial partners proposed that contingent-fee injury cases were the path to the Promised Land. The richest lawyers in the city are plaintiff's personal injury lawyers, after all. They get forty percent of some huge settlements. Why not us?"

"What did you say?" I ask.

"I said the reason they were so confident it was easy pickings was because the lawyers in this firm were all canvas backs themselves."

"Canvas backs?"

"They keep losing to these plaintiffs' lawyers and spend half their lives on their backs on the canvas. They posture and harrumph and then at the last moment fork over tons of money and persuade their clients that avoiding the risk makes it a good deal. No wonder they thought it was easy money. They were the competition."

"That must have made you popular."

"I'll say," he says. "So when Margaret brought this one in, they jumped on it as the test case, the one that would blaze a new trail for the firm. They called it 'raising our profile' as injury lawyers."

"It's not quite happening that way," I say.

"I'll say," he says again. "When someone finally took a good look at the expenses so far and realized what was going on they decided to abandon the whole project. You're sort of a sacrificial lamb in all this, though I expect you've come to that conclusion all on your own. Nobody expects you to win. They just want this to end as quickly and cheaply as possible."

"We may well get sued for malpractice," I say. "Quick and cheap may not be in the cards."

"They know that," he says. "That's why they were relieved to hear of Margaret's leaving. She's been angling for the judge thing for ages and it came across just in the nick of time. Can you imagine her as a malpractice defendant? Under a stiff cross-examination she would make Jack Nicholson look reserved."

"Why me?" I ask.

"Who knows?" Havens says. "People like you well enough. Half of them want to believe you can get us out of this somehow. The other half think of you as they think of every young person here, as cannon fodder. But there's also this. I think the consensus is that you'd be a more sympathetic presence in front of a malpractice jury than Margaret would have. You're so, well, civilized."

"Thank you," I say. "I think."

"You have to know," he says. "I can't sleep with myself, or my wife can't sleep with myself, with you not knowing."

Havens looks at his watch.

"It's going to be neither better nor worse in the morning," he said. "I'm going to stroll across to the Boston Harbor for a drink. Care to join me?"

"No thanks," I say. "Believe it or not, I've got work to do."

He stands and looks at me over the desk.

"You're up for partner in a month, aren't you?" he asks.

"I'm afraid so," I say.

"I remember it all too clearly," he says. "Back then it seemed like the peak of a mountain I'd spent my whole life climbing."

"It wasn't?"

"Just the beginning of a new and much more treacherous one," he says. "Do you have much money of your own? You look rich."

"Am I rich?"

"Yes, to put it bluntly," he says.

"My father owns a cheese shop in Toronto," I say.

"Damn," he says. "What we need is some real rich ones to share the liability."

"What liability?"

"Do you know how much they've borrowed to dress this place up like a Tibetan bordello?" he asks.

"I didn't know they'd borrowed money at all, quite frankly," I answer. "That's not exactly the sort of stuff they tell associates. And the Tibetan bordellos I've seen were quite modest."

"Twenty million dollars," he says gleefully. "Twenty million big ones. The philosophy behind it comes from that baseball movie: *If you build it, they will come.* Well they've built it and now it remains to be seen whether they will come. So far, not a lot of takers. And of course their timing has been exemplary."

He starts to laugh, and then to laugh harder.

"The saps," he says. "Olwine and Sheinburg carried them along like little sheep to the slaughter."

"Where did Harry Cabot stand on it?" I ask.

Since he is being indiscreet I might as well get answers to questions I've been wondering about.

"Cabot?" Havens says. "Cabot checked out of here years ago. He's just been waiting for his kids to get through college so that he can afford to talk the governor into making him a judge. I'm not sure his name isn't already in the ring. He went along. We all did. At the time it seemed unpatriotic to oppose them."

He begins to amble out of the office and I find myself walking beside him down the hallway.

"And what did we get for the money?" he asks. "Look at these columns."

He taps one and it sounds hollow.

"Fiberglass dressed up to look like granite. And these paintings. Garbage embellished to fake pedigree. Each marble conference table cost close to a hundred thousand dollars. Each fancy light fitting cost two thousand. There are sixty of them. This place was decorated by men driven by demons, I swear it."

Someone has fastened a bronze-colored plaque to a door that reads 'Break Center 4.'

"Who is all the grand speak aimed at?" he says. "Are we supposed to be impressing ourselves? I'll tell you one set of people who won't be impressed. Clients. They'll know who's paying for it all."

"I thought the same thing," I say.

We reach the elevator. "May I ask you one more question?" I say.

"Ask away," he prompts.

"Why do you stay?"

"For the same reason you do," he says. "The money. Where

else can an English major with no vocational skills, no ability in the sciences, no business acumen, no capital, no connections, and no entrepreneurial spirit, earn the kind of money we do. It's not distasteful most of the time, is it? You learn the rules eventually, guess a lot, win or lose, go for a drink, go home. It's not bad."

The elevator arrives.

"Goodnight, my hardworking friend," he says. "Do what you can to save our worthless bottoms."

The doors close and, among the fiberglass pillars, in a hallway lined with paintings and ornately carved light fixtures, I am alone. On the way to the coffee room I knock the pillars with my knuckles and they produce a hollow, muffled sound, rather like the sound of a tennis ball landing on a car roof, or a head hitting a plasterboard wall.

• • •

I need to mention one other thing before I get to the trial itself, the eye of the needle through which I must pass to go where I am going. What happened at the trial, which is of course the nub of the matter, what happened at the trial changed everything, including me.

But first I must get through this. I preface it with a disclaimer: I am not proud of it. It is something I am not proud of. Of which I am not proud.

I go to the typing pool and find Cindy working there. She is holding a paper up to the light, squinting at it as she tries to read it from different angles.

"Can you read this word?" she asks.

I go and stand beside her, really quite close, and try but I can not. I like the feeling, that sense that one is very, very close to someone else.

"That's what I hate about working up here," she says. "I'm used to Mr. Olwine's handwriting and I hate having to read anybody else's."

"Why are you working here then?" I ask.

"I need the money," she says.

"For anything in particular?"

"There's a few things I want," she says. "Not just one."

"Get someone to buy them for you," I suggest.

"There isn't anyone," she says disarmingly. "Just me."

"What time do you get off?"

"Ten," she says.

"Can I take you home?"

"Of course," she says.

• • •

I wait for her, though I have long since finished what I have stayed to do. The air conditioning has gone off, the air is heavy and stale. I read a newspaper in the library, and then a magazine in the reception area, and at five to ten I take the elevator to the typing pool.

She is reading *Cosmopolitan*.

"How long have you been doing this?" I ask.

"Since eight," she says. "There's nothing more to do but I'm not allowed to leave."

We leave separately and meet behind the building—secrecy, it seems, is my métier—and then we walk together to the parking lot. I hold the door for her and when I have let myself in and am sitting beside her I notice how she fills the car with the fragrance of perfume and a light, sensual perspiration reminiscent of old lipstick and leather. I glance at her knees, at her slender hands in her lap. She wears a thin band of gold on her wrist.

I look at her, see a glistening in her eyes.

"Thank you for offering this," she says.

"It feels nice to have you to myself and to know I don't have to

worry about Olwine or Kay or the girl in the pod next to you,"
I say.

"What took you so long?" she asks.

I look across at her, take her hand, kiss her. Her mouth is soft
and eager. She feels quite different than Maria. We spend the
night together.

• • •

Except it is not good, not at all, not in the least. How much
detail does one need? We go to her apartment. She invites me
in. What follows is all perfectly predictable and barren beyond
description. She is so shapely and lovely at a distance but close
up, how do I put this, there is an emptiness in me that drains life
from everything. She is firm and smooth and encouraging and
yet it is a practiced routine with its reciprocity, its compliance,
its positioning.

It has no heart. It has no nothing.

Why am I doing this?

Why am I here?

As I drift off I feel shadows of shame and of forbidden places
flickering through the room. I open my eyes, examine the things
that surround us as she purrs softly beside me, am a foreigner
in a place I do not want to be. How is it that a person can be so
fickle? Hours ago she was intriguing, innocent, harmless, fun,
and now the scales have dripped from my face like mud into a
pail. I am imprisoned by my own venality, stuck in a crushing
loneliness that grows by the second.

I would trade one kiss from Maria, one sentence, for a lifetime
of such aimless adventure.

"I have to go," I say finally.

It is two or three in the morning, some bad hour. Why did I
think this would solve anything? The light in the room is vague
and thin.

"Why?" she asks.

"I just do," I say.

"Not twice," she says. "You don't do this to me twice."

Excoriate. Judge. Scourge. I can do a better job of it.

Dumb. Dumb. Dumb.

XIV

I ARRIVE AT THE OFFICE A TANGLE OF CONTRADICTORY IMPULSES.
If Cindy and Maria cross my path simultaneously my systems
will overload and I will fall to the floor and lie like a fetus. Even
after its relentless slide I still have seventy-four thousand dollars in the stock market. If I sell my condominium at a fire sale
price, which may be necessary given the way things are, I will
clear another sixty. If I start now and drive west I will be in
California by the weekend. I will wear sandals and a loose fitting cotton shirt. I will find a seat in a bright restaurant serving
noodles and shrimp. I will feel Maria's absence but the place will
be so removed that the implausibility of it will mask the raw-
ness. I will make new acquaintances, find exotic lovers, walk on
deserted trails through moist and tropical landscapes.

If I do not hurry I will be late for court. The court has ordered
a final conference at which we will be asked to confirm that the
case is ready for trial. I would like to be able to shout that no, it
is not, it never will be, but of course I will stand, look respect-
ful, agree with Peter Hill that we are ready to start. We will
be assigned a trial judge. If I were the praying sort, this would
be my prayer: Some judges are settling judges, some judges are
trying judges, and the former outnumber the latter. I want one

of the former. I want a judge who will put the screws on Hill to come up with some money and then talk some sense into the parents so that they will adjust their expectations. I harbor no illusions. I do not want to be the next Clarence Darrow.

All I want is to be off the hook. Let the families get some money. Let Nibble get its share.

Let the volcano spew out its ashes, and then let those of us who live in its shadows reassemble what we can and get on with our lives.

. . .

Stan is right about Maria's change of heart. Each evening now I receive a memorandum from her. She leaves these in intraoffice envelopes on Kay's desk and I read them slowly, her synopses of scientific papers, her analysis of research, her lists of inconsistencies in the evidence. It is all make-work, not what I need, and I suppose I could let her spend the rest of the year laboring away in her office, scrawling notes on a yellow pad filled with doodles and unrelated phone numbers, faithfully producing nothing of value.

I am about to do something about this when she brings matters to a head herself. She enters my office, tentatively, somewhat shy.

"I'm wasting my time, aren't I?"

It is the first time she has been in my office since the Prom.

"I hadn't realized you were so conscientious," I say.

"Come on, Derek," she demands. "This is my job, like it or not, and I'm trying not to be a total screw up."

"Is that what's going on?"

"I don't have to explain things to you," she says. "First, because I don't have to, and second, because I don't want to. The fact is that I am breaking my ass trying to be useful and giving you my work is like pouring something down a bottomless hole. You don't acknowledge it, you don't tell me if I'm helping or not, I don't even think you've read a word I've written. It's pissing me off."

"Pissing you off is it, Princess?"

"Look here you faithless knucklehead," she says, walking around my desk and sitting on the corner next to me. "We're not playing that game today. I'm the same person I was before, and so are you. There's no reason to act as if I've done you some great wrong because I haven't. So stop moping and be normal."

"I'm not getting into this," I say. "What do you want from me?"

"What do I want from you?" she exclaims. "You drafted me into this loser case. I had to give up other work that may even have turned out to be interesting and now I have nothing else to do but work on this stupid thing and you refuse even to tell me what I'm supposed to be doing."

She is right, of course. It strikes me as she talks that going to Olwine and getting her assigned to the case was one thing, part of my campaign, and that ignoring her now, banishing her to her office and letting her waste her time like this, is another. If anyone else treated her this way I would be furious. Face it, I am still in love with her, always was, always will be.

"I do need help," I say.

"So?"

"Okay," I say.

She reaches over the desk and quickly touches the back of my hand.

"And one other thing," she says. "Whatever else may be true, I still think you're swell."

We look up just in time to see Olwine going by the open door. He hesitates, half turns, and then continues walking.

"Oh, Christ," I say.

• • •

We have to get to court and I begin gathering the papers I will need. In the old building trial bags, the heavy, square cases in which files were carried were stored in a closet under the internal stairway. Now, for the life of me, I can't find them anywhere.

I call Mrs. Buckles and ask her where they are.

"I have an inventory of those in Storeroom A," she says. "I can give you no more than two."

"We need at least five," I say. "And I don't know where Storeroom A is."

"Five is out of the question," she replies. "The new policy is to limit these bags to one per lawyer, or two in extenuating circumstances."

"Mrs. Buckles," I say, closing my eyes. "I'm going to court in a few minutes. The measure surely isn't how many cases you're allowed, but how many you *need*."

"For one thing," Mrs. Buckles retorts, "there are a finite number of these bags and you may be shocked to learn that there are other lawyers in this office besides yourself. For another, there is absolutely no need for another show of petulance on your part. If you have any problems with the procedure, perhaps you should take it up with Mr. Olwine."

"Why don't you," I say angrily, and instantly regret it.

There is a frozen pause.

"I'll take two," I say. "Miss Parma will be up for her two. Now where are they?"

"I'll get them," she says, "while you sign them out."

"Sign them out?"

"Be sure to include the client number, charge, and return date," she says.

"Someone's going to be charged for us carrying their papers to court in these bags?" I ask in amazement.

She ignores me and hangs up.

• • •

We take a taxi to the court, Maria and I. Kay has arranged for two messengers to accompany us. They carry in boxes the papers that do not fit into our precious bags. As it happens they are Brazilians, and dark skinned, and making our way into the building we resemble an expeditionary force off on some voyage of discovery, the bwanas up front. If they carried the boxes on their heads we might be mistaken for explorers off to find the source of the Nile.

I have never felt quite at home in this courthouse. It feels, always, very inbred, with groups of lawyers in huddles discussing whatever it is that they are there for, courthouse staff making their way up and down in the elevators. It all sometimes feels like some sort of conspiracy in which I have no part. Perhaps it is the Canadian in me, to feel so alien in such a prosaic place. I overhear someone complaining that his trial date has been postponed yet again, bumped somewhere into the indefinite future. A man in a Panama hat, a woman in a rumpled suit, three men in overalls, watch the Nibble & Kuhn contingent with suspicion, as if unless constantly monitored we will steal a rare commodity.

Several of the parents are here. They wait for me in a group outside the courtroom. We greet each other though once again they are wary, formal, in a few moments will be further unnerved by the mismatch in numbers, Maria and me and two Brazilian boys carrying boxes versus Peter Hill and his contingent of associates riffling through boxes of papers and men in dark suits whom I assume to be Morganic executives. Perhaps, if I am lucky, they are from an insurance company, better yet an excess insurance company. Whatever I may think of the merits of my claim, seven children with cancer could be, could potentially be if the stars align just right and I have good fortune beyond my lifetime experience, a very expensive matter.

I see that the assigning judge is William Ruggles. They say that he started out life as the governor's driver and that at some point he went to law school at night. After that, rumor has it, he made something of a living defending petty criminals and writing wills before cashing in on political connections from his driver days and finding himself a notch on the bench. People say different things about him, that he is not smart but that he is moderate, that he has a temper but that he has his measure of charm.

I do not know, off hand, whether he is a settling judge or not.

"Good morning, Peter," I say, and the phalanx around him looks across at me with a blank stare so synchronous it could be choreographed.

The parents know Peter Hill. Before I became involved he took their depositions, and as I think I have already suggested there is not a great deal of good feeling on their part. I think Margaret Kelly, in preparing them, must have attributed to Hill the vilest of motives whereas the truth of it is that he is just another lawyer, just another lawyer doing what he is paid to do. The camps gravitate to different ends of the courtroom, and then we wait. There is a lot of waiting in this line of work. The room slowly fills up. One court officer reads a newspaper in the witness stand. Another two chat by the door.

A woman enters from behind the judge's bench and takes her seat at the clerk's table. She picks up a telephone and dials, and then makes no effort to keep her conversation private.

"Look," she says. "The salesgirl told me that I could return it. Now you're telling me I can't."

She listens for a moment, makes an impatient gesture.

"Don't tell me you're different stores. It's the same exact store." She listens again.

"Well I'll come in at lunchtime then," she says, and slams the phone down.

"Having a bit of trouble, Betty?" Peter Hill says.

He wanders over to the table, sits on its edge.

"They don't know what they're doing," the clerk says.

"Nobody does any more."

"Ain't that the truth," Hill says, insufferably mellow and cordial. "How are things otherwise?"

"Can't complain," the clerk says.

A court officer comes out from behind the judge's bench and the courtroom falls silent, and then nothing happens. Shoes shuffle, someone coughs, a briefcase drops.

"He'll be here in a moment," I hear the clerk tell Peter Hill. "His wife's in the hospital this week and he's been on the phone a lot to the doctors."

"I hope she isn't too ill," Hill says.

His manner is solicitous, humble. This is not the fractious, strident Hill who has dogged first Margaret and then me every step of the way. This is the courtroom Hill, brimming with an assumed humility and a common touch. I take back that he is just another lawyer. He is a toady, a suck-up, a person who pretends an interest in courtroom clerks that is not genuine.

"Well," the clerk says, now sorting through a crumbling box of cards, "she's had her problems. But so has he," and she proceeds to discuss the judge, his heart attack the previous year, his shortness of breath, the pills he has to take, as if he were a case study in which she takes a benevolent interest.

"He'll be in soon," she says again and takes her little box of index cards out back into the judge's chambers.

The judge is finally announced by the court officer who continues to hold his newspaper in one hand as he mumbles the official salutation like an auctioneer.

"Be seated," he concludes.

Judge William Ruggles marches in, takes both steps onto his rostrum in a single stride, and sits heavily in his chair. He is an elderly, ruddy man, and tartan trousers and scuffed brown shoes show beneath his black robe. He apologizes for the delay, and to my surprise announces to the crowded court what the clerk has already told us, that his wife is ill and in the hospital but that, unlike himself, who had a heart condition—indeed who had a heart attack and still has to take all manner of medication and gets tired after lunch—she will be fine.

"What have we here?" he asks the clerk.

He looks up and surveys the crowded courtroom with what looks very much like disapproval.

"Looks like we've got a full house, Betty," he says.

And then we wait some more. The clerk calls the cases one by one, hands the judge the papers for each, and then, clearly unfamiliar with whatever it is he is being called on to decide, Ruggles listens to the lawyers speak until, at some tipping point, he makes up his mind and issues a ruling. It all seems arbitrary. It is easy to imagine Peter Hill and Margaret Kelly among this bunch, bickering about due dates and undue burdens and everything else under the sun.

Finally it is our turn. The clerk hands the judge a sheaf of papers among which I recognize a memorandum I have spent hours writing. I almost killed myself to have it delivered to the court by the deadline, and now it is clear that the judge has never seen it. There is silence as he flips through it, far too fast to be reading, and then he lays it out before him. He screws off the top of a pitcher on his desk, seems to have trouble aligning the spout, and pours himself a glass of water.

The whole courtroom watches, transfixed.

"Would counsel please introduce themselves," he says at last.

Peter Hill and I move beyond the bar, stand in the well of the court. The judge is perched on his bench, his gown riding up around his shoulders. He looks like a bird of prey sitting in a tree.

"Counsel," he says, pointing to me.

I know how much time the man has assigned to the other cases and that I have a half minute, at most, before he loses interest. The case is about pollution, I say, toxic chemicals that entered the ground water, and about seven little boys who have cancer because of it.

He nods, moves a paper or two around in front of him, and then, God bless him, says the words I have been praying for.

"What are the parties' positions on settlement?" he asks.

Peter Hill stands. His newfound humility is replaced by a grave mournfulness. Why does nobody see this charade for what it is?

"There was no run off of chemicals from the Morganic plant," he says. "The state has studied this issue several times. So have some of the best engineers and scientists in the country. Nobody has ever found that substances from my client's factory are present in the ground water or the Asheville swimming hole. There is also no evidence that even if they had, that these chemicals have caused cancer in anyone."

"I would be disappointed if that wasn't your position," the judge says sharply. "But my question was: What are the parties' positions on settlement?"

"Mr. Dover's predecessor made a demand of seventy million dollars," Peter Hill says, "which we rejected."

"What's your highest offer?" the judge asks with some impatience.

"Without admitting any responsibility, and purely to save the costs of trial, we are prepared to offer a hundred thousand dollars per family," Hill says. "Once the trial starts, the money will not be available."

Seven hundred thousand dollars. Nibble's share of that would be three hundred and twenty thousand dollars. If it were up to me I would take the money and run. It is not up to me.

"My clients reject that offer," I say.

"It certainly is low," the judge says.

I'm happy he is doing this, of course, thrilled, but how he can make this judgment is beyond me. If my case is as flimsy as I worry it is, Hill is offering far too much, and Ruggles knows absolutely nothing about the case to be making any judgment about its value at all. Seven hundred thousand dollars could be a king's ransom, given the facts, for all he knows.

"Several state surveys have found that there was no contamination of the ground water," Peter Hill is saying. "Under the circumstances, we believe the offer is reasonable."

"That's what I hate about this job," the judge shouts, suddenly energized. "Everyone postures with me. I spend weeks trying a case and then at the last moment everyone suddenly gets religion and I've wasted my time. Not only me. The Commonwealth. Betty. The court officers. The stenographers. Everyone."

God I love this guy. Keep going, judge. Ask for numbers. Move him up. Press my clients. Let's end this.

"With respect," Peter Hill says, "I can assure you that we have carefully evaluated the plaintiffs' situations, and that once the trial starts Morganic Continental will see it through to a jury verdict."

The judge stops writing, looks at the clerk over his glasses.

"They all say that at pretrial," he says.

Everyone in the courtroom now waits as the judge continues scribbling. For a moment it seems as if he has forgotten about us. Then he shuffles his papers and looks up.

"I have to cut you short here since I do have other commitments away from the courthouse," he says. "I'll be trying this one in my own session. Be here with witnesses and be prepared to pick a jury at nine a.m. on Monday."

He stands, gathers his things, and prepares to leave his bench. Not yet, judge, I want to say. Don't leave us. Try some more. But he is gone.

The courtroom comes to life and several of the men in suits walk toward Peter Hill. One puts his arm on Hill's shoulder and appears to be congratulating him on his firmness. He is particularly well groomed, this man, his leather shoes shine, the fabric in his suit flows in immaculate waves as he moves. His silver hair is carefully combed.

He has my money, that son of a bitch. Monday at nine A.M. it is, then.

• • •

Back at the office Kay knows me well enough to give me a wide berth, sits stolidly at her desk typing and fielding the occasional phone call. I hear her say something, and then Mrs. Buckles's voice, and then the latter enters my office.

"You neglected to enter the date on which you expect to return the trial bags," she says. "It is necessary to fill out all of the fields on the form if the system is to work."

I look at her incredulously. All the frustration and weariness of the day suddenly come to a head, close in on the muscular little woman with a poodle haircut standing on my carpet.

I stand and walk right over to her, to within inches of her.

"You may put down there that I will return the bags on June 27, 2027," I say. "Will that satisfy your system?"

For a moment she does nothing.

"You will hear more of this," she says at last and is gone.

XV

It is Saturday and the office is almost deserted. I run into one of the usually bow tied lawyers dressed, because it is the weekend, in khaki trousers, an L.L.Bean shirt, and a blazer. I know Maria is in. I know her by now, her habits, her sensibilities. She will not let me work alone this weekend.

And true enough, no sooner have I settled in behind my desk than her head appears around the door, my spirits rise, and she comes marching triumphantly in. She is carrying an armful of packages.

"What's all that stuff?" I ask.

"Clothes," she said. "I've been shopping. Jennifer told me about a sale in the Basement."

"How can you concentrate on buying clothes now?" I ask.

"Listen," she says. "Girls are like sharks. If they stop moving in search of new stuff, their wardrobes die. And you'd be looking at a pretty broken-down ensemble by the end of the first week of trial if I hadn't done some emergency shopping. I got great stuff. Do you want to see?"

"Just the act of reaching into those bags will draw Olwine into this room," I say. "And you already have more clothes than Carmen Miranda."

Maria stops what she's doing, reaches into a folder she is carrying, and hands me a sheaf of papers.

"What are these?" I ask.

"Everything you need, I think," she says, and leaves the room.

The papers include (without wishing to bore) motions *in limine,* motions for supplementary enquiry of jurors, motions to restrict, motions to quash, motions to exclude, everything I have mentioned to her I may need to start the trial.

I read them quickly. They are, for the most part, excellent.

• • •

She stays in the office all weekend and I know from the first moment that we are headed right back to where we were when we reached our impasse. It is lovely, warm, exciting, freeing, to have her near, Alfonso or no Alfonso, and now that my resolve is broken, it is broken entirely. So she is in and out of my office, forgetting her coffee cup, coming back for it, appropriating a corner of the carpet to sort things into untidy piles. It reminds me of when she first arrived and I took it upon myself to train her. We channeled our energies into the tasks at hand. Work had seemed almost enjoyable then.

On Saturday evening we order Chinese takeout and when it arrives we spread the containers across my desk and eat together.

"Just like old times," she says.

"Did I touch any part of you that first night in the copy room?" I ask. "Your arm or something. I can't remember and it's been bothering me."

"The mu shoos's inedible," she says.

There is a long silence and then I look up at the window and see that she is staring at my reflection. It is dark outside and our images in the glass are as clear as if the window were a mirror. There may be a bow tie or two on the other side of the floor, but otherwise the place is deserted.

She shakes her head.

"Oh God," she says.

"Don't do that," I say, looking at her reflection.

"Would you like me to submit my expressions for approval first?" she asks.

"That's one approach," I say. "I could think of others,"

We sit next to each other at my desk, look together into the window, at the untidy office, half-packed litigation bags, stacks of papers. She is wearing a T-shirt with an advertisement for olive oil on the front.

"How's Fonzie?" I ask.

"Alfonso. He's okay."

"I mean, how *is* Fonzie?" I ask again, this time less gently.

"Probably about the same as Olwine's secretary," she says.

I am an idiot to think I can keep a secret like that in a place as porous as Nibble & Kuhn. But it still shocks me to learn that she knows. Shocks and shames me.

"I'm not too proud of that," I say.

"I know," she says. "And I don't care, almost. If things were different I would care."

"How could they be different?" I ask.

"I don't know," she says. "Don't give up on me, please."

It is the most encouraging thing she has ever said to me. I hear it and try not to disturb the moment.

"I'm not sure I could if I wanted to," I say.

There is a long pause. We study our plates, she pushes a paper around, shakes her head.

"Neither could I, so I'm finding out," she says.

"Does Alfonso have a job?" I ask.

"I'm not sure he's looking for one," she says. "He has an offer to teach at Harvard for a year."

"Is this related to the de Bourbon Two Sicilies thing?" I ask.

"Maybe," she says simply. "His family built a lot of the buildings people study. Mine just owned orchards that became suburbs."

"Where is he living?"

"Still with us," she says.

"I'll never understand this," I say. "Is this a Spanish version of *Dallas*? How can all these adults live together in one house? How can Alfonso?"

"You're right. You don't understand."

"Explain it then."

"It's not a rite of passage in my family that everyone leave home and serve time in some insular little box in Harvard Square or the Back Bay," she says. "You make fun of the bow ties but the truth is that you share a lot of their preconceptions."

"How can you be an adult in your father's house?" I ask. "I set one foot in my parents' living room and we fall into all sorts of patterns I'm not that mad about any more."

She nods and keeps eating.

"That one's also inedible," she says pushing it toward me.

That night I kiss her. (I chronicle these events as if they were totemic. So be it. To me they are.) We have worked all day and it is almost midnight. I offer to take her home but she insists on calling a cab. I say I will wait with her and when I come to get her to go downstairs she is busy stuffing things into her bag.

"Ready?" I ask.

She nods and stands quite still. It is then that I take her in my arms and kiss her.

"This doesn't change anything," she says.

"Thanks for the admonition," I say.

"We can't do this again," she insists. "I mean it. It's not right."

"Thank you, Emily Post," I say and I do not stop.

She responds, in turn, as if drowning and brought up for air.

• • •

On Sunday she arrives in the office before me once again. I find coffee and a wrapped packet of almond cookies on my desk.

"Thanks for the cookies," I say when she comes in.

"My mother baked them," she says and then adds, "and Emma dropped me here this morning."

"Emma's back?"

"Yes," she says. "She wanted to come up and meet you and I almost let her, but I was sure we'd run into Olwine."

"He doesn't work weekends," I say.

"He would if this were the one day we were doing something," she says.

"Do your mother and sister know who the cookies were for?" I ask.

"Of course they do," she says. "My family isn't stupid."

"Who said they were?" I ask.

"Nobody," she says. "That was preemptive."

"And who are they for?"

She pauses.

"The lawyer I work for," she says. "The one I don't stop talking about, or so they say."

I celebrate tidbits. I've already said that.

And tomorrow the trial starts.

XVI

I ARRIVE AT THE OFFICE AT SIX THIRTY. I HAVE BEEN THERE HALF the night anyway and the papers are neatly packed in trial bags which are now lined up against the conference room wall. Everything is ready to go, the mounted charts with ground water flow patterns, the blown up copies of assays and tests, bags filled with deposition transcripts. There is a box with every article ever written by Dr. Wigworth, Morganic's hero, my nemesis. There are summaries of evidence, exhibits all organized and cataloged, everything physical that can be gathered and taken with us to court. But what will win this cannot be packed, cannot be further organized. Let's face it. What will win this, if it can be won, are savvy and quickness. I do not know, honestly, whether I have those.

We share a cab to the courthouse, Maria and I with our Gurkha troops and their line of bags and boxes following behind. I have arranged to meet those parents who will be attending outside the building, and a small committee of them awaits us on the sidewalk. They shake my hand with a grim civility. I introduce them to Maria and realize instantly that she will be an asset with the parents. They warm to her instantly, the women at least do, and begin to exchange pleasantries as I describe to one of the fathers who will be my first witness what to expect. Out of the corner of my eye I see her straightening one of the father's ties.

Through the glass panels of the courthouse door I can see that Peter Hill has already arrived and is waiting with his clients in the lobby. They are talking inaudibly and with their backs to us, as if a glimpse of their faces will betray some great and irretrievable secret. They are a sea of gray suits, two of the men who were in court for the pretrial, several others, a half dozen young bow tie types whom I guess are associates at Hill's firm.

"I'm pleased this isn't a matter of manpower alone," one of the fathers says solemnly. "They would overwhelm us."

Am I being too sensitive when I say I discern a critical note in this comment? I don't know what Margaret promised these people all those months ago, or even how this all started out. Maybe in the early days, when the firm was still behind her, Margaret had a half dozen associates of her own assigned to assist. There is evidence of it in the billing records. But now there does seem to be an imbalance, Peter Hill with his insurance adjusters and corporate representatives and a whole law firm behind him, lined up against Maria and me and our two Brazilian messengers who stand perplexedly against the wall waiting for instructions as to where to leave the boxes.

The parents size it all up with scarcely hidden discomfort. Everyone looks strained and uneasy, tuned to fever pitch, constantly on the verge of redirecting their grief into something else.

Anger at me would be a good place to start.

· · ·

When I first came to Nibble & Kuhn, back before the excesses at Triumph Plaza, after dinner at the firm Prom the senior associates used to put on skits about the firm and the idiosyncrasies of some of the partners. One year they put on a strange little show about lawsuits and I remember one vignette in particular that made people laugh. It was a song about someone who had lost both arms in an accident and couldn't settle his case because he wasn't able to sign the papers. Even as I laughed I remember wondering whether one didn't get a little too callous in this line of work. In a few hours I will begin eliciting testimony that will be, by design, heart-rending. The jury will hear about little children throwing up blood, dying in their parents' arms, mothers for whom no therapy can ease their grief. Two of the boys, I will show, are spending their last months, after the bone marrow transplants and the chemotherapy and the fevers and the confusion, simply wasting away to nothing. Maybe it's why trials make good television, sometimes. They do bring to a head, in a relatively concise manner, the essence of drama, conflicting versions of tragedy. But from the inside you have to wonder what role the truth plays in any of it.

Nobody will ever really know what role chemicals from that nasty factory played in these boys' illnesses, but one way or another it has all become irrelevant. What matters is what the twelve people who are about to be my jury can be made to believe. I feel bad for the parents, honestly I do even if it doesn't quite come across that way, but even if the factory is somehow tied to contamination of the swimming hole, and my doubts about this are unremitting, money will not fix the problem or purge anyone of their grief. What would a million dollars, a billion dollars, accomplish?

I do not start out, in short, with a missionary's zeal.

• • •

The courtroom is empty and so we go in and set the bags down by the lawyers' table. The Brazilians follow, set the boxes in a row, and go stand at the back of the room.

"Shall I tell them to go?" Maria asks, and I say she should.

She talks to them in Portuguese, they laugh, and then they disappear.

We settle down at our table, Maria and I, and then Peter Hill and three of the men who have been standing with him take seats at theirs. This really is about to start.

The judge's clerk enters the room and sits down.

"How are you all?" she asks.

"Not too bad," Peter Hill answers. "How is the judge's wife?"

How does he even remember to ask, I wonder. They say the best politicians never forget names and faces, little details about their constituents' families. Good trial lawyers too. I don't remember things like that. She was sick, someone did say something about that. I'd clean forgotten.

"Much better," the clerk says.

"All rise," a court officer shouts, and the door behind the partition springs open.

Judge Ruggles emerges and stalks to the bench.

"Hear ye, hear ye, hear ye," the court officer begins.

It is a different court officer from the last time. He is reading from a piece of paper encased in well-thumbed plastic. Everyone stands in silence until he is done.

"Well," Judge Ruggles begins.

The courtroom is quiet.

"Well," the judge says again, looking round. "I see you gentlemen have not been able to settle this case."

Silence from the lawyers.

Finally Hill and I rise.

"No," Ruggles says, waving us down. "I don't need a speech. The answer is either yes or no."

"No," Hill says.

"Very well," the judge says peremptorily. "Then let's empanel the jury and get this over with. How long is this trial going to last?"

Peter Hill is still standing.

"I would say a month, Your Honor," he says.

It is as if something inside the judge is erupting.

"A month!" he shouts. "I want to see you gentlemen in my chambers right now."

He stands.

"And without your respective entourages," he snaps from the doorway. "Just you, Mr. Hill, and you, Mr. Dover."

"Court is in recess," the officer wheezes, dropping his newspaper to the floor.

We cross the courtroom and are shepherded into chambers by a court officer.

"What's going on?" I hear one of the Morganic types, whom I vaguely recognize from the day I visited the plant, ask Peter Hill.

"He doesn't want to have his courtroom tied up with a month-long trial," Hill tells him. "My guess is you'll hear some yelling from in there as he begins twisting arms."

"Isn't conducting trials what he's here for?" the man asks.

"This is standard procedure," Hill says. "Often cases do settle because a judge bullies the lawyers as the trial's about to start. This is a busy court. They count on cases settling or there'd be no way they could handle them all."

Oh, glory be, I think. Another chance to avoid this. The freedom at the other side of the needle's eye seems golden.

"Seventy million dollars," the man snorts. "We could buy the whole of Dana Farber and pay to find a cure for cancer for what these ambulance chasers want."

• • •

The morning is wasted as we posture at each other, Hill and I, there in the fug of the Suffolk County Courthouse. I can't make another demand unless Hill gets serious, but he raises his offer from seven hundred thousand to seven hundred and seventy, and despite my desperation I quietly decline to make a new demand. It is clearly pointless but the judge is relentless. By lunchtime, however, it is obvious we are getting nowhere and he sends a message from his chambers that a jury pool will be brought up to the room at two, and that the trial will start then and there.

"He's going to be a in sweet mood, for sure," I say to Peter Hill as we hear the message.

"You're not doing your clients any favors by taking such a hard line," Peter Hill says.

"Oh, lighten up," I say.

And so we start the trial.

• • •

I am not going to do what I could do at this point, despite the temptation. Lawyers, even recovering lawyers, tend to dwell on their moments in the sunshine. We pick a jury in short order— Judge Ruggles isn't Judge Ito and Massachusetts isn't California—and by late afternoon we are ready to start.

I stand up, straighten my jacket, walk over to the jury box. I remember looking back and seeing Maria, her face bright and open, and realizing that I had worked so hard, prepared so carefully, in part because I wanted to do well with her watching. Our jury is unexceptional, a collection of housewives and students and three people in middle management, and they seem open and ready to listen. I greet them, thank them for their service, and suddenly that they are this odd legal construct, a jury, falls away and I see twelve rather ordinary people sitting in a two rows in a strange wooden box waiting to hear what I

am about to tell them. They'll listen if I make sense. Somehow
at the moment most lawyers seem to dread, it all seems rather
simple.

I start by telling them that this is the only opportunity that
the families I represent will ever have to state their case, to
have their claim heard, and if they deserve it, to get redress.
Once this case is over, I say, once this jury has heard everything
and made their decision, Morganic will go its way, the families
will go theirs, and justice will have been done. It's a remarkable
thing, I say, really, that we can agree on this as a way to sort out
deeply held differences, peacefully and fairly, and finally. I tell
them that we, the families and I, and even Peter Hill and his client, agree on this one thing, and agree firmly. We are here for
justice, and we believe we will get it.

Whether I actually believe all this I cannot say. I did then, as
I stood there, and I do recall that several of the faces seemed
to register recognition, to acknowledge that I had made some
sense. Maybe I had.

And then I tell them a story. It's about seven boys living in an
outlying suburb who spend their summers playing in a sweet-
smelling swimming hole not far from their homes. I describe
each boy, give a few details of each family, and suddenly I find
I am rather enjoying this, telling the story, that for all the trim-
mings, the bluster, the falsity, it is, after all, what I need to do.
I talk about the swimming hole, show them a picture of it,
describe how for several summers they swim in it almost from
dawn to dusk until one morning, a Tuesday morning, one of
the boy's mothers notices a small mark on her son's arm and a
nightmare begins that ends here, in this room, today.

I am not, I suppose, cut out for hand wringing. When I am
done describing the symptoms, the treatments, the lost years,
the lost lives, I tell them that I am not in search of their sympathy, that the case must be decided on the evidence only, and
then I pass into the gray area of things, and I tell them that I

am passing into the gray area of things, what we can know for sure and what we can't know for sure but need them to decide. I touch on the possibility that chemicals can move through the ground, and they can, and that more likely than not they did in this case, and that the chemicals I am talking about are known to cause cancer, and that they did here, and that in the end no one can say with certainty what causes a cancer cell to appear, but that they can say with probability what did, and that the evidence will lead them to that place in this case.

I finish. The jury is respectfully silent. They watch me as I return to my table. The suits at Hill's table do not look happy. It looks as if they would have preferred to be placed in stocks and to have had rotten eggs thrown at them than to listen to me.

Maria leans over as Peter Hill makes his way out front to deliver his opening.

"I believe for the first time," she whispers. "I do."

I decide as I watch him that I don't much like him, but I suppose I'd be something more than I am if I did. I mean, it is supposed to be a form of combat and one wouldn't get very far in it if one were constantly suffused with affection for one's adversary. Hill is masterful, of course, his themes carefully planned. It occurs to me that one of the people sitting with his entourage may even be a jury consultant. Certainly he was passing notes furiously during the selection process. Hill says what one would expect him to, that simply because a claim has been brought does not mean that it has merit, that one would be less than human if one didn't sympathize with the families whose children had become ill, but that, and here he agrees with me, the case must be decided on facts, and not on sympathy.

The courtroom is overheated. Every so often a radiator punctures the air with a loud hiss. I am watching the jurors. They had started out looking at him skeptically, but that is changing. I also see things like Hill's knuckles resting on the podium. They are white, the color of paper.

"You will not hear one word of testimony that any of the chemicals from the Morganic factory actually ended up in the ground water or the swimming hole," he says, "and only guesswork that these chemicals could cause cancer even if they had."

He begins to list the studies that have been done on the swimming hole and as he does I can see that he is having an impact. I mean, Dr. Endicott P. Wigworth, Dean of the Harvard School of Public Health, for heavens' sake. Who else would one look to for the definitive word on what may and may not pose a public health hazard? Of course there are a couple of state surveys of the site too, and Hill is not inaccurate in saying they don't reach the same conclusion as my own Dr. Finkbiner does, and he then spends a few moments talking about Dr. Finkbiner, and what he says is not flattering.

"Bear in mind too," Hill says, "that the two boys who have died both had siblings who died of other kinds of cancer, and well before their families even moved to Asheville. Of course we are all saddened by youngsters with cancer," he says.

He waits for effect.

"Of course we are."

He pauses again. The room is dead silent. It seems as if even the hum of the fluorescent lights is still for a moment.

"But if that were the only test," he says, "whether we are able to empathize with people in distress, no justice would ever be possible because justice requires a more difficult balance. We have confidence you will make the right decision."

Hill's bow ties have been scrambling about with his exhibits. Others in his group are busily taking notes. Suddenly everything is perfectly silent and he walks slowly back to his table.

And that is that for the day.

Four twenty by my watch and the court officer, who is still reading the same newspaper—he could have memorized it by now—suddenly looks intently at Ruggles, jumps up, and makes an announcement with all the enthusiasm of a call to victory,

"Court is in recess until nine thirty tomorrow. All rise."

● ● ●

I am ghoulishly tired. There is something about being so vigilant, scrutinizing every word that is being said, worrying whether I am missing something, that has left me unnaturally exhausted. Maria calls the Brazilians and they return to the courthouse, and our little expedition makes its way back to the office, the gringos up front, the entourage and the boxes behind. Something about reaching the great still hallways of Nibble & Kuhn is reassuring. We can eat, regroup, plan for the morning. It is friendly territory. Tomorrow the parents get their chance.

There is a note on my chair from Olwine. He wants to see me, and although it is past five, I find him still here. I also walk past Cindy. She makes a point of ignoring me.

"You wanted to see me," I say.

He is writing at his desk, its surface clear except for the pad before him, a book or two and a glass of water. He makes a point of looking at his watch as I walk in and then looks back at his papers.

He addresses me without again lifting his eyes, slowly, methodically, without putting down his pen.

"Mrs. Buckles tells me," he says, "that she is encountering an extraordinary degree of resistance from both your secretary and yourself in connection with the implementation of certain new procedures."

I freeze where I stand, cast about for something to say. I had assumed, moron that I am, that he wanted to know how the first day of trial had gone. I had assumed he was somewhat interested, given what was at stake. I was wrong.

"Is that what you want to see me about?" I ask.

I am smoldering, resentful, on the verge of an outburst.

"Actually, no," he says. "I am receiving a series of bills for expenses you are incurring in this matter, from people apparently preparing exhibits, and from a series of expert witnesses. I specifically said you were not authorized to incur expenses exceeding one hundred dollars."

"Did you think the experts were gong to testify for free?" I burst out.

"I'm not sure what to make of your tone," he says, and this has a very rapidly sobering effect on me. "I gave you the terms of reference for the prosecution of this case," he says, "and you appear to be disregarding them."

"Tony," I say slowly and carefully. "Expert witnesses do not testify for free. In fact, in the case of the people Margaret hired, money seems to be all that drives them."

"Some people take responsibility for their actions," he says, and this is now either a threat or a *non sequitur*, something of which I suppose I can make what I choose, "and some never do."

He shifts his gaze dreamily to the window.

"I find the latter particularly inappropriate in an associate."

"I think that's quite unfair, Tony," I begin but he raises his hand.

"Please," he says. "I am not going to debate this with you."

For a moment there is something resembling an impasse. Of course it is I who capitulate. To allow the silence to continue would be defiance.

"I'd better get back to my desk, then," I say.

It occurs to me that either he doesn't know I'm on trial, or doesn't care. He must know. He doesn't care.

"Do that," he responds.

• • •

I sit at my desk raging, first at Tony Olwine, then at Mrs. Buckles, then again at Olwine. Just as I begin to calm down, to steel myself for the night's work, Stan comes charging into my office.

"Guess what," he says.

"I'm not in the mood to fuck around, Stan," I say.

"No. Guess," he demands.

"I can't," I say and then I add, sounding even to myself like a child, "Does anybody in this firm care that I'm on trial?"

"No," he says. "Not this trial. I just got off the phone with Farida. I asked her to marry me and she accepted."

"That's nice," I say. "Who's doing your prenup?"

"Is that all you can say?" he demands.

"Listen you poor lost soul," I say. "You've known her for all of four weeks, the partnership vote is less than a month away, things are so odd I wonder whether any of us will have jobs by December, I'm in the middle of a trial that may end up with me getting my head handed to me along with a summons for a malpractice lawsuit, and you don't have enough work to do. So congratulations."

"So we're doomed," he says brightly. "It occurs to me that I don't actually care as much as I thought. Aren't you happy for me?"

"Of course," I say.

"I'm meeting her for a drink," he says. "Come and join us."

"You're meeting the girl you've just asked to marry you and you want me to tag along?" I ask.

"Sure," he says.

"You're in even worse shape than you appear to be," I say. "I have work to do."

But I do feel better.

XVII

A TRIAL ACQUIRES A RHYTHM, BECOMES A WORLD ALL OF ITS OWN. There is a lot of waiting, a great deal of repetition, tedious sessions with the judge out of the hearing of everyone else. There is a touch of ritual, very rare moments of humor (a witness fumbles for his glasses; a juror points out that they are on top of his head). Slowly the story begins to unfold as over the next few days each of the parents walks solemnly to the witness stand, says his piece, steps down somehow relieved and purged. I know, as does Peter Hill, that I am just setting the stage for the real showdown. Until the experts take over—get to the heart of it, whether all this pain can be laid at Morganic's feet—all we have is pain, not liability.

And pain there is. It is not easy to watch parents talk about the illnesses and deaths of their children. If it were theater it would be riveting, but it is not. I try to be subtle in how I go about it, how I lead them one by one through the normal years and then approach the swimming hole, reference the smokestack in the distance to which nobody paid any attention at all, the calm before the storm. They answer my questions evenly, speak in self-effacing monotones, when the judge addresses them they rear back in the chair as if the force of his words alone were

enough to bend their backs. For the most part Peter Hill cross
-examines mildly and respectfully.

Only once does he uncoil. When one of the father's has given
a graphic account of his child's illness, instead of doing his usual
routine, asking about other illnesses in the family, other expo-
sures to harmful substances, he allows a hint of nastiness to
surface.

"It's true, isn't it," he says, "that you saw very little of your son
in the years before he became ill?"

We know it's true. We all, those of us on stage, know what is
coming.

"And it's true," he continues, "that you and your wife spent
some time in court arguing about child support in the years
before he became ill?"

I had toyed with the idea of bringing this out myself, blunting
the impact of what is coming. I know, of course, that the father
weeping about his dying son on the witness stand hasn't paid
child support for two years and is involved in separate proceedings that could land him in jail. I have decided to leave it. If Peter
does not get this exactly right, he will not emerge unscathed
himself.

A child is ill, play it however you will.

"Would you tell us the status of that matter?" Hill drones on.

Whatever. There is something completely ordinary about it
and something quite odd at the same time. It's like some antique
play, in a way, with the jury sitting day after day like a mute
Greek chorus off to the side, and the judge, Ruggles Zeus, ruddy
faced, never much of a success in law practice, the Governor's
friend, high up on his Olympus size bench presiding over it all
as he stares straight ahead. What he thinks, truly, I cannot say.
Whether he thinks, truly, I cannot say.

In front of him is the clerk, worried already about her Christmas shopping, on the phone and in one squabble after another
with store clerks during each recess, a court officer with a sub-

way map of burst capillaries in his nose reading what may be the same newspaper day after day there in his little box off to the left.

"All rise," and then "All be seated," and with a sigh of exhaustion he collapses into his box and settles down to another tough day.

And then us, Maria and me, Hill and his small army of associates who come and go from the spectators' gallery, snort indignantly when the testimony is not to their liking, rustle up a wind with their nods of agreement when it is. One of Hill's team, scarcely more than a boy, sits with his long legs folded under the table, like a schoolchild's under an undersized desk. There is something too relaxed, too presumptuous about his affect. Maybe the jury notices. Maybe they don't.

The witnesses mount the stand one by one, the parents, the doctors, a retired town inspector who several times cited the factory for violations of waste disposal rules. The violations have nothing to do with chemicals and Margaret and Peter Hill have already argued about whether it is relevant. Now Ruggles waves it all in over Peter Hill's objections. I suspect that the inspector was petty and meddlesome, that whether there were the right kind of ties on the plastic bags in which Morganic disposed of lunchroom waste has nothing to do with anything, but like Morganic chemicals, I will throw it up and let what leaches leach.

The inspector is humble and doddering on the witness stand. Only I know that when I called to confirm that he would be in court he told me that he would not come at all, a subpoena requiring him to do so notwithstanding, unless I agreed to front him a sizeable check for his "expenses."

Maybe a jury can sense these things. Maybe not.

I think the jury is becoming a little inured to all of it.

Soon Dr. Finkbiner and the warbling Dr. Krishnapatnaram will either take us over the bar or sink the ship without a trace.

...

There is a lime green memorandum, something I haven't seen for a while, on my desk. Mrs. Buckles is quite transparent. She is, apparently, trying to convince everyone that there has been a slight course correction, a minor change in approach in a carefully orchestrated master plan that is working superbly. There are going to be lay offs, in other words, of many of the new coordinators and associates facilitators and assistant administrators, my own Shannon Bertucci among them, who have just been hired. It is all described as a "Force Enhancement," a Great Leap Forward, something that has just occurred to the firm as a marvelous idea.

"This really is the last straw," Kay says coming into my office as I read.

I have hardly had time to hang up my coat.

"What is?" I ask.

"Do they really think we're ninnies?" she says. "All those poor food service and audio visual employees who've just been hired are now being frog marched from the building. I mean, they're people aren't they? People."

"What do you mean frog marched?" I ask.

"I mean what I say," she says. There is something new in her tone, not disrespectful but so soaked in irony that I think her personality may be breaking new ground. "They were given one hour's notice and escorted from the building."

"Why would they need to be escorted from the building?" I ask.

"Who knows?" she says. "They were told that it was in the best interests of the firm for them to be exterminated, and therefore in their best interests because as loyal employees they would have the firm's interests at heart, and then they were given one hour's notice and after that taken by the scruffs of their necks and summarily pitched into the street."

"I think they're short of money," I say. "I'm not defending them, of course."

"They didn't see this coming?" she asks. "Even the secretaries saw this coming. The only difference is that instead of firing or terminating them, they enhanced them."

There is, as I say, a new air to her, a wry smile on her face, something I have not seen before.

"I even overheard some of the young lawyers saying that there were going to be lay offs of associates, and that they were pulling back offers they've already made to some of last year's summer class. I find that hard to believe. They wouldn't do that, would they?"

There is nothing I can say to reassure her.

• • •

The corridors, which in the old building had been alive with activity and which even at Triumph Plaza not too many weeks before had been filled with busy administrators darting about with their clipboards, are very quiet.

"You've got to come see something in the library," Stan says as he ambles into my office.

"I'm busy," I tell him. "I've got a thousand things to do. Tomorrow I put Dr. Krishnapatnaram on the stand."

"God I love that man's name," Stan says. "But come anyway."

"What's up there?" I ask, making no effort to move.

"It's like a men's club," he says. "All the older partners are sitting around chatting, reading the newspaper. You've simply got to see it. It's quite quaint really."

"It's pathetic," I say.

"Several of the old coots are actually trying to do legal research," he says. "Snatching basic billable hours from first year associates. You have to come and see them snuffling through the books. I didn't have the heart to point out to some bald codger with reading glasses that we do our research on the computer these days and that some of the books he's looking in haven't been updated for years."

"I would like to see this," I say. "Maybe some other time."

"The end is nigh," Stan says. "I feel it. It's time to pull the rip cord."

"Chew through the umbilical cord more likely," I say.

"You don't get it, do you?" he says. "You claim to be a cynic and a clear thinker but you're actually a fuddy duddy deep down. In thirty years you're going to be a bald coot doing research in the library on a computer that hasn't been oiled in a decade."

"You don't oil computers," I say, but he's not wrong.

Not completely.

XVIII

Dr. Vijayananda Krishnapatnaram shows up for court all dressed up and ready to go. I have spoken to him on the phone at length, have almost become reconciled to his rather strong accent—it is as if he has marbles in his cheeks and must roll the words around them before they emerge—but I am not prepared for his appearance. He is pencil thin, very dark, and there is not a natural fiber on his body. He is also dressed entirely in brown, shiny brown pants, a broad brown nylon tie, and a brown jacket that appears too large for him and is covered in large squares.

He looks like a chocolate bar with hair, which is greased down, all except for a thick sprout that stands up at the crown like broccoli.

"Good morning," he says, his voice quite thin and eager. "Are we going to get them today?"

I shake his hand and say something vague. Get them today is one thing I am becoming somewhat doubtful we are going to do.

"We're going to do our best," I say.

"One other thing," he says, and there is something either tentative in his voice or it is his accent, the way his voice warbles on it. "I quoted a fee of two hundred and fifty dollars an hour at the

217

beginning, but I neglected to mention that for trial testimony my fee adjusts upward."

He says this as if it were a natural phenomenon, like if you put a kettle on a stove it will boil.

"How much upward?" I say.

Bear in mind that we are standing outside of the courtroom and that my little brown pirate is about to be my star witness. Maria, in a gesture of futility, asks him if he'd mind if she straightened his tie and he agrees with an odd little gurgle.

"Oh, five hundred dollars would be in the range," he says.

In the range! I can't wait to present Olwine with this invoice.

"Hear ye, hear ye," and we're off to another day.

• • •

Judge Ruggles does not disguise his reaction to my witness. He is taken aback, and interjects himself into proceedings immediately.

"Please tell the ladies and gentleman of the jury your name," I say.

"Dr. Vijayananda Krishnapatnaram," he says and Ruggles, hiking his gown up over his shoulders and hunkering down on his bench so that he again looks like a vulture about to swoop says, "Wo, wo, wo, doctor. Can you say that slowly."

The jury smiles and turns back to the doctor expectantly. Something mischievous injects itself into this. They look too inclined to enjoy themselves.

Dr. Krishnapatnaram repeats his name slowly and spells it for the court reporter as the judge raises his eyebrows. I am apparently now allowed to continue.

"You are a medical doctor?" I ask.

"Yes, that I am," he says.

I would be the first to admit that you have to listen carefully to follow things. This is not going well.

"Where do you practice medicine, doctor?" I ask, and here comes the Beverly Hills, Mississippi, part I have been worrying about, and another interjection from the judge, "Beverly Hills where?"

I notice that already my collar is chafing and that my brow feels clammy. Look, I don't want to come across as racist because I'm not, and perhaps I'm overly sensitive because he is my own witness, but I can't help wondering, as I ask my questions and he answers them, whether there isn't something ludicrous about this scene. I ask him something, if it's even faintly complex he prefaces his answer with "My goodness," once even with "My goodness gracious," and as he putters along, his tuft of vegetable hair sticking up, a slip of a man in a shining brown suit talking something close to rubbish in mangled English, I feel like I'm on the deck of a sinking ship. The jurors have no idea what to make of him, no clue, none whatsoever. You can see it on their faces: bemusement, puzzlement, worst of all, a deep, deep skepticism.

I'm still on his credentials. For Ruggles to accept him as an expert I have to show that he really does know his subject, that appearances aside, he is a knowledgeable cancer specialist. He describes his background, first at the University of Tamilnadu and then at the Poona Medical University, and that done we begin to talk about the field of oncology, how he has spent years studying and treating cancers, and maybe the jury is hearing this, has had enough time to put aside the surreal image I have brought to them and to listen to the substance of things. You don't need to look like Robert Redford to speak sense.

Hill isn't objecting to anything, and neither would I. I almost wish he would, but why would he interrupt, add something coherent to a flow of weightless words. Substantively Dr. Krishnapatnaram is not doing that badly, though I am, really, drenched in the perspiration of failure.

What was Margaret thinking?

• • •

We break for lunch and Maria goes downstairs to get me a sandwich while I read over my notes. She is trying to be, I suppose, sympathetic and supportive, but there is only so far a person can go.

"He's doing what he has to," she says. "I'm just not sure he would be my first choice if I were sick."

"How about your last?" I say.

"Are you okay?" she asks. "Is there anything I can do?"

She is concerned, I can see, not about the case but about me. From time to time I look across and see her, her yellow pad on her lap, taking notes, watching the jury, looking at me. When I catch her eye I feel, for just an instant of course, as if I have just walked through my own front door.

"We could dash out and buy plane tickets to Burma," I say. "We'd be there before court convenes tomorrow morning."

• • •

The jury returns from lunch looking well-fed, if nothing else. They rattle into the jury box, retake their assigned seats, look eagerly about. The court officer recalls Dr. Krishnapatnaram and they watch him carefully—too carefully, but then this is my witness, as I say, and I may be being sensitive—as he resumes the stand.

"You're still under oath," the court officer says, and the doctor replies, "Goodness yes."

We are at the crux of things. He describes how he has studied the medical records of the boys, has reviewed state surveys of the site and the report Dr. Finkbiner has written regarding the chemicals present in the ground water.

"And have you been able to form an opinion, doctor," I ask, "as to whether the chemicals found in the Asheville swimming hole can cause cancer in human beings?"

Now Hill objects, but the judge tells him to wait.

"Mabbit," he says. It's how he overrules objections. "He may have it," is what he means.

"Goodness yes," Dr. Krishnapatnaram answers. "These chemicals definitely can cause cancer in human beings, and did in these boys."

Now Hill leaps up but even before he opens his mouth Ruggles is on the case. There are limits to how much an expert can wing things, and he is suspicious.

"Is that just your personal opinion," Ruggles asks, "or is there good published scientific data to back you up?"

"It is my personal opinion," the doctor says, "and there is most certainly good science to back it up, my goodness."

"Perhaps now would be a good time to tell us what that scientific data consists of," Ruggles says.

"There are at least two published articles on which I rely," the doctor says. "Both of them may be found in the *Sri Lanka Journal of Medicine*."

"The what?" Judge Ruggles, leaning over the bench, wrinkling his brow, asks.

"The *Sri Lanka Journal of Medicine*," Dr. Krishnapatnaram says. The judge looks blank and I decide to intervene.

"A medical journal published in Sri Lanka," I say and then, who knows why I do it, I add: "It's a country next to India. The articles the doctor is referring to have both been furnished to the defense."

I think Ruggles may explode the way his face reddens and then darkens.

"I know where Sri Lanka is, counselor," he hisses. "What I wonder about it why this witness had to go all the way to the end of the earth to find support for his opinion."

Dr. Krishnapatnaram senses that his ethnicity is being slighted.

"The *Medical Journal of Sri Lanka* is a highly respected journal,

Sir," the doctor snaps, his head wagging from side to side with each syllable and, God help us, wagging his finger. "Its articles are peer-reviewed at the highest levels. The highest levels, goodness gracious," he adds for emphasis. "They meet the highest standards of science."

The judge is taken aback, the jury in some kind of shock.

"In the case in point," the doctor helpfully adds, "by reviewers at the University of Pondicherry and at my own medical school, the Poona Medical University."

"I have no doubt," the judge says at last, his hands tied, and he gives me a long and meaningful look over his glasses.

• • •

I am done by three thirty, and just as Peter Hill rises from his chair the judge must nod to the court officer—I don't see it, but I assume this is what happens—who jumps to his feet and shouts joyfully that court is in recess until tomorrow morning.

Dr. Krishnapatnaram comes up to me as soon as the courtroom is clear.

"I am free to go back to Mississippi, no?" he says.

"I'm afraid not," I say. "Mr. Hill has to cross-examine you still."

"You mean I have to stay another night?" he asks.

"Yes," I say. "My secretary will see to your hotel."

He thinks it over for a moment.

"If I have to stay a day beyond what was anticipated, my fee for tomorrow will have to be doubled," he says.

"Of course it will," I say.

• • •

"You're not going to believe this," Lioce has written on a note which is lying on my chair. "I've been fired. Have a nice evening."

I go looking for him and find him in his office.

"It's actually liberating once it's happened," he says.

"What happened?" I ask.

"Sheinburg called me in," he says. "He went on and on for about seven hours about what an asset I was to the firm and how great I had done and I thought either he was about to give me an award or he was about to fire me, and in the end he made me an offer I could refuse."

"Your note said that you'd been fired," I say.

"He offered me a spot as a permanent associate here, at three quarters my present salary," he says. "I listened for a while and then his words stopped coming and all I could see were his lips moving, his inflated blue lips saying things that made no sense."

"What did you do?"

"What do you think I did?"

"What?"

"I told him he was deluded," he says. "I've already called around and found I can share an office with a group of guys I went to law school with, secretary, library and all, for eight hundred bucks a month."

"You're actually going to do that?" I say.

"Done it already," he says. "Apparently Sheinburg didn't take well to my manner and I've been ordered to be out of the building by five p.m."

"That's gracious," I say. "Eight years of your prime and then a march to the door."

"Who cares?" he says. "Honestly. I would not have anticipated how easy this is. My new office is great, near Faneuil Hall. It's small, but one wall is exposed brick and there's this rickety little staircase to a kind of loft they use as a library. Trust me, I don't mind. It's liberating."

"It sounds good," I say uncertainly.

He is making it sound as if, all told, I should congratulate him rather than commiserate. I'm not so sure. It is at once my greatest fear and my most elusive aspiration, to step off a cliff and yet be free rather than free falling.

"I tell you," he says, "even if they make you a partner, when you see this place you'll be tempted. Its human size, friendly. I even think I can take a few clients that will prevent us from starving to death for the first few months. And we'll get other clients."

"And you're paying for this with what?" I ask.

"Listen," he says. " I'll tell you something else. With the overhead these clowns have committed to, they're on a death spiral. We can service the same clients for half as much and still make a decent living."

"If we could persuade them to throw in their lot with two losers, a typewriter, and an office."

"Did you say 'we?'" Stan says.

"Just daydreaming," I say.

"Just think of it," he says. "No more Olwines, no more Cabots, no more Buckleses, no more Sheinburgs, no more Triumph Plazas. Just think of it."

"Calm down," I say. "No more food. No more rent money. I have obligations."

"Think all you want," he says. "The offer's open for you indefinitely. And we'll eat, I promise.

I've already signed the lease, rented the computers, subscribed to the library service. If you don't make partner, or even if you do and Olwine's secretary gets you indicted for sex crimes, you just walk across the street and you're all set."

"It's that simple," I say.

"It's that simple," he replies. "I've already received an office warming gift."

"From whom?"

"Maria. She went out and bought me a plant as soon as the little busy body heard about it from someone."

Without Lioce, Nibble & Kuhn promises to be a heartless place indeed.

XIX

Dr. Krishnapatnaram shows up for court in exactly the same clothes he wore yesterday which raises all sorts of questions I would rather not answer. He sits up in his box, my possibly pungent little champion, his broccoli still sprouting, and looks quite eager. He has no idea, I think, none whatsoever, about what he is now in for.

I'm not going to get into what happens next because, quite frankly, one doesn't have to have any legal training, or much imagination for that matter, to imagine it. Things were left so shaky after Dr. Krishnapatnaram's supposedly friendly evidence that there's no point going through the methodical devastation of Peter Hill's cross-examination.

It is excruciating.

Yes, it's true, Dr. Krishnapatnaram doesn't have much of a medical practice.

Yes, that is a flyer he had printed up and had someone place on parked cars down there in Beverly Hills, Mississippi. (Just how did Hill get this gem, I wonder. And seriously, what kind of oncologist puts flyers on car windshields? I think for an instant of Margaret Kelly. I don't feel homicidal anymore. I am beyond that.)

Yes, it's true, Dr. Krishnapatnaram agrees, he offers his services on the Internet and elsewhere as an expert witness.

Yes, it's true too that he has never turned down a case he's been asked to testify in.

"A remarkable coincidence," Hill says sarcastically. "Every lawyer who has ever contacted you has a rock solid case of malpractice?"

"Certainly yes," Dr. Krishnapatnaram says. "There's a lot of it going around."

Hill even gets the doctor to describe his sandbagging fee structure, one amount before the trial starts, another once it's underway.

"Let me get this straight, Dr. Krishnapatnaram," he says.

He walks to the edge of the courtroom, takes off his glasses, walks back to the center.

"You told Mr. Dover only yesterday morning that you were increasing your charges to five hundred dollars an hour?"

There is silence. Some members of the jury look at me strangely. It might be sympathy or it might be scorn.

"Not increasing, my goodness," the doctor says bobbling his head. "That is my fee."

It doesn't help.

"But you only told him yesterday morning," Hill shouts, "just as the trial was about to begin and he had no alternative but to call you," and with this proposition too the doctor has to agree.

Hill shakes his head slowly, his gesture of sadness at how low our society has sunk, I would imagine, and then moves on. Ruggles watches it all with an incredulous detachment.

"These medical articles from Sri Lanka," Hill begins, and then, truthfully, I tune out.

Dr. Krishnapatnaram knows nothing of the methodology they employ, has no chemistry background himself. It turns out as well that he knows nothing about the quality of medical research in Sri Lanka, but boy, is he ferocious in defending its quality.

"The science of astronomy itself was invented in south Asia," he says at one point, as if this somehow proves his case.

Honestly, I'm trying not to listen. It doesn't matter to the doctor that there are at least fifty articles from well-known American institutions that flatly refute his. Nothing moves Dr. Krishnapatnaram. He admits it. There is nothing Hill could show him, no research, no science, no amount of evidence, that would change his mind. He clings tenaciously to his views, talks in circles when challenged, and in the end seems unembarrassed by a morning that would put lesser men into therapy.

When Hill is done I have no redirect. What possible line of questioning could rehabilitate this fulminating little dervish? Well, at least we're half way through my expert presentation.

•••

It is late afternoon when Dr. Maxwell Finkbiner takes the stand. At least he does look the part. He is quite tall, appropriately dressed, sports an M.I.T. ring, bold and blue, on his finger. "Please tell the jury your name," I say.

"Maxwell W. Finkbiner," he answers steadily. "F-I-N-K-B-I-N-E-R," he repeats, spelling it out for the court reporter.

Believe it or not, up there in the witness box the man's stutter diminishes. He presents himself with confidence, in a loud and clear voice, only occasionally has difficulty with consonants. He faces the jury as he speaks, puts things simply, is quite likeable. Perhaps it will all work out, somehow. He is a graduate of M.I.T., after all, even if it was a long time ago. In his youth he published real papers on a variety of subjects.

He is describing his research now for the jury. He manages to mention Harvard four times, and then Stanford twice, emphasizes how research on toxic substances, their migration in soil, is very much a part of his background and specialty. He describes his visit to the factory, how carefully he took his soil samples, how he selected the laboratory to which he sent them for analysis, what he found, what these findings mean. He uses phrases like "statistical strength" and "confidence level" as if they were talismanic, and agree with him or not, he has the jury's undivided attention.

My spirits, in short, revive.

"And Dr. Finkbiner," I finally ask, "at my request did you investigate whether any of the chemicals used in the Morganic factory, and which you have also now testified you detected in the soil outside of the factory, are also to be found in the Asheville swimming hole?"

"I did," he says gravely. "I most certainly did."

"And what did you find?" I ask.

"I found," Dr. Finkbiner says, "that there were traces of the chemicals used in the plant, the ones already discussed by Dr. Krishnapatnaram as being cancer causing, in the Asheville swimming hole."

Praise the Lord. I think this case may survive Peter Hill's efforts to have Judge Ruggles throw it out before it gets to the jury. I won't say I return to Triumph Plaza triumphant. I will say I have regained a shred of hope. Even one of the parents nods knowingly as we leave for the evening.

• • •

First thing in the morning, we are all back in the courtroom, the jury too, all trundled into its box, and it is Hill's turn to cross examine. He uncurls, arises from behind his table like a genie out of a bottle, carefully straightens a pile of books before he begins.

"How many times have you testified in court, doctor?" he asks.

"A number," Dr. Finkbiner says. "Perhaps forty or forty-five."

"Or fifty or fifty-five?" Hill suggests.

"Possibly," Dr. Finkbiner says.

"Sixty or sixty-five?" Hill suggests.

"One tends to lose track," Dr. Finkbiner tells him.

"One does," Hill agrees. "And how many depositions have you given?"

"More than that," Finkbiner answers.

"Would two hundred be an exaggeration?" Hill suggests.

"Not necessarily," Dr. Finkbiner says.

"Three hundred?" Hill asks.

"About that," the doctor says thoughtfully.

"And of course you're being paid for all this testimony, aren't you?" he says.

"Of course."

"You told the jury yesterday about the research you did and the papers you published, but you haven't done any research or published any papers for almost twenty years now, have you doctor?"

Finkbiner tries to answer that he has written reports for lawyers, produced papers required by judges, but Hill is having none of it.

"Did you hear my question?" he asks. "Outside of the courtroom, you have not done any scientific research, or written any scientific papers, for many, many years."

The doctor tries to argue, but the judge intervenes.

"Doctor," he says, leaning over the bench. "Try to answer the question. It's not a complicated one."

"No," Dr. Finkbiner says and, to my dismay, his stutter appears to be returning.

"And in the courtroom, at least, you've offered yourself as an expert on a wide range of subjects, haven't you?" Hill presses.

"I'm not sure what you mean by wide range," Dr. Finkbiner says.

This is not working for me. I have suggested he answer these questions simply and quickly. I mean, he *is* an expert for hire. He *has* testified a lot. He *has* made a lot of money giving evidence on a lot of subjects. What's the point of drawing it out. The members of the jury aren't imbeciles.

"Well," Peter Hill says, "you've testified as an expert on drain cleaners?"

"Yes."

"Carbon monoxide?"

"Yes."

"Coffee?"

"Yes."

"Asphalt?"

"Yes."

"Laundry detergents?"

"Yes."

"You once gave an opinion that fumes from a molasses plant in New Jersey interfered with animal husbandry on a neighboring farm?"

"I certainly did," Dr. Finkbiner says.

"You've testified as an expert on sugar?"

"Yes."

"Tobacco?"

"Yes."

"Gasoline?"

"Yes."

"Whiteout?"

"Yes."

"Glue?"

"Yes."

"Radioactive fuels?"

"Yes."

"Smokestacks?"

"Yes."

"Lead paint?"

"Yes."

"You've held yourself out as an expert on fetal alcohol syndrome?"

"Yes."

"On propane?"

"Yes."

"And on chlorinated water."

"Yes."

"And benzene?"

"Yes."

"And a host of other substances."

"I would say so," Dr. Finkbiner says in a confident monotone.

"You're an expert on just about everything, aren't you?" Hill says.

I object.

"Well," Ruggles says thoughtfully. "It sounds like everything. Mabbit."

"No," Dr. Finkbiner says. "But insofar as they are materials and substances which, in their interaction with organic matter, precipitate responses at the cellular level . . ."

"Doctor," Hill interrupts. "You're an expert on each of these substances, and a hundred or two other I haven't yet mentioned?"

"As I was saying," Finkbiner begins.

Ruggles leans over the bench.

"Just answer the question," he admonishes. He could be addressing a small child. "It's not that difficult when you really try."

"Now doctor," Peter Hill says, moving on without giving him the chance. "The swimming hole in Asheville is up a rather steep hill from the factory, isn't it?"

I know this is coming, know what Finkbiner's views are, but somehow it comes across as a bit of a bombshell. It gets the jury's attention. Even the judge leans forward, looks across and regards me with a stern eye.

"Yes," Dr. Finkbiner says. "And we took soil samples from several places on the factory grounds away, and uphill, from the factory. I found traces of the subject chemicals in all of our samples, even the one I analyzed that was farthest uphill from the building."

"How far uphill from the factory did you get?" Ruggles intervenes.

He is not meant to be questioning the witness but one can tell that he is trying to picture this.

"Ten feet," Finkbiner says.

"That's it," the judge interrupts. "You never got more than ten feet from the building."

"I wasn't authorized to analyze additional soil samples," Dr. Finkbiner says, glancing briefly at me. "But in the end it wasn't necessary. There are important and immutable principles of hydraulics involved here."

"And what are those immutable principles?" the judge demands.

I think Ruggles is beginning to see my case as something less than credible and me as a basket case. Maybe he wants to bring it to an end, one way or another. Maybe it all is simply a matter of macabre fascination.

"If water can go even one foot uphill," Finkbiner says, "who is to say it can't go ten or a hundred or a thousand. Clearly there are subterranean hydraulic forces at work here. There is no other explanation."

"Subterranean hydraulic forces," the judge splutters.

"Oh," Finkbiner says casually. "Such things have been well documented."

"Subterranean hydraulic forces," the judge repeats.

"Absolutely, subterranean hydraulic forces," Finkbiner tries to say, but he is flustered now and his stutter is firmly in place and with a vengeance. He gets so lost in the consonants that it takes him a very long time to say it. Waiting for him to say "subterra-nean" is gruesome. Fortunately he leaves Dr. Krishnapatnaram out of his answer or we'd be here until breakfast.

"With regard to your testimony that the chemicals used at Morganic traveled uphill," Hill continues, relentless, like an army moving through a breach, "that's not a theory you've pre-sented in any place outside of this courtroom, is it?"

"Subterranean hydraulics is well accepted by geological engi-neers," Dr. Finkbiner says, "and documented by me in this case."

As he answers he smiles, and nods at the jury. I note that no one smiles back.

"Point me to a single scientific article that says it's an accepted geologic principle," Hill demands. "Just one article that says that water can flow uphill."

"I don't have a bibliography memorized," Dr. Finkbiner says. "But I proved it here, myself, using standard hydraulic principles."

"For the jury to accept your testimony, they would have to believe that water can flow uphill," Hill says.

"Under certain circumstances it does," the doctor says solemnly.

"Uphill," Hill repeats.

"It does."

He pauses for a few seconds, is about to say something, and then he changes his mind and waits. There is a long silence in the courtroom.

"Uphill?" he says one final time.

"Objection," I say.

Judge Ruggles looks at me over his glasses. His robe is now so high at his back that he looks like he is peering out of a cave.

"Sustained, Mr. Dover," he says. "For what it's worth."

I would have preferred a "Mabbit."

"I have no more questions," Hill announces, and returns to his table.

Maybe the jury missed some of this, heard some of it, still has to make up its mind. All I know is that my witness has been torn to pieces. I don't care what anybody says. Except in a courtroom, water doesn't flow uphill.

"The plaintiff rests," I say to the judge.

• • •

"You've put on a very thin case," Ruggles says to me when the room is empty. "But it's probably enough to send to the jury and that's where it's going to be decided. They may understand what you're saying even if I'm not sure I do. Stranger things have happened."

He stands and starts to leave. Just as he reaches the door to his chambers he pauses, looks over his shoulder, and adds a final thought.

"Stranger things have happened," he repeats. "Though not many."

XX

S<small>EEN ONE WAY</small>, M<small>ARIA SITTING ON THE EDGE OF MY DESK, HER HAND</small> on my arm, leaning toward me as we discuss the case, is innocuous. That is not, of course, how Olwine sees it. He is walking down the hall and happens to pass just as Maria has finished listening to me heap curses on Maxwell Finkbiner and is saying, "You poor duck."

We look up and there, framed in the doorway, he stands and not only Olwine. The stolid Mrs. Buckles is at his side.

"We would like a word with you," he says icily.

• • •

Three minutes earlier and this would not have happened. I am sitting at my desk rereading some of the publications I am sure Dr. Endicott Wigworth will be relying on, and for the life of me I can't see how I am going to score any points against him on cross-examination. I mean, unlike my witnesses—or, as I've taken to saying, Margaret's witnesses because there is nothing about them of which I want to claim ownership—Dr. Wigworth is what he is supposed to be. His list of publications runs to thirty pages, his career is filled with nothing but eminence, and his opinions in this case do make sense.

If I try to discredit Dr. Wigworth on his own turf, I will be annihilated.

I expect everyone feels this way from time to time, so beaten down that everything becomes bleak. As much as I keep saying to myself that this Rosemary's baby is the conception of Margaret Kelly and Tony Olwine, I do own some of the farce, don't I?

"You don't," Maria says, her hand on my arm and she leans over to look into my face. "You poor duck," she adds as Olwine appears at the door.

"We'd like a word with you," he says.

Without waiting he and Mrs. Buckles enter my office as if reclaiming territory.

"Please," I say mildly, gesturing to the chairs.

Maria gathers her papers from the desk and beats a hasty retreat. A sense of impending doom has swept into the room. Mrs. Buckles closes the door and they sit down.

"I do not take kindly," he says, slowly and deliberately, "to being misled."

He is holding his reading glasses, swinging them slowly as he speaks.

"Neither would I," I say. "Who has misled you?"

"Please," Olwine says. "What Mrs. Buckles and I witnessed a moment ago confirms the essence of what has been alleged, and makes this rather more serious than it might otherwise have been."

His tone is now so contemptuous there can be no doubt that his antagonism is deep, complex, and personal. I am surprised how little thought I have given to what I would say if the affair between Cindy and me, or anything touching on Maria, ever became an issue. For a moment I wish I had rehearsed an indignant response. Instead all I do is raise an eyebrow. There is something lurid in this, embarrassing to be in this room with these two oddities discussing such things.

"I still don't know what you're talking about," I say, though of course I do. "Perhaps you might supply a few details."

He looks at me scornfully, and then lays his glasses carefully on the corner of my desk.

"The details are tawdry and unimportant," he says. "And you are not doing yourself credit by your manner. I have observed first hand instances where the tenor of your relationship with at least one, and one supposes therefore other, of the female lawyers in this office has not been appropriate, and more to the point have actually raised this matter with you once before, apparently to no avail. When you requested assistance on the Morganic matter I assumed it was done in good faith, that you needed assistance, and that you had reason to believe that the lawyer you requested had the requisite qualifications and experience to perform the legal tasks, the legal tasks," he repeats, "that were required. Perhaps you have lost sight of the fact that the women who work in this office are not a commodity available to you for your personal purposes, as much as you may wish it. I was also informed several weeks ago that you had entered into inappropriate relations with another employee of this firm, and now I see that you think nothing of it, of entering into inappropriate relationships at will." Perhaps because it is all so bleak I find myself almost energized by this exchange, almost angry.

"Isn't this something that might have waited?" I say. "I'm in the middle of a trial, with an expert witness to cross-examine in the morning."

"It is because you are in the middle of a trial that the firm will refrain from taking the steps I consider unavoidable at this juncture," he says. "I would also suggest that you not forget yourself."

I am losing the fight to retain my equanimity.

"This is absurd," I say.

The injustice of it overwhelms me, takes me to the edge, though only to the edge, of my self control. Olwine looks as if he is a machine that has been unplugged. He sits still for a moment, retrieves his glasses, allows them to dangle between his fingers. Then he stands.

"I have long since learned," he says, especially quietly, "to disregard everything that is said to me in a raised voice. You should have no doubt that the intemperance of your response will not in any way deflect us from our focus or the gravity of these issues."

He walks to the door, Mrs. Buckles in tow, allows her to leave first and then turns back for a parting shot.

"As you should long since have learned," he says, "that we do not, at Nibble & Kuhn, countenance the inappropriate treatment of others."

Now that, coming from Olwine, should be engraved somewhere. I see my things in boxes ready to be taken home, someone else in this lifeless office, someone else dictating to Kay, someone else taking instructions and riding in the dreary elevators and working late into the night. I would almost welcome being fired today if it also meant I could escape the rest of the trial, but the way it works whatever happens at Nibble & Kuhn, if I don't show up in court in the morning I risk getting disbarred.

I feel quite numb, really. The mere act of standing up is not physically possible. I stay at my desk, eventually resume my work, keep on until the sky begins to turn pink at dawn. I leave and go home to shower, change, and to catch an hour of sleep before court begins once again. Oddly enough, being dog tired may be a good thing, may function like a cheap narcotic.

To tell the truth, I start the day feeling more than a little nauseated.

XXI

THE FIRST TWO HOURS OF THE DAY ARE TAKEN UP WITH PETER HILL trying to persuade the judge to throw the case out then and there.

"Your Honor," he keeps saying, "the court can take judicial notice of the fact that water doesn't flow uphill."

"Finkhauser, or whatever the man's name was, testified that he found water that had migrated up the hill," Ruggles, that prince of the law, says. "The jury can believe it or they needn't. It's not my job to decide on credibility."

Hill has already handed the judge a stack of photocopied cases. He keeps citing them, but it is clear that the judge has absolutely no plans to read them. I know, and Peter Hill knows, why that is. Why make a ruling and risk being reversed by the appeals court when it is already as clear as day that the jury is going to find in Morganic's favor anyway and without risk to Judge Ruggles.

To say nothing of the fact that if he doesn't rule he won't have to write an opinion.

• • •

Peter Hill's first witness is the plant manager. He is not one of the coterie of men in suits who have surrounded Peter Hill since the beginning of the case. Instead he shows up for his turn on the witness stand dressed pretty much as if brought from Central Casting, in a corduroy jacket and trousers, light blue shirt, red tie. He has not been in a courtroom before, he says shortly after Hill has introduced him to the jury, and for the first few moments he appears to be overwhelmed by it all. He is also a little breathless and I remember with a measure of satisfaction that Morganic is not some impregnable leviathan that is predestined to plow right over me. These are people. They make mistakes.

I may find one or two.

He starts out by explaining what is made at the Asheville factory, and for the first time it all begins to sound quite reasonable. They make the mainframes for children's toys, he says, but also plated shower heads and automobile parts that look like chrome but are far from merely cosmetic. The chrome plated plastic is lighter than metal and thus its use allows for lighter cars and better fuel mileage. He mentions global warming. All that is missing is an American flag.

"Are there environmental regulations that apply to what you do in the Asheville factory?" Hill finally asks.

"Oh, yes sir," he says. "In terms of the environment, we are the second most heavily regulated industry in the United States."

"And the first?" Hill asks.

"The nuclear power industry," the man says earnestly.

He then begins to discuss the regulations that apply to the factory and shows himself to have an almost encyclopedic knowledge of them. He knows every relevant rule, every subpart of every rule; what can be used and what cannot, what can be carted over the highways and what cannot, where each ounce of toxic materials originates, where it goes as waste.

There are times when it is bad to bore a jury, times when it serves a purpose. Now it serves a purpose. Hill lets them see how exhaustive the process of waste disposal is, how finicky, how much time and effort go into complying with the rules. What difference does it make that OSHA requires workers handling the sealed vats to wear gloves and goggles, and how thick the gloves and goggles have to be, but this witness leaves none of it out, and even as the jurors attention appears to be wandering, it is with a sense of confidence that with this man they are in good hands.

Frenzy and boredom run thickly together. I am alert to any transgression, any sign of overreaching, but Hill plays it straight down the line. Straightforward questions, straightforward answers, a well-primed machine functioning as it should. It occurs to me as I listen to him that he is entirely credible, that I must tread carefully when my turn comes to ask questions. The jury must like him. I do.

"Your witness," Hill finally declares.

The judge turns to me and asks if I have any questions and when I say that I do he looks surprised. I expect he would take odds that I will make no headway, and he would make some money if he did. The witness turns to me with an open face as I approach the podium. When I introduce myself and he responds, "Pleased to meet you, sir," my instinct is to sit down.

But I need to at least try. He readily agrees that some of the documents I now show to him, papers Peter Hill long ago produced to Margaret Kelly as part of the pre-trial exchanges, show citations by OSHA for infractions. I am prepared to go at him if he tries to minimize them, and the truth of it is that individually they are minor, but he does not, takes full responsibility for their existence.

"Oh, yes," he says, seeing one of them and blushing deeply. "I haven't seen this one for a while. Where did you find it?"

He is genuinely curious, amused that I have it, as if I have caught him out on something about which he is particularly embarrassed.

"I sure slipped up on this one," he says. "Spent the week-end remedying it too. Can't have leaking pipes in the lady's bathroom."

He could coach little league, this guy, barbecue burgers for the neighbor's kids, fix intractable problems in his neighbors' cars. Hell, I'd like to take him home and have him answer a few questions about my own building's furnace.

· · ·

Ruggles returns from lunch, takes his seat on the bench.

"Who's your next witness?" he asks Hill.

"Dr. Endicott Wigworth," Hill says. "Of the Harvard School of Public Health."

Ruggles raises his eyebrows, why exactly I couldn't say although I could hazard a guess. He crouches over his papers, his black robe again creeping up the back of his head.

"Dr. Wigworth then," he says.

When Dr. Wigworth takes the stand it feels a bit as if the Almighty himself has entered the courtroom.

"Please state your name for the record, sir," Hill says.

"Endicott P. Wigworth," he answers steadily as if his name itself is a credential.

He does look impressive. He is, how could he be anything other, a graduate of Harvard College, Yale Medical School, the Harvard School of Public Health. I'm not sure the members of the jury have ever seen anyone quite so accomplished. I'm not sure I have. He has written three textbooks, for Christ's sake, on waterborne carcinogens, on environmental hazards to chil-dren, on the toxic nature of certain chemicals. He is involved in several large studies funded by the federal government on environmental hazards posed by Superfund sites, is a consultant to the Commonwealth of Massachusetts on the Woburn toxic site, the State of New York on cleaning up Love Canal, and is an occasional guest on *Nightline* and CNN. It goes on and on.

"Have you ever testified in a courtroom before?" Hill asks.

"Only once," the man says.

I wonder whether the jury breathes a sigh of relief. Between Dr. Finkbiner and Dr. Krishnapatnaram they must wonder whether there is such a thing as a scientist who does not somehow also fancy himself a lawyer.

"Could you describe that case briefly," Hill asks.

"About a year ago," he says, "I happened to be standing on a corner when a bus's brakes failed and it ran into a group of people. I was called at the trial as a fact witness."

"I remember that case," Ruggles says, coming to life and leaning over the bench. "Strange case. Driver fell asleep or something."

"That's correct, Your Honor," Dr. Wigworth says, starting something of a love fest with the judge. "If an accident like that has to happen, I suppose it's just as well that it happen outside the Massachusetts General Hospital. There were five of us giving first aid within seconds."

"Yes, yes," Ruggles says. "I remember."

Hill might just as well have Marcus Welby on the stand.

• • •

But the Welby thing does wear thin. He is not very likeable, in the end, Dr. Endicott Wigworth. I am sure, if one digs a bit, one will find traces of him on a Mayflower manifest and on the membership lists of the Algonquin and University clubs.

Let me describe him: Very tall and lanky, salt-and-pepper hair, a dull green Harris tweed jacket with leather at the elbows, tortoise shell half glasses, preternaturally big eyebrows. You will see him, or you would have, had you waited long enough on Brattle Street in Cambridge, walking his dog. I would have put money on it. You would have found him reading the *New*

York Times over coffee in a bakery on Mount Auburn Street though it will be, I will put money on this too, a borrowed newspaper or one left behind by someone else. Dr. Wigworth would consider it an imprudent use of resources to buy one himself. There is something about him that is so patrician, so set in its way, so oblivious to the rough edges of the world, that it is annoying. Even his work in public health begins to smack, at least it does to me, of *noblesse oblige.* Maybe the jury sees it my way, though as yet they show no signs of it.

He speaks in a seminary monotone, has a whiskey voice, raises and lowers his inhumanly thick eyebrows as he talks although this is associated with no particular change in emotion or emphasis. Every so often he sweeps a cord of salty hair off his forehead.

"How does one study whether a chemical might cause cancer?" Hill asks and the jury gets a short but careful lecture on double-blind studies, retrospective case control studies, the science of epidemiology, the importance of independence in research.

"Have there been studies on the link between the kind of chemicals used in the Asheville factory and cancer?" Hill asks, and once again the answer is a discussion of the articles that have been written on the subject, several by Dr. Wigworth himself.

"Is it possible for a scientist to say, to a reasonable degree of certainty," Hill asks, "that any particular case of cancer was caused by these substances?"

"Absolutely not," Dr. Wigworth replies with conviction. "There are many recognized causes of cancer, but the substances you have just named are not among them."

And then the doctor goes through each child's medical history, shows what other risks there were, why it is more likely that some of these other risks, not chemicals from the Morganic plant, caused the problems.

"One young man had a younger brother who died of cancer

before this family ever moved to Asheville," he says. "And a mother who had a mastectomy at thirty-one. These are risk factors for cancer, far more likely, I would say, to point to the conditions that might cause cancer in a child than his environment in the last four years of his life."

"Did you in fact visit the Asheville factory?" Hill asks.

"I certainly did," Dr. Wigworth replies. "I also spent considerable time at the swimming hole in question."

"What did you do there?" Hill asks.

"We took numerous samples, on several days, of the water in the hole," he says. "Indeed, I have brought them with me."

He turns and opens his bag, and from it he extracts two sealed beakers. They contain water, appear quite clear, unexceptional.

"What are those?" Hill asks.

"A sample taken from the swimming hole on December 24," he says. "And water taken from my kitchen faucet at home. They are labeled."

"The day before Christmas," Judge Ruggles says knowledgeably, and everyone nods at his comprehensive insight on calendar issues.

"So it was," Dr. Wigworth agrees.

"Did you analyze them?"

"Yes, we certainly did," Dr. Wigworth says. "Would you like me to tell you what we found?"

"Please do," the Judge interjects.

He is leaning over the bench and smiling. He is enjoying this.

"These samples both contain trace amounts of certain chemicals," he says. "Some of these chemicals are related to chemicals used in the Asheville factory. Some are not. But one thing is certain. The swimming hole water is as clean, and as free of dangerous chemicals, as the drinking water that comes out of my faucet in Cambridge."

"How much more do you have?" Ruggles asks, sitting back in his chair and smiling.

"I'll be done in five minutes," Hill says.

Ruggles nods and returns to his writing. With rare exceptions he lives up there in a kind of grumpy detachment, growling about settlement, ruling on objections, treating the jurors with an old-fashioned courtliness. His rulings are not always right, in my opinion, but at least they are as often wrong in my favor as in Hill's.

"Do you have an opinion to a reasonable degree of scientific certainty as to what it was that caused the cancer in these little boys," Hill asks.

"I do."

Like marriage vows, almost, in their solemnity.

"And what is that opinion?"

"No one will ever know," the doctor says. "But whatever it was, the water in the swimming hole is irrelevant to the analysis. That is the only honest answer."

"That is all," Hill says.

Without warning the court officer stands and shouts that we are in recess. It is just past three.

"Is that the end of the trial day?" I ask.

Ruggles peers down from his perch.

"How much do you have?" he asks.

"An hour or two, at most," I say.

"If it's one hour I'll allow your motion to reconvene after a five-minute bathroom break. If it's two I'll deny it," he says.

The jury snickers.

"One hour," I say trying to sound sporting. All in a day's work. Right ho.

"Motion granted," the Ruggles rules.

• • •

What happens next, honest to God, I couldn't make up. I fall into it unwittingly. It changes everything.

"Dr. Wigworth," I say, "may I see those two beakers."

He says I certainly may, lifts them out of his bag, places them carefully on the ledge in front of the witness stand.

"One comes from your faucet, and one, on the day before Christmas, from the hole?"

"That is what I have testified," he says.

"Dr. Finkbiner was there with you, wasn't he?" I say.

"Yes," he says. "It was an outing organized by the lawyers. A very cold outing, I might add."

People smile. Judge Ruggles appears not to be listening.

"You didn't test this water yourself, did you?" I ask.

"No," he says. "My testimony is based on the results of testing done by a lab at the Harvard School of Public Health."

"You've read, surely," I say, "the analysis done by a laboratory at Dr. Finkbiner's request."

"I have," he says.

"And that analysis finds more than trace amounts of chemicals in the swimming hole water, doesn't it?" I say. "In fact, harmful chemicals."

Where I am going with this I cannot say. It is all I have.

"I disagree," he says. "This water," and he holds up the beaker, turns it slowly in the dull light of the courtroom, "is, as I have just said, as pure as Cambridge drinking water."

There's a scene in that movie *Erin Brokovich* where Erin, who is a paralegal in a law firm that is suing an electric utility for polluting water, offers some corporate stiffs who have come to her office glasses of water to drink. As they're about to drink she drops on them that the water comes from a well they have been insisting is not contaminated, and they get all flustered and put the glasses quickly down. I don't have a lot in common with Julia Roberts—I don't have anything in common with Julia Roberts—but what a fine idea she had that day.

I'm going to do the same thing.

"You would drink it?" I suddenly find myself saying as Peter

Hill jumps up and objects.

Ruggles, disturbed from his torpor, raises his eyes and glares at me.

"He doesn't have to drink anything," Ruggles says.

"So then you wouldn't be comfortable drinking it, notwithstanding that you've told the jury that it is as pure as Cambridge tap water," I press on.

Suddenly it descends on me that I have Dr. Wigworth in something of a dilemma. Of course he doesn't have to drink anything, but he said it, and it's out there, and either he's being honest or he's being disingenuous.

"I didn't say that," he says. "I said it was pure."

"I see," I say. "You'd agree that in all likelihood boys swimming in the swimming hole swallowed water from time to time?"

"Perhaps," he says.

"In other words they drank it," I say.

"Perhaps."

"Would you?"

Again Hill erupts, again Ruggles steps in, and for what it's worth I've now had my Julia Roberts moment and am ready to move on. I didn't ask for this, in fact I'd rather we move on quickly, but I do want the jury to see that for all the mentions of Harvard and the Massachusetts General Hospital, the eloquence and the big words and the lofty opinions, Dr. Wigworth would just rather not, is simply not prepared, to put his money where his mouth is, so to speak, to allow past his pursed Cantabrigian lips the same water he has just sworn under oath to a jury was harmless for my seven little working-class boys. There is, at this point, a noticeable shine on Dr. Wigworth's forehead.

"This is quite improper," Hill says and then adds, "For one thing, I object to the witness drinking the evidence."

"The doctor did bring it up," Ruggles says.

Dr. Wigworth lifts the beaker off the ledge, holds it up again to the light.

"Hold on doctor," the judge says firmly, now looking nervous. Wigworth's hand is trembling slightly, though maybe it is always like that. "You don't have to do anything of the kind."

The jury is riveted. This impasse is my first unambiguously good moment of the trial. Everyone knows it. Wigworth knows it. In some strange, distorted, way, his credibility, everything he has said, is on the line. Even the court officer puts his newspaper down. Jump, jump, the crowd below says.

"Let's move on," I say.

I have made my point. I mean if he drinks it, that's that. Even if he does get cancer years from now, it's not going to do me any good.

"You can put the beaker down, doctor," I say. "I'm almost done."

There is something thick in the air now, a sense of disappointment I think it is, and directed at Dr. Wigworth. Hill must sense it. The doctor certainly does. He shifts in his chair, actually reaches, inadvertently it seems, for the real glass of drinking water that has been standing at the edge of the witness box the whole time. I start to mumble my way into my next question, pause, gesture to him to go ahead and take his refreshment. He looks at me over his glasses, openly hostile. Things can't get any better than they are at this moment.

And then they do. Without warning Dr. Wigworth replaces the water glass and lifts the beaker of evidence to his mouth. Even as the judge is saying "I wouldn't do that, doctor," Wigworth tilts back his head and takes a long slow sip, and then, as I say, honest to God I couldn't make something like this up, he drops dead, right there, dead on the floor in the middle of the courtroom. Drops like a bag of beans. Such is the dynamic of the thing that my first thought as I watch this unfold is not that I may have had a hand in the death of a human being, but that the trial has to be over, that somehow I have been saved.

It is, for a moment at least, as unreal as the trial itself, nothing more momentous, indeed, than a piece of evidence. It is, at that instant, a fortuitous death. No hard feelings. Rest in peace.

Maria seems too caught up in it to appreciate the gravity of what has just happened.

"Killer cross-examination," she whispers in my ear as she stands, her body held against my back by the press of the crowd. The crowd softens but she remains where she was, closer than she needs to be. I feel her breast against my back, held deliberately against my back, in court, in Judge Ruggles's court. Her thigh presses against my mine. It is a caress.

I reach back and touch her. For a moment she does not move.

XXII

THE TRIAL IS OF COURSE NOW OVER, THOUGH NOT AS OVER AS PETER Hill would like it to be.

Let me skip past the uproar, the sudden explosion of activity with court officers and first-aid workers and even the judge crouching beside the witness in his black robe, seeming to forget that although it is still his court room, the Judicial Nominating Committee did not give him powers to issue rulings either to emergency medical workers or to nature.

"Dr. Wigworth," he demands. "Dr. Wigworth. Would you kindly respond, sir."

"Would you mind moving," an emergency worker says, and the judge, brought suddenly back to the reality of his impotence, stands up and moves away from the very blue former witness.

There is, of course, no precedent for this. The jury has piled out of the box, stepped where they are expressly forbidden to step, into the well of the court, mingle and exchange expressions of astonishment with each other and with the small flood of people that has somehow sensed the excitement and come into the courtroom. And then, just as suddenly, the swinging door to the courtroom opens to allow the medical technicians to wheel the former Dr. Wigworth out, and we are left,

an amorphous mob mingling about in no particular order and
without purpose.

Ruggles is now surrounded by court officers and after a brief
exchange one of them decides to restore a semblance of order.

"Order in the court," he shouts, and even those who hear him
aren't quite sure, in practical terms, what this requires them to
do.

The judge, meanwhile, straightening his robe, returns to the
bench and pounds his gavel.

"Would the jury kindly return to the box, the lawyers to their
tables, and the spectators to their appropriate seats behind the
bar," he orders, and then he stands waiting as the mob gradually
sorts itself out.

Peter Hill, I see, is in the middle of a furious conference with
his suits. He disengages from them reluctantly and returns to
stand behind his table.

"Your Honor," he begins, but Ruggles silences him.

He turns to the jury and asks the impossible of them. He asks
them to put aside for the rest of the day the issues raised in this
trial, not even to discuss with their families what they have just
witnessed, tells them that the lawyers have some work to do in
light of what has just happened, and orders them to report for
continued service at nine a.m.

Peter Hill stands once more and asks for a conference outside
of the jury's hearing.

"You'll have that when they're gone," Ruggles says impatiently.

"There's something I would like to raise before they leave,"
he says.

"No," Ruggles insists. "Sit."

What Hill wants, of course, and he gets right down to is as
soon as the last juror has disappeared, is a mistrial. I would
say, under the circumstances, that this is not an unreasonable
request. Indeed I would say that it is almost compelled.

To my astonishment, Ruggles disagrees.

"I told him not to do it," he says. "You and he brought this on yourselves. You must have known what he was going to testify, and he said the water could be drunk safely and without anxiety. Apparently it couldn't be drunk without anxiety, now, could it? If the glove fits, you must acquit, or whatever it was that lawyer said."

"But whatever it was Dr. Wigworth became ill from," Hill says, and I suppose he clings on to some hope that the man will recover though I suspect that people who are as blue as Dr. Wigworth and who don't breath despite numerous electric shocks and poundings do not have an optimistic prognosis, "has nothing to do with the case."

"I would agree with that," Ruggles says. "And will so instruct the jury."

He turns to me. "You're not claiming the well water actually killed him, are you Mr. Dover?" he asks and it's odd because he's suddenly my ally, suddenly sees the future quite differently than he did just moments ago. "You're not claiming that are you?" this beacon of law and reason repeats.

"No, of course not judge," I say agreeably.

"Well, then," Ruggles says in a manner that is clear he will countenance no further discussion. "First thing in the morning I will give the jury a report on the man's condition, and if he has expired I will share with them what we are told is the reason. I will also make clear that there is no allegation in this case that the water in question can cause whatever acute illness the man may have succumbed to. But we have three weeks invested in this trial already, a great deal of everyone's time and resources, and I see no reason to turn back. This jury will understand."

"I don't think they will," Hill insists, but it is futile.

"As I see it," the judge says, suddenly standing and beginning to gather his papers, "you have two choices Mr. Hill."

"What are they?" Hill asks uncertainly.

"You can continue with this trial at nine thirty tomorrow

morning, and if the appeals court later says I was wrong, well so be it, or you can gather up your claims adjusters and clients and whoever it is you have behind you in the courtroom, and you can pay these boys some serious money."

"Court is in recess," yells the officer.

There follows a lot of backward and forward. Ruggles orders that the families be given the jury room to work in, and Peter Hill and his suits hover about in the lobby on cell phones and using the phone bank. There is a lot of posturing and calculating and arguing, and numbers bandied about that make my head swim. I don't quite believe myself when I say to him, in all seriousness as we talk privately in a corridor, that Margaret's demand of seventy million dollars, or ten million a family, remains our position, but he takes me seriously, agrees to convey it again to his clients and their insurers, and with only one concession by me.

I make the concession he requests.

Yes, I say, I will. I will persuade the families that this number may be too high and that we should entertain the notion of finding middle ground.

Yes, I will.

XXIII

PERHAPS IT IS SIMPLY BECAUSE THE EVENT IS A WELCOME RELIEF from the dreariness of it all. The firm is deathly quiet and it has always been something of a tradition at the old Nibble & Kuhn building that when someone wins a jury verdict or has a particularly good result in court everyone comes out of their offices when they return to applaud and pepper them with questions. But there is an edge of hysteria to this reception. People hearing about it second- and third-hand come down from other floors to see what is going on, and pretty soon almost the whole firm is crowded in a large circle around me, listening, laughing, seeking to share the victory as if they had won it themselves. There is almost a taste of the old Nibble & Kuhn, the pre-Mrs. Buckles place, a college of sorts, at times even a dorm. Perhaps because it is so alien to them, the administrators are wholly absent in this celebration.

Forty percent of thirty-five million dollars divided among forty partners results in . . . well someone else will have to do the math because I can't bear to. In doing it, though, do remember to subtract from the money available for distribution to the partners the $5,000 I have been told will be mine, come Christmas, as a bonus. I care rather less about not getting anything than about who will.

I field the questions, the admiring comments, with good enough humor. Strangely it is not exhilaration I feel so much as relief, like the day I passed the Bar Exam or received an offer to work at Nibble & Kuhn. At such times it has always seemed more like a process of running in place, or of dodging a bullet. I have fended off disaster, for me and perhaps for the firm too, and for whatever reason I take no particular pride in any of it. A man is dead too, but that suddenly seems to have happened in a place so remote and unreal that it scarcely registers.

Of all the people in the room Maria must surely best under-stand how I feel. I scan the crowd of Nibble lawyers for her more than once, but in all the tumult in the courthouse, and then the signing of the papers and entering the agreement into the record and then supervising the Brazilians who arrive to get the boxes, we have gone our separate ways.

"Oliver Wendell Ruggles he isn't," someone says and not to be outdone, launches into his own story concerning Ruggles, but I tune him out.

"No mistrial," someone else says. "That's reversible error for sure."

The discussion moves away from me and I stroll back to my office. I find a note on my chair from Mrs. Buckles:

Kindly complete this form regarding the duration of your intended use of the trial bags presently checked out to you, it says.

• • •

I am pleased to look up and see Richard Havens sauntering into my office.

"Oh boy, my friend," he says, "have you brought home a cas-ket of humble pie."

"What do you mean?" I ask.

"Well, you won, didn't you?" he says. "One moment everyone is distancing themselves as you get thrown to the wolves, the next everyone is trying to explain that they didn't mean exactly that, that this brilliant idea was actually theirs all along. A lot of it has to do with money"—and here's where he tells me about the way it's to be split and my proposed rich bonus—"but a lot has to do with taking credit. Oh," he says, "it's rich. Rich. And I couldn't be more delighted for you."

"Thank you," I say.

"May I take you for a drink and dinner?" he asks. "And bring your young lady, if you have one. On me. Or your young man. Anyone you want. Bring them."

"That's okay," I say.

"Well round up that young lawyer in any event," he says. "Don't take no for an answer."

"What young lawyer?" I ask.

"The one who can't take her eyes off you, my friend," he says loudly.

I would like nothing better than to go home, to take off my suit, perhaps to take a walk by myself along the river. It has been weeks since I have had an evening so free, and the prospect of walking aimlessly along the Esplanade in the dusk is as alluring as anything I can contemplate. When I was a very young lawyer there was some novelty to business dinners. Now I will take a tuna melt in my own kitchen, in my real clothes, any day. But I allow myself to be dragooned into this dinner and who would I be bluffing if I did not admit the reason.

It's not a subtle matter. Perhaps, I am thinking, Maria will reappear.

• • •

I am thrilled to see, when the group that Richard Havens has collected begins to gather in the foyer, that Maria is indeed there. She does not relish occasions like this any more than I do, but I see her standing with a couple of bow ties and when she sees me her face comes alive in a way that I know belongs to me. Now anything is worth it. I cherish everything about her, everything, from her white linen suit to her hair clip with its huge plastic pearls to her oversized bag. She is, suddenly and unexpectedly, more familiar to me than anything else in sight. Anything else, indeed, anywhere.

"My mom says this bag makes me look like a ragamuffin," she has said about the bag she carries now. "She wants to buy me a briefcase."

"Why don't you let her?" I ask

"Carry a briefcase," she says. "Me? Can you just picture it?"

And I can't.

I have the strange sense as we sit in the restaurant Richard Havens has chosen that everything is out of focus. Maria, at the other end of the table, appears to be fully engaged in conversation with the bow ties, but I know her well enough, catch her eye often enough, to sense the strain in her animated gestures. I recall the fragrance of her clothes at the end of the day, the shape of her dark profile as she sits in the car beside me, the feel of something being within reach and yet beyond holding. I wish it were I who were sitting next to her.

I could go into some detail about this supposed victory dinner but I'll spare myself. It was both predictable and surprising. I mention it at all only because of this...

She has ordered lobster and has pulled off the legs. The rest is untouched. A bow tie sitting next to her is showing off, talking about some impossibly remote villa from which he and his fiancé have just returned. She looks at me and her face twitches, for in instant, into a grimace. Perhaps Havens notices because he turns to her almost immediately and asks, "And where do you spend your vacations?"

"In Spain," she says. "My grandfather lives there."

"Do you have much family there?" he asks.

"A huge family," she says. "Cousins, aunts, uncles, cousins of aunts and uncles. It goes on forever."

We exchange a glance, Maria and I. She knows, of course, that I will not betray her.

"Are you married?" Havens asks. "I seem to recall that you had a young man at that ghastly firm function."

"No," she says quickly.

I watch this exchange, intrigued. She looks down, moves her fork, starts to say something and then thinks better of it.

"But my parents think I'm engaged," she adds suddenly.

The bow tie sits forward in his chair.

"Your parents think you're engaged and you're not?" he asks incredulously.

"'How could that be?" I say. "How could your parents think you're engaged and be mistaken? One would think that either you are or you aren't."

I have jumped in without much thought, but it is an opportunity that will not come again. She looks across at me blankly. It reminds me of the two-track conversations in the old days with Kay as our audience. Now we face each other from opposite ends of a long table.

"I'm not telling everyone my business," she says, trying to strike a balance between indignation and lightheartedness. "Things got out of hand."

"But then who finally decides whether you're actually engaged or not?" I ask. Perhaps the others are taking note of my sudden interest. Perhaps not. It really doesn't matter. "I mean," I add, "there comes a time when there's not much room for ambiguity."

A waiter thrusts his way between chairs to the table. He removes a plate or two, straightens some cutlery. Everyone awaits her answer.

"That time obviously hasn't come yet," she says seriously. "I expect I'll know when it does."

She is still holding on to her flippant tone, her airy way, bantering with me. I am not bantering with her.

"And how will you know?" I ask firmly.

I am holding her eye, and she mine, and the others at the table can think what they will, but this is between Maria and me and what they think means nothing at this moment. There is a burning in my chest, anger now and resentment, and a longing deeper than I can tolerate.

"I can't say," she says. "I just know I will."

"What's going on here?" Havens interrupts. The man may be a drunk but he is not a fool. "This is supposed to be a celebration."

"For sure," she says as she gets up from the table and makes her way to the ladies' room.

XXIV

I HAVE NOT SENT THE MORGANIC FILE TO ARCHIVES. THERE IS NO
particular reason why I have kept the boxes lined up the way
they are against the wall. Kay has offered several times to help
me pack them into properly labeled folders and to send them
off, but I have said no. Sometimes I just sit and stare at it all, the
charts and the photographs, the boxes, the folders, even an easel
still where I propped it behind the door.

The fall is now here, there is no doubt about it. Soon it will
be time to break out tweed suits and wool sweaters. The leaves
are turning and the graying skies and the crisp breezes suggest
freshmen and newness and traffic jams at Kenmore Square.
There is something invigorating about it, fresh year, clean slate,
new start. The heart of fall in the city of Boston, tinged as it is
with orange trees, the smell of wood smoke, waves of newcom-
ers, is fresh and bracing. In the morning a mist hangs over the
river and dew coats the grass.

I am busy, perhaps busier than I have ever been, treated with
an odd new respect it is difficult to process. It is a combination,
of course, of the television coverage that followed the trial, most
of it far from subtle, numerous newspapers stories, several articles in the national lawyer journals, and what this has all come

to mean for the firm. Dr. Wigworth's death is always central to the story, but somehow I am given credit for the outcome, as if his decision to give himself a heart attack was somehow part of a strategic master plan. It's nonsense, of course, and I've laid out the facts here; this is not false modesty. Somewhere in the mix Dr. Krishnapatnaram, with whom we are in a fee fight, not because of his actual charges but because of the premium he is now demanding, and Dr. Finkbiner, are seen as bit performers, yeomen scientists who did what they had to so that an accomplished young lawyer could pull off his stunning coup.

Nibble's new publicity coordinator comes excitedly into my office at least twice a day with suggestions that we do this or that we do that. The most recent of them is that we hire a penguin from the Aquarium and bring it to the firm, and that I pose for photographs standing next to it for use in a release that reads something like: *The penguin isn't the only one who cares about our environment.*

"Mrs. Beveridge," I say. "Not in this lifetime, nor if I die and am reincarnated as a penguin, would I appear in a photograph like that."

She mutters something about my inability to seize an opportunity and staggers out of my office on her pointy *Arabian Nights* shoes, but the sea change in the firm's fortunes, and my own, is palpable. I am on, should I say this, can I with a straight face, the firm's new screening committee, which is charged with deciding which of the numerous toxic tort referrals we will take, and which we will decline. But each time someone considers sending a new case to Nibble the referring lawyer seeks reassurance that I personally, me, Derek Dover, master trial lawyer, will handle it.

Dollar signs dance like sugar plum fairies in the partners' dreams.

And the benchmark for which new cases Nibble will decide to take? Well, they have to be at least as strong as the claims we had in Morganic.

Isn't that a howl?

• • •

On the night of the partnership vote I leave the office early and walk into the city. My coat is still in my office and it is chilly, but I walk faster until I am warm. The Common is filled with people walking home, students, old-timers, a few who obviously have nowhere else to go. I walk across one of Olmsted's little bridges, through the great gates on Arlington Street, past the Taj. This is the door I came through after leaving Maria. Here is where my car was parked. This is where I stood and waited, wondering if she would turn and run after me. She did not.

This is a city of which I have been enamored since I was a child, and not only because my mother was born here. I remember visiting when I was in high school and being awed by it, by the young people everywhere, by the sense of anticipation and possibility in the air, by the profound beauty of life in a place filled with parks and universities and museums and bow-fronted houses. There are roofs here made of copper, a sheen of patina over them, bell towers and loggias, secluded private gardens. When I finally found a job here, and an apartment overlooking what I believe to be the most beautiful boulevard in North America, Commonwealth Avenue, it was like living in a dream. It's hard to describe this but at first, and several times every day, the thought of where I was would dawn on me and I would become suddenly, irrationally, exuberantly, happy. Boston was my home, the law was my profession, anything was possible.

I have walked countless times past these statues and monuments, through the Common with its ponds and gazebos, approached with a sense of endless possibility my elegant office in the shadow of the gold-domed State House. I have been working toward this night ever since I came to believe that a partnership in Nibble & Kuhn marked the apogee of my aspirations, a

point after which I would be able to view the future with confidence and certainty and the past with satisfaction. And yet
something is also perfectly wrong. Those moments of exuberance are a distant memory. I recall them, but that is not to say
that I can feel how they were.

• • •

Kay is gone. Not for the day. Forever. She seems to have had
an epiphany of her own of sorts, finally came clean about something that made me realize how much less I know than I think
I do. I return to my office from some firm meeting or other. It
is late in the afternoon and I find that her desk is clear of everything, completely empty. She is sitting sedately with her hands
folded in her lap.

She says nothing as I approach, simply stands and follows me
into my office.

"May I have a word with you please," she says.

"Of course."

She closes the door, approaches the desk and sits in one of the
client chairs across from me.

"I have two things I want to tell you, Derek," she says.

I must say that starting with the day she told me about the
firings the tone of our interaction has shifted. Calling me by
my first name is a part of it. An almost maternal concern for my
well being, not within the firm but somehow beyond that, has
become apparent.

"The first is that I've given my notice," she says.

She had looked pale out there in the open, but now color is
returning to her face.

"I don't want you to think it has anything to do with the silliness that seems to have come over this firm in the past few
months," she adds. "In fact, I would say that in retrospect I welcome the silliness. It has been clarifying."

"What do you mean?" I ask.

"It's a matter of realizing what one wants from life," she says. "I seem at last to have learned what everyone around me appears always to have known, and that is that adherence to duty is not necessarily its own reward. I am surprised that this is true, but it seems that it is."

"I suppose I can't disagree with you," I say.

"It's not only that, of course," she continues. "The second thing I want to tell you about concerns Miss Silversmith and me. I have been disingenuous with you for these past few years, in fact with everyone, and that too, especially in this day and age, seems to me an anachronism whose time is past. Miss Silver-smith—Emma—and I have known each other since we were in college. We formed a bond that has now lasted for many years. For a long time the sort of friendship we have was looked upon very narrowly, as you know, but it's enough now. Living one's life on disparate tracks is not good for the soul."

I am speechless, literally. I do not know what to say. It does not reflect well on me that my first thought is that I will gloat with Maria about how wrong she was, and how absolutely con-fident she was in her wrongness. I am also struck by the coinci-dence that Kay's partner's name is the same as Maria's sister's. But then something else takes hold of me. It takes courage to do what Kay has just done. When I do tell Maria, if I tell Maria, it will not be in the context of a joke.

"What are you going to do for your next act?" I finally ask, smiling.

"That's the easy part," she says. "We have talked for years about one day going off on a great adventure, and that day is now. We are going, you see, to places where little old ladies like ourselves are curiosities."

I shake my head in wonder.

"Emma and I were up almost all night talking about it," she says. "We found ourselves becoming so excited about or lives,

about our good fortune, about how things have a way of turning out, that I came in this morning with a kind of confidence I
haven't had before. I just realized, maybe I'm slower than most,
that life is finite. Now that I know it, really know it, each day
neglected is a particular kind of sin, a slap in the face to nature."

I say nothing.

"And as for all the silliness," she says standing up, "all those
poor boys and girls coming in now in their expensive clothes
and with their expensive tastes, they look half scared to death
if you ask me, which you haven't. I don't know how it all got
this way, but if anyone can change things around here you can.
Either way, working with you has been a privilege and I wish
you nothing but success and satisfaction."

"You're leaving now?" I say. "Right now?"

I recognize in my voice a tone I once used on my mother as
she left for her bridge games.

"Right now, dearie," she says. "Emma is waiting downstairs
and Tom is taking us out for a drink to celebrate."

"Things will never be the same," I say.

"Things won't be the same, but perhaps they'll be better," she
says. "I've put my things in a bag, and my tea cup I've left on a
shelf in the break room. I did take down my notes. It's someone
else's turn to keep it tidy."

I look at her and, truthfully, well I have never considered
whether she is or once was beautiful, but she looks radiant. The
pallor has disappeared and a small, irrepressible smile keeps
creeping across her lips. I feel as if I have just come to know
her. I think of her walking out of the building and into the
street, to Tom's cab there waiting by the curb with Emma sitting demurely in the back, of Tom who has brought her to work
every day for decades now opening the door one last time and
Kay climbing in to sit beside her partner, of the cab pulling away
from the sidewalk, of two hats visible through the rear window,
two little white bowls, like daisies, side by side in the glass. They

will look much the same sliding by in a gondola, in the back of an old Austin taxi somewhere in Scotland, peering at a giraffe through the sunroof of a striped jeep on an African plain.

The hats bob and sway and then are swept away, two little monuments of order in a loud and disorderly street.

• • •

Now I feel like a cup of good coffee, the really rich, freshly ground, imported stuff my father sells, and a soft, newly baked, pastry. I find a café I have not been in before and place an order, sit by the window and watch the people walk by. In the semi-darkness I feel at ease. I once placed so much stock in this decision that the firm is making tonight that I have not really thought very much about what lies beyond it. But now, standing on the crest and able to look down, I see for the first time a host of vague objects scattered about the future and it occurs to me that they are not as unlike those that have lain scattered about the past as I might once have believed.

I take my time, order a second cup of coffee, pay the bill only when it has been lying on the table for ten minutes and the waitress has asked me for a third time whether I want a refill. Only as I rise do I begin to feel some pressure, a vague sense of panic.

I walk briskly back to my office to keep my vigil. On my desk is a note from Maria. It says, simply: *I hope you make it (if you want to). Whatever does or doesn't happen, you are the love of my life.*

I hold it, caress it, kiss it. Then I fold it and put it in my pocket.

• • •

They send Richard Havens down to get me. There is something cynical about this, sending a man who I know is in disfavor. Perhaps they think that Havens of all of them will best give me the sense that there is a place in the firm for all types, that there is an element of humor, even, in the firm's decisions. But Havens says little, merely invites me to go with him upstairs to the Alfred Nibble Conference Center.

"Come along," he says. "The big moment has arrived."

If he is trying to muster a measure of camaraderie, his manner lacks conviction. He walks steadily ahead, not turning back, not talking again, up the marble stairs, along the boulevard with its urns and paintings, past the trophy case filled with firm memorabilia, under the diamond shadows of two sets of chandeliers. Outside the cherry wood door to the conference room we both pause.

"Go on in, then," Havens says. "It's what you've been waiting for, isn't it?"

I open the door, the heavy door behind which the great meeting of the partners is in progress. The first people I see as I enter are Cabot and Sheinburg sitting side by side on a platform. Cabot was told several days ago that his judicial appointment has been approved and it seems as if this has brought a new gravity to him, has struck him like arthritis, causing him to move about the firm just a little more slowly, to ponder a second longer before he speaks. He turns toward me, smiles his new, ponderous smile, and then turns away. David Sheinburg watches me eagerly. I think Stan is right when he says that the most dangerous place in America may be the space between David Sheinburg, perverse master of the deal, urinated on by his dog, and a dollar bill that happens to be lying on the ground.

I see Olwine at a podium near the bank of windows, and also Mrs. Buckles at a table by Olwine's side, and then I see them all, the whole partnership, forty men and a handful of women waiting expectantly for the pageant to unfold. They sit like schoolboys in their straight rows, row by row to the back of the auditorium, surrounded by their fake pillars and their fake paintings of fake ancestors, fake ferns and plaster of Paris painted to look like marble. Sitting so neatly now they truly do resemble boys resting from their scrapping, taking momentary refuge among the spoils of their schoolyard games.

Olwine at the podium is wearing a dark suit that looks a bit like an undertaker's, positively funereal. He might just as well be wearing a stovepipe hat and have come as Abraham Lincoln. He begins to speak and I hear the voice but the words just wash over me, leave no impression at all. I am facing the entire room and see the partners now in a different context than I ever have. Their attention is focused on Olwine, tormentor, sadist, closet romantic, and their affect suggests a belief that he can somehow lead them out from the thicket and back into prosperity. But the flock. Look at the flock. They are mouthpieces and regulation readers and orators, town meeting members and justices of the peace and committeemen, treasurers and delegates and panelists, a room filled with people who have built nothing, invented nothing, cured nothing, created nothing. Olwine is an unmitigated bore and yet watch them lap it up, laugh politely, shift their bottoms comfortably in their seats.

Now he is concluding a lofty speech about something or other—my name does keep coming up—but his voice is especially thin, weightless, almost lost in the soft buzz of the lights and the rustle of air from the vents. And then he is done and I realize that I am expected to speak, to accept what they are offering with something akin to gratitude.

I have no idea what I might say and so I say nothing.

Olwine shifts at the podium.

"Well," he says, a trace of impatience in his voice.

Draped behind him is a big banner with the words "Nibble Knows" emblazoned across it. Babbet catches my eye and winks. He has shaved off his beard, must have decided that it was time to change his nondescript appearance into another no more prepossessing. He has a round, yellow face, a square chin with a dimple in the center. I marvel at how an institution can achieve a measure of eminence—or at least the appearance of a measure of eminence—even as its constituent parts are ciphers, worse than ciphers. Who would have guessed that just the act of walking into this ornate room would prick me awake as it has. They are impotent, but so am I, liar to juries, groveler, parasite, abuser of women, impotent as a eunuch when it comes to the only woman who matters.

"Oh, for heavens' sake," I say. "Of course not."

A great stillness sweeps the room and then a groundswell of disapproval begins, abruptly muffled by the slamming of the door. What I will remember most vividly later are not the strange looks I get from Cabot or the sudden pallor of Sheinburg sitting next to him, but rather the impassivity of Olwine, his face a mask of stone.

· · ·

There is now no doubt what I have to do. My coat is still in my office but I leave it there, know that in all probability this means that I will never see it again, it and my stupid prints, my monogrammed coffee mug, my ugly laminated diplomas.

Before I leave the building I call Stan at his new office. An answering machine picks up after three rings.

"I guess I owe you ten bucks," I tell it.

It is cold outside, still windy, but I barely feel it as I walk over the expressway and then cross the bridge to the parking lot. It is almost eight, a good time, a good evening.

XXV

Sometimes, Wigworth-like, fate intervenes. And sometimes, it seems, you have to *schlep* it, kicking and screaming, into the arena.

My thoughts of her at home always place her on a chair, surrounded by her family, in an ornate room lit by candles. They sit around the long oak table, her parents at each end, Emma with her curly dark hair and dusky skin on one side, Maria on the other. They are always eating, sampling pieces of the dishes she sometimes mentions, braised oysters with garlic, warmed prosciutto, figs wrapped in veal. Alfonso drifts in and out of focus, sometimes there, sometimes not. Tonight he will be there, his fair hair and classic features larger than life.

That is good too.

Perhaps she once wanted Alfonso, was convinced that he fit her plans, met her expectations, could make her happy, and yet he is not enough for her in the real world, the world outside of the fairy tale of the Bourbons and however many Sicilies they all once owned. If he was, she would never have allowed things to get so out of hand, would not have challenged me to tip the balance as she has. That is what she has done, after all. And if I am wrong, so be it. Royal dowagers may rust away in Palm Beach and Madrid, but what else remains of the autocracy, of their nineteenth century ways, is an anachronism. What can they do to me, after all? What can they do to her? Circumcise her? Ship her off to North Africa to spend the rest of her life wearing a long black dress and doing menial chores.

Not Maria. But whatever it is this persona of mine, so squeamish, so risk averse, so lawyer like, is stifling me.

Sometimes, as I say, fate intervenes. Sometimes you have to *schlep* it in, kicking and screaming.

• • •

There is not much traffic on the Massachusetts turnpike and soon I am in Wellesley and approaching her parents' house. If she just knew what was about to break, sitting there so unaware, she would jump, wave her hands in frenzied gestures, hyperventilate, call me a lost soul. It wouldn't be the first time. But my progress is inexorable, Route 9, Cliff Road, closer and closer.

My determination does not come from knowing what I will do, let alone say, when I get there, but from the need to go there itself, to leave this cloister of passivity. I want her.

If she wants me, now and without reservation, it is her moment. If she does not, it is her moment too. And now I am on her block, and then, with my heart in my mouth, turning into her driveway for the second time in my life, up and around, to a standstill beneath the imposing oak tree except that this time there are cars parked there and lights on throughout the house. No one accosts me. There are no hostile shouts. Somewhere through the trees, within the yellow lights, people are eating, enjoying their last seconds before a storm descends.

The gravel makes exaggerated sounds as I cross it, and then I am at the front door and looking for the bell. It rings, deep and echoing and for a few moments there is silence though I am very aware of my heart, my heart and my lungs, and then

there are footsteps. The door opens and whoever else I might be
expecting would be there, it is Maria herself.

For a moment she just stands there, her face frozen, cast in
plaster. Her hand remains on the handle, her legs in mid stride,
her eyes wide.

"*Loco perdido*," she says.

"Good evening," I say.

"What the . . ." she begins.

She is either on the verge of laughing, or on the verge of running. She becomes appreciably paler.

"What *are* you doing here?" she whispers.

"I came to see you," I say, filled now with energy, almost
beyond the reach of anxiety.

"I mean it," she whispers urgently, and a trace of a smile lights
her face. "What crazy, misplaced, misguided, misbegotten
notion brings you here?"

"Thanks. I will come in," I say, and step into the hall.

"Please," she says. "Please don't do anything dumb."

Now she is panicked, whatever pleasure she may have felt
in seeing me is quite gone. She holds me back by the fabric of
my shirt and is about to say something—I'm not sure even she
knows what—when someone else comes into the hall. I know
instantly who it is.

"Hello, Emma," I say, and hold out my hand.

I will know this woman, I know I will, for all of my life. I
like her instantly, see so much that is familiar in her. It is not
that she and Maria look alike, because they do not, but there is
something startlingly similar about them. Emma is beautiful,
has the same dusky skin as Maria does, and almond-shaped
eyes, long dark hair.

She reaches around her sister who continues to block me half-
heartedly, and shakes my hand. She examines my face carefully,
and then her sister's.

"This is Derek, my boss," Maria says.

"I'm not her boss," I say.

"I know who you are," Emma says. Something in the way she says it speaks worlds. "Did you know he was coming?"

"Of course not," Maria says. "Do you think I'm crazy. Go," she says, turning to me.

"No," I say. "Let's go inside instead."

"Are you nuts?" she pleads, but she is laughing now, has abandoned hope that the event will pass, that nothing will come of it.

"Well," Emma asks, quite seriously. "Are you nuts?"

"No."

"Then come in," she says calmly. "I've been wondering about you for months. We were just having coffee."

She stands aside to let me in, gestures ahead.

"Did you make partner?" Maria asks.

"Yes and no," I answer. "I turned them down."

"Now I know you've gone off your rocker," Maria says. "You'd better come in. Just don't make trouble."

"I'm here to make trouble," I say. "Come with me and I won't go in."

"*Aiyaiyai*," Maria wails even as she pushes me, slightly but unambiguously, ahead of her and into the room.

• • •

So that is her father, handsome, expansive, comfortable looking, in shirt sleeves. I would not have recognized him there, drinking a glass of wine, from his cameo appearance in the road. Her mother, similarly unrecognizable in a wool skirt and sweater, remains poised, perhaps even a little amused at the confusion. The house is warm, filled with moving shadows, the aromas of rich food.

Only Alfonso, who rises to shake my hand, is exactly as I remember him. Sweep of fair hair, long straight nose, narrow face.

"Tonight's a big night at the firm," Maria says as she introduces me. "Derek was offered a partnership."

I can let her explain me away, I suppose. She is trying hard enough to do it, is about to begin an earnest discourse on the politics of Nibble & Kuhn. The air is thick, sleepy, the offered coffee smells good. I feel how easily I could be seduced by it all, by the warmth and the comfort, the wholly familiar chatter.

"That's a big honor, to be offered a partnership at a firm like Nibble & Kuhn," her father says gesturing to a chair. He has a very slight accent, English more than Spanish, a deep voice. "Maria says it is a very fine firm."

"She does?" I say, momentarily distracted.

"She has also mentioned that you are a skillful trial lawyer," he says.

That she has mentioned me here, that there has been a time when I have been discussed at this table, produces a feeling of pleasure that is almost physical. So I have an unexpected choice now, the chance to disguise this as nothing more than some burst of exuberance, impetuous perhaps, but manageable. The air begins to settle, some measure of understanding to set in among the people in the room. The thought occurs to me that it is now or never, that even if Maria forgives me for allowing it to pass I will never forgive myself.

"The reason I'm here has nothing to do with partnership," I say. "I'm here to ask Maria to come away with me."

There is silence for only a moment.

"Where were you planning on going?" her mother asks.

She turns to Maria, who shrugs and looks at me.

"Where were we planning on going?" she asks wryly.

"They really don't know anything about us, do they," I say.

"Nope," she says. "Although you're rapidly becoming unforgettable."

"Is this some kind of a prank?" her father asks.

"It isn't," Emma says quietly and they all turn to face her.

Alfonso stands up and leans on the back of his chair.

"Come away where?" he asks calmly.

He seems to understand something of it all, he and Emma too even as her parents remain quite at sea.

"This is not the sort of intrusion we welcome," her father says slowly.

"Come away where?" Alfonso asks again.

He is measured, self possessed. He looks like the kind of person one should take seriously, mature, trustworthy. I have no answer to this. Come away from here, is what I mean, away from this place and these people, just away, and with me. Nothing more.

"Perhaps you are making a fool of yourself, young man," her father says. "Perhaps you should leave and let Maria explain whatever needs to be explained."

"You're not making a fool of yourself," Maria says softly. "And I'd like you to stay."

Even Emma looks astounded. The truth is that I have no idea what comes next. It had seemed inevitable at the time, on the walk to my car, on the turnpike to Wellesley, that I come, but now that I am here, surrounded by them all, in the confusion of it all, the confusion that I have created, the logic of my actions is elusive.

"So why are you here?" Maria's father asks.

There is suddenly an edge to it, a sense that he could become very angry very quickly, and the answer to his question, just as suddenly, becomes obvious. I had thought for a moment, in the car, on the road, that my daring at Nibble had somehow emboldened me, made me reckless, filled me with an aggression born of waiting and frustration. But it is not that. It is that now that my life at Nibble is over the logic of things has changed and nothing will be the same again. In the morning we will begin a drift away from this moment, Maria and I, back to where we were before we met, before Nibble in its lumbering, prickly way brought us together, gave us our moment, held us in crisis, and how we begin will determine how we continue. I have with Maria a bond that goes all the way to the center of my soul, mine and hers, and I know that she knows it too. Tomorrow brings a risk of losing something that I suspect comes just once in a lifetime.

Suddenly I feel unspeakably bold.

"I won't be at Nibble in the morning," I say. "It's now or never."

For a few seconds the room is quiet, the silence broken only by a crack from the fire, a distant sound from the street. Maria isn't smiling but there is a sort of ironic look on her face, somehow hapless, somehow pleased.

"I think I may have invited him," she says.

Her mother looks at Alfonso, at her husband.

"But you're engaged," she says. "These things don't happen unless you let them."

"I must have let them," Maria says, and then she turns to Alfonso, tries to take his hand, but he pulls it back. "We've been together our whole lives and I love you like a brother. But this is the boy I'm in love with."

Alfonso looks straight down at the table, speaks in a monotone.

"I suppose," he says bitterly, "all things considered, I need time to think too."

"Why don't you just tell us what's going on," her mother suggests.

She has a deep voice, a nice voice. I like her, wish I had been one of them all along and not an imposter storming in on their quiet night.

"I'll tell you some other time," Maria answers. "But in the meantime I have to go talk with this boy. I've kept him waiting for a long time."

She begins to lead me past them, toward the door. The air in the room is perfectly still.

"Too long," she says to me.

• • •

We walk from the house together, past my car, down the road, sniff in the scents of wood smoke and pine. I feel as if I could take off and fly, like on the first day of summer vacation, before I took within myself, right inside, expectations and burdens that arc not natural. I had a teacher once, when I was a boy but it is still vivid, who took the whole class on an imaginary trip around the world, made us keep diaries of experiences we never actually had, write descriptions of places we never actually visited and would never actually go. The adventure is still inside me, covered only with a dust of knowledge so evanescent as to be irrelevant. A person's got to think about what he does in his life, I think. You can't just do it because you're doing it. Law, law school, and most everything else can be a good thing for some people, I suppose, but for me it has been a place to park myself, to go on autopilot, to wait things out while I look for whatever else it is in life that may be satisfying.

That can't be right.

"You sure know how to make a big entrance," Maria says as we walk down the driveway.

Perhaps a newspaper. A school class of my own, ripe for adventures in ancient Egypt and nights in Dar es Salaam. Or the Peace Corps.

"Take me to the piazza in your grandfather's village," I say. "We can wait until it rains and watch the people slip."

"They paved it over last year," she says.

Perhaps we will learn to grow things or we will set out into the sunset and end up teaching English in Kuala Lumpur or somewhere else equally unlikely. If we have babies, and I hope and trust that we will, I hope that we will bind them up in cloth like the Zulu women do and bundle them on our backs, wear boots, own a jeep. But whatever it is I am sure of only one thing: whatever it is, it will have to make immediate sense here and now, make sense to me or I will not spend one moment doing it. There is too much to choose from for a fate like that.

"You did hear that I'm no longer gainfully employed," I say as we reach the street.

"Wanna hear a coincidence?" Maria asks.

"What?"

"I have five million dollars in a trust fund," she says. "Exactly the same amount that you won for each of those boys."

"Speaking of people called Emma," I say. "Do *you* wanna hear a coincidence?"

Acclaim For David Schmahmann's First Novel
EMPIRE SETTINGS

"Schmahmann's portrayal of South Africa, past and present, is as poignant—and as nuanced—as his delineation of the characters and their relationships."
—*The Los Angeles Times*

"Teaches us volumes about hello and goodbye, holding on and letting go."
—*The Christian Science Monitor*

"All of Schmahmann's characters . . . long for a past that can no longer exist—a longing [he] elucidates with bittersweet grace."
—*The Baltimore Sun*

"It bristles with tension and suspense and is remarkably authentic. You can smell the sea and the decay, and almost touch the people, who are so real."
—Desmond Tutu, Archbishop Emeritus and Nobel Laureate

"Lyrically written."   —Calvin Reid, *Publishers Weekly*

"A powerful, engrossing story about a time and place that many would rather forget . . . the author is masterful at manipulating the various voices. He creates the personalities and circumstances of each character through their speech patterns . . . and expressions of guilt and grief, bigotry and ambiguity, fury and tenderness."
—*Knight Ridder Newspapers*

"This brilliant first novel . . . examines the forces that combine to bring lovers together and, often, to keep them apart."
—*American Way Magazine*

"Schmahmann is adept at blending the personal and the political, and his story manages memorably to evoke his country's terrible past even as it portrays the tragic difficulties of its present struggles."
—*The San Francisco Chronicle*

"A marvelous and painful psalm . . . [that] tells more about the twisted results of racism than any non-fiction report could."
—*The Providence Journal*